c

49

CHARLIE CHAN CARRIES ON

Charlie Chan Carries On

"Murder like potato chip," said Charlie Chan to his old friend Chief Inspector Duff of Scotland Yard, "cannot stop at just one."

Duff had all too much reason to appreciate the truth of that saying, for he had come to Honolulu following a trail which began, one foggy night in London, when an American millionaire was found murdered in the ultra-respectable Broome's Hotel. The killer, it seemed, must be one of a small, elite party which was making a round-the-world tour.

So Duff had joined the tour, and the murderer had killed again and again—in Nice, in San Remo, in Yokohama.

He had just been telling Charlie about it when a bullet struck him down, there in Charlie Chan's own office. Never was there so intolerable an affront to the Honolulu Police Force and to its most celebrated detective.

"Tell him," Charlie whispers to the surgeon, "that Charlie Chan has sailed for San Francisco and will have guilty man before boat reaches shore of mainland. Make it in the form of a promise, and say it comes from one who has never yet smashed promise to a friend."

Charlie Chan Carries On is probably the best, the most satisfyingly mature, book in all this famous series; a gripping story, a clever detective puzzle and, at the centre of it, the often imitated but still inimitable figure of Charlie Chan himself.

CHARLIE CHAN
CARRIES ON

by

Earl Derr Biggers

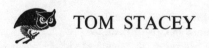 TOM STACEY

This edition published 1972 by
Tom Stacey Reprints Ltd.
28-29 Maiden Lane, London WC2E 7JP
England

ISBN 0 85468 122 1
Printed in Great Britain by
Biddles Ltd., Martyr Road, Guildford, Surrey

CONTENTS

CHARLIE CHAN
CARRIES ON

CHAPTER I

RAIN IN PICCADILLY

CHIEF INSPECTOR DUFF, of Scotland Yard, was walking down Piccadilly in the rain. Faint and far away, beyond St. James's Park, he had just heard Big Ben on the Houses of Parliament strike the hour of ten. It was the night of February 6, 1930. One must keep in mind the clock and the calendar where chief inspectors are concerned, although in this case the items are relatively unimportant. They will never appear as evidence in court.

Though naturally of a serene and even temperament, Inspector Duff was at the moment in a rather restless mood. Only that morning a long and tedious case had come to an end as he sat in court and watched the judge, in his ominous black cap, sentence an insignificant, sullen-looking little man to the scaffold. Well, that was that, Duff had thought. A cowardly murderer, with no conscience, no human feeling whatever. And what a merry chase he had led Scotland Yard before his final capture. But perseverance had won—that, and a bit of the Duff luck. Getting hold of a letter the murderer had written to the woman in Battersea Park Road, seeing at once the double meaning of a harmless little phrase, seizing upon it and holding on until he had the picture complete. That had done it. All over now. What next?

Duff moved on, his ulster wrapped close about him. Water dripped from the brim of his old felt hat. For the past three hours he had been sitting in the Marble Arch Pavilion, hoping to be taken out of himself by the pictures on the screen. The story had been photographed in the South Seas—palm-fringed shores, blazing skies, eternal sunshine. As he watched it Duff had thought of a fellow-detective, encountered some years before in San Francisco. A modest chap who followed the profession of man-hunting against such a background. Studied clues where the trade-winds whispered in flowering trees and the month was always June. The inspector had smiled gently at the recollection.

With no definite destination in mind, Duff wandered along via Park Lane to Piccadilly. It was a thoroughfare of memories for him, and now they crowded about him. Up to a short time ago he had been divisional detective-inspector at the Vine Street station, and so in charge of the C.I.D. in this fashionable quarter. The West End had been his hunting preserve. There, looming in dignified splendour through the rain, was the exclusive club where, with a few quiet words, he had taken an absconding banker. A darkened shopfront recalled that early morning when he had bent over the French woman, murdered among her Paris gowns. The white façade of the Berkeley brought memories of a cruel blackmailer seized, dazed and helpless, as he stepped from his bath. A few feet up Half Moon Street, before the tube station, Duff had whispered a word into a swarthy man's ear, and seen his face go white. The debonair killer wanted so badly by the New York police had been at breakfast in his comfortable quarters at the Albany when Duff laid a hand on his shoulder. In Prince's restaurant, across the way, the inspector had dined every night tor two weeks, keeping a careful eye upon a man who thought that evening clothes concealed successfully the sordid secret in his heart. And here in Piccadilly Circus, to which he had now come, he had fought, one memorable midnight, a duel to the death with the diamond robbers of Hatton Garden.

The rain increased, lashing against him with a new fury. He stepped into a doorway and stared at the scene before him. London's quiet and restrained version of a Great White Way. The yellow lights of innumerable electric signs blurred uncertainly in the downpour, little pools of water lay shining in the street. Feeling the need of companionship, Duff skirted the circle and disappeared down a darker thoroughfare. A bare two hundred yards from the lights and the traffic he came upon a grim building with iron bars at the ground-floor windows and a faintly burning lamp before it. In another moment he was mounting the familiar steps of Vine Street Police Station.

Divisional Inspector Hayley, Duff's successor at this important post, was alone in his room. A spare, weary-looking man, his face brightened at sight of an old friend.

"Come in, Duff, my boy," he said. "I was feeling the need of a chat."

"Glad to hear it," Duff answered. He removed the dripping hat, the soggy ulster, and sat down. Through the open door into the next room he noted a group of detectives, each armed with an evening paper. "Rather quiet evening, I take it?"

"Yes, thank heaven," Hayley replied. "We're raiding a night club a bit later—but that sort of thing, as you know, is our chief diversion nowadays. By the way, I see that congratulations are again in order."

"Congratulations?" Duff raised his heavy eyebrows.

"Yes—that Borough case, you know. Special commendation for Inspector Duff from the judge—splendid work—intelligent reasoning—all that sort of thing."

Duff shrugged. "Yes, of course—thanks, old man." He took out his pipe and began to fill it. "But that's in the past—it will be forgotten to-morrow." He was silent for a moment, then he added: "Odd sort of trade, ours, what?"

Hayley gave him a searching look. "The reaction," he nodded. "Always feel it myself after a hard case. What you need is work, my boy. A new puzzle. No period for reflection between. Now, if you had this post——"

"I've had it," Duff reminded him.

"So you have—that's true. But before we dismiss the past from our minds—and it's a good plan, I agree with you—mayn't I add my own humble word of praise? Your work on this case should stand as an example——"

Duff interrupted him. "I had luck," he said. "Don't forget that. As our old chief, Sir Frederic Bruce, always put it—hard work, intelligence and luck, and of these three, luck is the greatest by far."

"Ah, yes—poor Sir Frederic," Hayley answered.

"Been thinking about Sir Frederic to-night," Duff continued. "Thinking about him, and the Chinese detective who ran down his murderer."

Hayley nodded. "The chap from Hawaii. Sergeant Chan—was that the name?"

"Charlie Chan—yes. But he's an inspector now, in Honolulu."

"You hear from him then?"

"At long intervals, yes." Duff lighted his pipe. "Busy as I am, I've kept up a correspondence. Can't get Charlie out of my mind, somehow. I wrote him a couple of months ago, asking for news of himself."

"And he answered?"

"Yes—the reply came only this morning." Duff took a letter from his pocket. "There's no news," he added, smiling.

Hayley leaned back in his chair. "None the less, let's hear the letter," he suggested.

Duff drew two sheets of paper from the envelope and spread them out. For a moment he stared at those lines typed in another police station on the far side of the world. Then, a faint smile still lingering about his lips, he began to read in a voice strangely gentle for a Scotland Yard inspector:

"REVERED AND HONOURABLE FRIEND.—Kindly epistle from you finished long journey with due time elapsed, and brought happy memories of past floating into this despicable mind. What is wealth? Write down list of friends and you have answer. Plenty rich is way I feel when I know you still have space in honourably busy brain for thoughts of most unworthy C. Chan.

"Turning picture over to inspect other side, I do not forget you. Never. Pardon crude remark which I am now about to inscribe, but such suggestion on your part is getting plenty absurd. Words of praise you once heaped upon me linger on in memory, surrounded always by little glow of unseemly pride.

"Coming now to request conveyed in letter regarding the news with me, there are, most sorry to report, none whatever. Water falls from the eaves into the same old holes, which is accurate description of life as I encounter it. Homicides do not abound in Honolulu. The calm man is the happy man, and I offer no hot complaint. Oriental knows that there is a time to fish, and a time to dry the nets.

"But maybe sometimes I get a little anxious because there is so much drying of the nets. Why is that? Can it be that Oriental character is slipping from me owing to fact I live so many years among restless Americans? No matter. I keep the affair hidden. I pursue not very important duties with uncommunicative face. But it can happen that I sit some nights on lanai look-

ing out across sleepy town and suffer strange wish telephone would jangle with important message. Nothing
doing, to quote my children, who learn nice English
as she is taught in local schools.

"I rejoice that gods have different fate waiting for
you. Often I think of you in great city where it is your
lot to dwell. Your fine talents are not allowed to lie
like stagnant water. Many times the telephone jangles,
and you go out on quest. I know in heart that success
will always walk smiling at your side. I felt same when
I enjoyed great privilege of your society. Chinese,
you know, are very psychic people.

"How kind of you to burden great mind with inquiry
for my children. Summing up quickly, they number
now eleven. I am often reminded of wise man who said:
To govern a kingdom is easy; to govern a family is
difficult. But I struggle onward. My eldest daughter
Rose is college student on mainland. When I meet
for first time the true cost of American education, I
get idea much better to draw line under present list
of offspring and total up for ever,

"Once more my warmest thanks for plenty amiable
letter. Maybe some day we meet again, though appalling
miles of land and water between us make thought sound
dreamy. Accept anyhow this fresh offering of my kind
regards. May you have safe walk down every path where
duty leads you. Same being wish of

"Yours, with deep respect,
"CHARLIE CHAN."

Duff finished reading and slowly folded the missive.
Looking up, he saw Hayley staring at him, incredulous.

"Charming," said the divisional inspector. "But
—er—a bit naïve. You don't mean to tell me that
the man who wrote that letter ran down the murderer
of Sir Frederic Bruce!"

"Don't be deceived by Charlie's syntax," Duff
laughed. "He's a bit deeper than he sounds.
Patience, intelligence, hard work—Scotland Yard has
no monopoly on these. Inspector Chan happens to be
an ornament to our profession, Hayley. Pity he's

buried in a place like Honolulu." The palm-fringed shore he had seen at the cinema flitted before his eyes. "Though perhaps, at that, the calm man is the happy man."

"Perhaps," Hayley answered. "But we'll never have a chance to test it, you and I. You're not going, are you?" For Duff had risen.

"Yes—I'll be getting on to my diggings," the chief inspector replied. "I was rather down when I came in, but I feel better now."

"Not married yet, eh?" Hayley inquired.

"Married no end," Duff told him. "Haven't time for anything else. Married to Scotland Yard."

Hayley shook his head. "That's not enough. But it's no affair of mine." He helped Duff on with his coat. "Here's hoping you won't be long between cases. Not good for you. When the telephone on your desk—what was it Chan said?—when it jangles with an important message—then, my boy, you'll be keen again."

"Water," Duff shrugged, "dropping from the eaves into the same old holes."

"But you love to hear it drop. You know you do."

"Yes," nodded the chief inspector. "You're quite right. As a matter of fact, I'm not happy unless I do. Good-bye, and luck at the night club."

At eight o'clock on the following morning, Inspector Duff walked briskly into his room at Scotland Yard. He was his old cheery self; his cheeks were glowing, a heritage of the days on that Yorkshire farm whence he had come to join the Metropolitan Police. Opening his desk, he ran through a small morning mail. Then he took up his copy of the *Telegraph*, lighted a good cigar, and began a leisurely perusal of the news.

At eight-fifteen his telephone jangled suddenly. Duff stopped reading and stared at it. It rang again.

sharply, insistently, like a call for help. Duff laid down his paper and picked up the instrument.

"Morning, old chap." It was Hayley's voice. " Just had a bit of news from my sergeant. Sometime during the night a man was murdered at Broome's Hotel."

"At Broome's," Duff repeated. "You don't mean at Broome's?"

"Sounds like an incredible setting for murder, I know," Hayley replied. "But none the less, it's happened. Murdered in his sleep—an American tourist from Detroit, or some queer place like that. I thought of you at once—naturally, after our chat last evening. Then, too, this is your old division. No doubt you know your way about in the rarified atmosphere of Broome's. I've spoken to the superintendent. You'll get your orders in a moment. Hop into a car with a squad and join me at the hotel at your earliest."

Hayley rang off. As he did so, Duff's superior came hastily into the room.

"An American murdered in Half Moon Street," he announced. "At Broome's Hotel, I believe. Mr. Hayley has asked for help, and suggested you. A good idea. You'll go at once, Mr. Duff——"

Duff was already in the doorway, wearing hat and coat. "On my way, sir."

"Good," he heard the superintendent say as he dashed down the stairs.

In another moment he was climbing into a little green car at the kerb. Out of nowhere appeared a finger-print expert and a photographer. Silently they joined the party. The green car travelled down the brief length of Derby Street and turned to the right on Whitehall.

The rain of the night before had ceased, but the

morning was thick with fog. They crept along through an uncertain world, their ears assailed by the constant honking of motor horns, the shrill cries of whistles. To right and left the street lamps were burning, pale, ineffectual blobs of yellow against a gloomy grey. Somewhere back of the curtain, London went about its business as usual.

The scene was in striking contrast with that the inspector had witnessed at the cinema the night before. No blazing sunlight here, no white breakers, no gently nodding palms. But Duff was not thinking of the South Seas. All that was swept from his mind. He sat hunched up in the little car, his eyes trying vainly to pierce the mist that covered the road ahead—the road that was to lead him far. He had completely forgotten everything else—including his old friend, Charlie Chan.

Nor was Charlie at that moment thinking of Duff. On the other side of the world this February day had not yet dawned—it was, in fact, the night of the day before. The plump inspector of the Honolulu police was sitting on his lanai, serenely indifferent to fate. From that perch on Punchbowl Hill he gazed across the twinkling lights of the town at the curving shore line of Waikiki, gleaming white beneath the tropic moon. He was a calm man, and this was one of the calmest moments of his life.

He had not heard the jangle of the telephone on Inspector Duff's desk at Scotland Yard. No sudden vision of the start of that little green car had flashed before him. Nor did he see, as in a dream, a certain high-ceilinged room in Broome's famous London hotel, and on the bed the for-ever motionless figure of an old man, strangled by means of a luggage strap bound tightly about his throat.

Perhaps the Chinese are not so very psychic after all.

CHAPTER II

FOG AT BROOME'S HOTEL

To speak of Broome's Hotel in connection with the word murder is more or less sacrilege, but unfortunately it must be done. This quaint old hostelry has been standing in Half Moon Street for more than a hundred years: it is strong in tradition. Samuel Broome, it is rumoured, started with a single house of the residential type. As the enterprise prospered, more were added, until to-day twelve such houses have been welded into a unit, and Broome's not only has a wide frontage on Half Moon Street, but stretches all the way to Clarges Street in the rear, where there is a second entrance.

The various residences have been joined in haphazard fashion, and a guest who walks the corridors of the upper floors finds himself in a sort of mystic maze. Here he mounts three steps, there he descends two more, he turns the most eccentric corners, doors and archways bob up before him where he least expects them. It is a bit hard on the servants who carry coals for the open fires, and hot water in old-fashioned cans for the guests who have not been able to secure one of the rare bathrooms, installed as a half-hearted afterthought.

But do not think that because it lacks in modern comforts, a suite at Broome's is easily secured. To be admitted to this hotel is an accolade, and in the London season an impossible feat for an outsider.

Then it is filled to overflowing with good county families, famous statesmen and writers, a sprinkling of nobility. Once it accommodated an exiled king, but his social connections were admirable. Out of the season, Broome's has of late years let down the bars. Even Americans have been admitted. And now, this foggy February morning, one of them had got himself murdered upstairs. It was all very distressing.

Duff came through the Half Moon Street entrance into the dim, hushed interior. He felt as though he had stepped inside a cathedral. Taking off his hat, he stood as one awaiting the first notes of an organ. The pink-coated servants, however, who were flitting noiselessly about, rather upset this illusion. No one would ever mistake them for choir-boys. Almost without exception they seemed to date back to the days when Samuel Broome had only one house to his name. Old men who had grown grey at Broome's, thin old men, fat old men, most of them wearing spectacles. Men with the aura of the past about them.

A servant with the bearing of a prime minister rose from his chair behind the porter's desk and moved ponderously towards the inspector.

"Good morning, Peter," Duff said. "What's all this?"

Peter shook a gloomy head. "A most disturbing accident, sir. A gentleman from America—the third floor, room number 28, at the rear. Quite defunct, they tell me." He lowered his quavering voice. "It all comes of letting in these outsiders," he added.

"No doubt," Duff smiled. "I'm sorry, Peter."

"We're all sorry, sir. We all feel it quite keenly. Henry!" He summoned a youngster of seventy who was feeling it keenly on a near-by bench. "Henry will take you wherever you wish to go, Inspector. If I may say so, it is most reassuring to have the inevitable investigation in such hands as yours."

"Thanks," Duff answered.   "Has Inspector Hayley arrived?"

"He is above, sir, in the—in the room in question."

Duff turned to Henry. "Please take these men up to room 28," he said, indicating the photographer and the finger-print man who had entered with him. "I should like a talk first with Mr. Kent, Peter. Don't trouble—he's in his office, I presume?"

"I believe he is, sir. You know the way."

Kent, the managing director of Broome's, was resplendent in morning coat, grey waistcoat and tie. A small pink rose adorned his left lapel. For all that, he appeared to be far from happy. Beside his desk sat a scholarly-looking, bearded man, wrapped in gloomy silence.

"Come in, Mr. Duff, come in," the manager said, rising at once. "This is a bit of luck, our first this morning. To have you assigned here—that's more than I hoped for. It's a horrible mess, Inspector, a horrible mess. If you will keep it all as quiet as possible, I shall be eternally——"

"I know," Duff cut in. "But unfortunately murder and publicity go hand in hand. I should like to learn who the murdered man was, when he got here, who was with him, and any other facts you can give me."

"The chap's name was Hugh Morris Drake," answered Kent, "and he was registered from Detroit —a city in the States, I understand. He arrived last Monday, the third, coming up from Southampton on a boat train after crossing from New York. With him were his daughter, a Mrs. Potter, also of Detroit, and his granddaughter. Her name—it escapes me for the moment." He turned to the bearded man. "The young lady's name, Doctor Lofton?"

"Pamela," said the other, in a cold, hard voice.

"Ah, yes—Miss Pamela Potter. Oh, by the way, Doctor Lofton—may I present Inspector Duff, of Scotland Yard?" The two men bowed. Kent turned to Duff. "The doctor can tell you much more about the dead man than I can. About all the party, in fact. You see, he's the conductor."

"The conductor?" repeated Duff, puzzled.

"Yes, of course. The conductor of the tour," Kent added.

"What tour? You mean this dead man was travelling in a party, with a courier?" Duff looked at the doctor.

"I should hardly call myself a courier," Lofton replied. "Though in a way, of course I am. Evidently, Inspector, you have not heard of Lofton's Round the World Tours, which I have been conducting for some fifteen years, in association with the Nomad Travel Company."

"The information has escaped me," Duff answered dryly. "So Mr. Hugh Morris Drake had embarked on a world cruise, under your direction——"

"If you will permit me," interrupted Lofton, "it is not precisely a world cruise. That term is used only in connection with a large party travelling the entire distance aboard a single ship. My arrangements are quite different—various trains and many different ships—and comparatively a very small group."

"What do you call a small group?" Duff inquired.

"This year there are only seventeen in the party," Lofton told him. "That is—there were last night. To-day, of course, there are but sixteen."

Duff's stout heart sank. "Plenty," he commented.

"Now, Doctor Lofton—by the way, are you a medical doctor?"

"Not at all. I am a doctor of philosophy. I hold a large number of degrees——"

"Ah, yes. Has there been any trouble on this tour before last night? Any incident that might lead you to suspect an enmity, a feud——"

"Absurd!" Lofton broke in. He got up and began to pace the floor. "There has been nothing, nothing. We had a very rough crossing from New York, and the members of the party have really seen very little of one another. They were all practically strangers when they arrived at this hotel last Monday. We have made a few excursions together since, but they are still—— Look here, Inspector!" His calmness had vanished, and his face was flushed and excited beneath the beard. "This is a horrible position for me. My life work, which I have built up by fifteen years of effort—my reputation, my standing—everything is likely to be smashed by this. In heaven's name, don't begin with the idea that some member of the party killed Hugh Drake. It's impossible. Some sneak thief—some hotel servant——"

"I beg your pardon," cried the manager hotly. "Look at my servants. They've been with us for years. No employee of this hotel is involved in any way. I'd stake my life on it."

"Then someone from outside," Lofton said. His tone was pleading. "I tell you it couldn't have been anyone in my group. My standards are high—the best people, always." He laid his hand on Duff's arm. "Pardon my excitement, Inspector. I know you'll be fair. But this is a serious situation for me."

"I know," Duff nodded. "I'll do all I can for you. But I must question the members of your party as soon as possible. Do you think you could get them together for me in one of the rooms of the hotel?"

"I'll try," Lofton replied. "Some of them may be out at the moment, but I'm certain they'll all be in by ten o'clock. You see, we are taking the eleven o'clock from Victoria, to connect with the Dover-Calais boat."

"You *were* taking the eleven from Victoria," Duff corrected him.

"Ah, yes, of course—we were leaving at that hour, I should have said. And now—what now, Inspector?"

"That's rather difficult to say," Duff answered. "We shall see. I'll go upstairs, Mr. Kent, if I may."

He did not wait for an answer, but went quickly out. A lift operator who was wont to boast of his great-grandchildren took him up to the third floor. In the doorway of room 28, he encountered Hayley.

"Oh, hello, Duff," the man from Vine Street said. "Come in."

Duff entered a large bedroom in which the odour of flashlight powder was strong. The room was furnished in such fashion that, had Queen Victoria entered with him, she would have taken off her bonnet and sat down in the nearest arm-chair. She would have felt at home. The bed stood in an alcove at the rear, far from the windows. On it lay the body of a man well along in years—the late sixties, Duff guessed. It did not need the luggage strap, still bound about the thin throat of the dead man, to tell Duff that he had died by strangulation, and the detective's keen eyes saw also that the body presented every evidence of a frantic and fruitless struggle. He stood for a moment looking down at his newest puzzle. Outside, the fog was lifting, and from the pavement below came the notes of *Silver Threads among the Gold*, played by one of the street players that haunt this section of London.

"Divisional surgeon been here?" Duff inquired.

"Yes—he's made his report and gone," Hayley replied. "He tells me the chap's been dead about four hours."

Duff stepped forward and removed, with his hand-kerchief, the luggage strap, which he handed to the finger-print man. Then he began a careful examination of all that was mortal of Mr. Hugh Morris Drake, of Detroit. He lifted the left arm, and bent back the clenched fingers of the hand. As he prepared to do the same with the right, an exclamation of interest escaped him. From between the lean stiff fingers something glittered—a link from a slender, platinum watch-chain. Duff released the object the right hand was clutching, and it fell to the bed. Three links of the chain, and on the end, a small key.

Hayley came close, and together they studied the find as it lay on Duff's handkerchief. On one side of the key was the number "3260," and on the other the words: "Dietrich Safe and Lock Company, Canton, Ohio." Duff glanced at the blank face on the pillow.

"Good old boy," he remarked softly. "He tried to help us. Tore off the end of his assailant's watch-chain—and kept it, by gad."

"That's something," Hayley commented.

Duff nodded. "Perhaps. But it begins to look too much American for my taste, old chap. I'm a London detective, myself."

He knelt beside the bed for a closer examination of the floor. Someone entered the room, but Duff was for the moment too engrossed to look up. When he finally did so, what he saw caused him to leap to his feet, giving the knees of his trousers a hasty brush in passing. A slender and attractive American girl was standing there, looking at him with eyes which, he was not too busy to note, were something rather special in that line.

"Ah—er—good morning," the detective said.

"Good morning," the girl answered gravely. "I'm Pamela Potter, and Mr. Drake—was my grandfather. I presume you're from Scotland Yard. Of course you'll want to talk to one of the family."

"Naturally," Duff agreed. Very composed and sure of herself, this girl was, but there were traces of tears about those violet eyes. "Your mother, I believe, is also with this touring party?"

"Mother is prostrated," the girl explained. "She may come round later. But just at present I am the only one who can face this thing. What can I tell you?"

"Can you think of any reason for this unhappy affair?"

The girl shook her head. "None whatever. It's quite unbelievable, really. The kindest man in the world—not an enemy. It's preposterous, you know."

Up from Clarges Street came the loud strains of *There's a Long, Long Trail A-Winding*. Duff turned to one of his men. "Shut that window," he ordered sharply. "Your grandfather was prominent in the life of Detroit?" he added, to the girl. He spoke the name uncertainly, accenting the first syllable.

"Oh, yes—for many years. He was one of the first to go into the automobile business. He retired from the presidency of his company five years ago, but he kept a place on the board of directors. For the past few years he has been interested in charitable work—gave away hundreds of thousands. Everybody honoured and respected him. Those who knew him loved him."

"He was, I take it, a very wealthy man?"

"Of course."

"And who——" Duff paused. "Pardon me, but it's a routine question. Who will inherit his money?"

The girl stared at Duff. "Why, I hadn't thought of that at all. But whatever isn't left to charity will, I suppose, go to my mother."

"And in time—to you?"

"To me and my brother. I fancy so. What of it?"

"Nothing, I imagine. When did you last see your grandfather? Alive, I mean."

"Just after dinner, last evening. Mother and I were going to the theatre, but he didn't care to go. He was tired, he said, and besides, poor dear, he couldn't enjoy a play."

Duff nodded. "I understand. Your grandfather was deaf."

The girl started. "How did you know—oh——" Her eyes followed those of the inspector to a table where an ear-phone, with a battery attached, was lying. Suddenly she burst into tears, but instantly regained her self-control "Yes—that was his," she added, and reached out her hand.

"Do not touch it, please," Duff said quickly.

"Oh, I see. Of course not. He wore that constantly, but it didn't help a lot. Last night he told us to go along, that he intended to retire early, as he expected to-day would be tiring—we were all starting for Paris, you know. We warned him not to oversleep —our rooms are on the floor below. He said he wouldn't, that he had arranged with a waiter to wake him every morning just before eight. We were down in the lobby expecting him to join us for breakfast at eight-thirty, when the manager told us—what had happened."

"Your mother was quite overcome?"

"Why not—such horrible news? She fainted, and I finally got her back to her room."

"You did not faint?"

The girl looked at Duff with some contempt. "I don't belong to a fainting generation. I was naturally terribly shocked."

"Naturally. May I step out of character to say that I'm frightfully sorry?"

"Thank you. What else can I tell you?"

"Nothing now. I hope very much that you can arrange for me to see your mother a moment before I go. I must, you understand. But we will give her another hour or so. In the meantime, I am meeting the other members of your travel party in a room below. I won't ask you to come——"

"Nonsense," cried the girl. "Of course I'll come. I'm no weakling, and besides, I want a good look at the members of this party. We haven't had time to get acquainted—the trip across was rather trying. Yes, I'll be there. This thing is too meaningless, too cruel. I shan't rest until I know what is behind it. Anything I can do, Mr.——"

"Inspector Duff," he answered. "I'm glad you feel that way. We'll hunt the answer together, Miss Potter."

"And we'll find it," she added. "We've got to." For the first time she glanced at the bed. "He was so—so kind to me," she said brokenly, and went quickly out.

Duff stood looking after her. "Rather a thoroughbred, isn't she?" he commented to Hayley. "Amazing how many American girls are. Well, let's see. What have we? A bit of chain and a key. Good as far as it goes."

Hayley looked rather sheepish. "Duff, I have been an ass," he said. "There was something else.

The surgeon picked it up from the bed—it was lying beside the body. Just carelessly thrown there, evidently."

"What?" Duff asked tersely.

"This." Hayley handed over a small, worn-looking bag of wash-leather, fastened at the top with a slip cord. It was heavy with some mysterious contents. Duff stepped to a bureau, unloosed the cord, and poured the contents out on the bureau top. For a time he stared, a puzzled frown on his face.

"What—what should you say, Hayley?"

"Pebbles," Hayley remarked. "Little stones of various shapes and sizes. Some of them smooth— might have been picked up from a beach." He flattened out the pile with his hand. "Worthless little pebbles, and nothing else."

"A bit senseless, don't you think?" murmured Duff. He turned to one of his men. "I say—just count these, and put them back in the bag." As the officer set about his task, Duff sat down in an old-fashioned chair, and looked slowly about the room. "The case has its points," he remarked.

"It has indeed," Hayley answered.

"A harmless old man, making a pleasure trip around the world with his daughter and grand-daughter, is strangled in a London hotel. A very deaf, gentle old soul, noted for his kindnesses and his benefactions. He rouses from sleep, struggles, gets hold of part of his assailant's watch-chain. But his strength fails, the strap draws tighter, and the murderer, with one final gesture, throws on to the bed a silly bag of stones. What do you make of it, Hayley?"

"I'm rather puzzled, I must say."

"So am I. But I've noted one or two things. You have too, no doubt?"

"I was never in your class, Duff."

"Rot. Don't be modest, old chap. You haven't used your eyes, that's all. If a man stood beside a bed, engaged in a mortal struggle with another man, his shoes would disturb the nap of the carpet to some extent. Especially if it were an old thick carpet such as this. There is no indication of any such roughing of the carpet, Hayley."

"No?"

"None whatever. And—take a look at the bed, if you please."

"By Jove!" The eyes of the Vine Street man widened. "I see what you mean. It's been slept in, of course, but——"

"Precisely. At the foot and at one side, the covers are still tucked into place. The whole impression is one of neatness and order. Was there a struggle to the death on that bed, Hayley?"

"I think not, Duff."

"I'm sure there was not." Duff gazed thoughtfully about him. "Yes—this was Drake's room. His property is all about. His ear-phone is on the table. His clothes are on that chair. But something tells me that Hugh Morris Drake was murdered elsewhere."

CHAPTER III

THE MAN WITH A WEAK HEART

AFTER this surprising statement, Duff was silent for a moment, staring into space. Kent, the hotel manager, appeared in the doorway, his round face still harassed and worried.

"I thought perhaps I might be of some help here," he remarked.

"Thank you," Duff replied. "I should like to interview the person who first came upon this crime."

"I rather thought you might," the manager answered. "The body was found by Martin, the floor waiter. I have brought him along." He went to the door and beckoned.

A servant with a rather blank face, much younger than most of his fellows, entered the room. He was obviously nervous.

"Good morning," said Duff, taking out his notebook. "I am Inspector Duff, of Scotland Yard." The young man's manner became even more distressed. "I want you to tell me everything that happened here this morning."

"Well, sir, I—I had an arrangement with Mr. Drake," Martin began. "I was to rouse him every morning, there being no telephones in the rooms. He preferred to breakfast below, but he was fearful of oversleeping. A bit of a job it was, sir, to make him hear, him being so deaf. Twice I had to go to the housekeeper for a key, and enter the room.

"This morning, at a quarter before eight, I knocked at his door. I knocked many times, but nothing happened. Finally I went for the housekeeper's key, but I was told it had disappeared yesterday."

"The housekeeper's key was lost?"

"It was, sir. There was another master key downstairs, and I went for that. I had no thought of anything wrong—I had failed to make him hear me on those other mornings. I unlocked the door of this room and came in. One window was closed, the curtain was down all the way. The other was open and the curtain was up, too. The light entered from there. Everything seemed to be in order—I saw the ear-telephone on the table, Mr. Drake's clothes on a chair. Then I approached the bed, sir—and it was a case of notifying the management immediately. That—that is all I can tell you, Inspector."

Duff turned to Kent. "What is this about the housekeeper's key?"

"Rather odd about that," the manager said. "This is an old-fashioned house, as you know, and our maids are not provided with keys to the rooms. If a guest locks his door on going out, the maids are unable to do the room until they have obtained the master key from the housekeeper. Yesterday the lady in room 27, next door, a Mrs. Irene Spicer, also a member of Doctor Lofton's party, went out and locked her door, though she had been requested not to do so by the servants.

"The maid was forced to secure the housekeeper's key in order to enter. She left it in the lock and proceeded about her work. Later, when she sought the key, it had disappeared. It is still missing."

"Naturally," smiled Duff. "It was in use, no doubt, about four o'clock this morning." He looked at Hayley. "Deliberately planned." Hayley nodded. "Any other recent incidents around the hotel," he continued to Kent, "about which we should know?"

The manager considered. "Yes," he said. "Our night-watchman reports two rather queer events that took place during the night. He is no longer a young man and I told him to lie down in a vacant room and get a little rest. I have sent for him, however, and he will see you presently. I prefer that you hear of these things from him."

Lofton appeared in the doorway. "Ah, Inspector Duff," he remarked. "I find a few of our party are still out, but I am rounding up everybody possible. They will all be here, as I told you, by ten o'clock. There are a number on this floor, and——"

"Just a moment," Duff broke in. "I am particularly interested in the occupants of the rooms on either side of this one. In 27, Mr. Kent tells me, there is a Mrs. Spicer. Will you kindly see if she is in, Doctor Lofton, and if so, bring her here?"

Lofton went out, and Duff stepped to the bed, where he covered over the face of the dead man. As he returned from the alcove, Lofton re-entered accompanied by a smartly-dressed woman of about thirty. She had no doubt been beautiful, but her tired eyes and the somewhat hard lines about her mouth suggested a rather gay past.

"This is Mrs. Spicer," Lofton announced. "Inspector Duff, of Scotland Yard."

The woman stared at Duff with sudden interest. "Why should you wish to speak with me?" she asked.

"You know what has happened here this morning, I take it?"

"I know nothing. I had breakfast in my room, and I have not until this moment been outside it. Of

course, I have heard a great deal of talking in
here——"

"The gentleman who occupied this room was
murdered in the night," said Duff, tersely, studying
her face as he spoke. The face paled.

"Murdered?" she cried. She swayed slightly.
Hayley was quick with a chair. "Thank you," she
nodded mechanically. "You mean poor old Mr.
Drake? Such a charming man. Why—that's—
that's terrible."

"It seems rather unfortunate," Duff admitted.
"There is only a thin door between your room and
this. It was fastened at all times, of course?"

"Naturally."

"On both sides?"

Her eyes narrowed. "I know nothing of this side.
It was always locked on mine." Duff's little stratagem
had failed.

"Did you hear any noise in the night? A struggle
—a cry, perhaps?"

"I heard nothing."

"That's rather odd."

"Why should it be? I am a sound sleeper."

"Then you were probably asleep at the hour the
murder took place?"

She hesitated. "You're rather clever, aren't you,
Inspector? I have, of course, no idea when the
murder took place."

"Ah, no—how could you? At about four this
morning, we believe. You have heard no one talking in this room within—say—the last twenty-four
hours?"

"Let me think. I went to the theatre last
night——"

"Alone?"

"No—with Mr. Stuart Vivian, who is also in our

party. When I returned about twelve everything
was very quiet here. But I did hear talking in this
room—last evening, while I was dressing for dinner.
Quite loud talking."

"Indeed?"

"It seemed, as a matter of fact, to be almost—a
quarrel."

"How many people were involved?"

"Only two. Two men. Mr. Drake and——"
She stopped.

"You recognized the other voice?"

"I did. He has a distinctive voice. Doctor
Lofton, I mean."

Duff turned suddenly to the conductor of the party.
"You had a quarrel with the dead man in this room
last evening before dinner?" he asked sternly. Distress was evident on the doctor's face.

"Not precisely—I wouldn't call it that," he protested. "I had dropped in to acquaint him with
to-day's arrangements, and he began at once to criti-
cize the personnel of the party. He said some of our
members were not of the sort he had expected."

"No wonder he said that," put in Mrs. Spicer.

"Naturally, my reputation is dear to me," Lofton
went on. "I am not accustomed to that kind of
criticism. It is true that this year, owing to bad
business conditions at home, I have been forced to
accept two or three people who would not ordinarily
be taken. But whatever their station in life, they are
quite all right, I'm certain. I resented Mr. Drake's
remarks, and no doubt the conversation became a bit
heated. But it was hardly the type of misunder-
standing that would lead to anything"—he nodded
towards the bed—"like this."

Duff turned to the woman. "You heard none of
that conversation?"

"I couldn't make out what was said, no. Of course I didn't particularly try. I only know they seemed quite intense and excited."

"Where is your home, Mrs. Spicer?" Duff inquired.

"In San Francisco. My husband is a broker there. He was too busy to accompany me on this tour."

"Is this your first trip abroad?"

"Oh, no, indeed. I have been over many times. In fact, I've been around the world twice before."

"Really? Great travellers, you Americans. I am asking the members of Doctor Lofton's party to gather in a room on the ground floor at once. Will you be good enough to go down there?"

"Of course. I'll go immediately." She went out.

The finger-print man came over and handed the luggage strap to Duff. "Nothing on it, Mr. Duff," he remarked. "Wiped clean and handled with gloves after that, I fancy."

Duff held up the strap. "Doctor Lofton, have you ever noted this strap on the luggage of any of your— er—guests? It appears to be——" He stopped, surprised at the look on the conductor's face.

"This is odd," Lofton said. "I have a strap identically like that on one of my old bags. I purchased it just before we sailed from New York."

"Will you get it, please," the inspector suggested.

"Gladly," agreed the doctor, and departed.

The hotel manager stepped forward. "I'll see if the watchman is ready," he said.

As he left the room, Duff looked at Hayley. "Our conductor seems to be getting into rather deep water," he remarked.

"He was wearing a wrist-watch," Hayley said.

"So I noticed. Has he always worn it—or was there a watch on the end of a platinum chain? Nonsense. The man has everything to lose by this. It may wreck his business. That's a pretty good alibi."

"Unless he is contemplating a change of business," Hayley suggested.

"Yes. In that case, his natural distress over all this would be an excellent cloak. However, why should he mention that he owns a similar strap——"

Lofton returned. He appeared to be slightly up-set. "I'm sorry, Inspector," he remarked. "My strap is gone."

"Really? Then perhaps this one is yours." The detective handed it over.

The doctor examined it. "I'm inclined to think it is," he said.

"When did you last see it?"

"On Monday night, when I unpacked. I put the bag into a cupboard, and haven't touched it since." He looked appealingly at Duff. "Someone is trying to cast suspicion on me."

"No doubt about that. Who has been in your room?"

"Everybody. They come in and out, asking ques-tions about the tour. Not that I think any member of my party is involved. The whole of London has had access to my room the past five days. The maids, you will recall, asked us not to lock our doors on going out."

Duff nodded. "Don't distress yourself, Doctor Lofton. I don't believe you would be such a fool as to strangle a man with a strap so readily identified. We'll drop the matter. Now tell me—do you know who has that room there?" He indicated the con-necting door on the other side. "Room 29, I fancy."

"That is occupied by Mr. Walter Honywood, a very fine gentleman, a millionaire from New York. One of our party."

"If he is in, will you please ask him to step here, and then return to the task of gathering up your people below?"

After the doctor had gone, Duff rose and tried the door leading from Drake's room into number 29. It was locked from the side where he stood.

"Great pity about the strap," Hayley commented softly. "It lets Doctor Lofton out, I fancy."

"It probably does," Duff agreed. "Unless the man's remarkably subtle—it's my strap—naturally I wouldn't use it—it was stolen from my cupboard—no, men aren't as subtle as that. But it's rather unfortunate, for I don't feel like making a confidant of the conductor now. And we shall need a confidant in that party before we are finished——"

A tall, handsome man in his late thirties was standing in the doorway leading to the hall. "I am Walter Honywood, of New York," he said. "I'm frightfully distressed about all this. I have, you know, room 29."

"Come in, Mr. Honywood," Duff remarked. "You know what has happened, I perceive."

"Yes. I heard about it at breakfast."

"Please sit down." The New Yorker did so. His face was a bit florid for his age, and his hair greying. He had the look of a man who had lived hard in his short life. Duff was reminded of Mrs. Spicer—the deep lines about the mouth, the weary, sophisticated light in the eyes.

"You knew nothing about the matter until you were told at breakfast?" the detective inquired.

"Not a thing."

"That's odd, isn't it?"

"What do you mean?" An expression of alarm flashed across Honywood's face.

"I mean—in the next room, you know. You heard no cry, no struggle?"

"Nothing. I'm a sound sleeper."

"You were sleeping, then, when this murder took place?"

"Absolutely."

"Then you know when it took place?"

"Well—well, no, of course not. I was merely assuming that I must have been asleep—otherwise I should no doubt have heard——"

Duff smiled. "Ah, yes—I see. Tell me—the door between your room and this was always locked?"

"Oh, yes."

"On both sides?"

"Absolutely."

Duff lifted his eyebrows. "How do you know it was fastened on this side?"

"Why—why, the other morning I heard the floor waiter trying to rouse the old gentleman. I unlocked the door on my side, thinking we could reach him that way. But his side was bolted."

Honywood's man-of-the-world air had deserted him. He was perspiring, and his face had turned a sickly grey. Duff watched him with deep interest.

"I seem to have heard your name somewhere."

"Perhaps. I'm a theatrical producer in New York, and I've done a little of that sort of thing in London. No doubt you have heard also of my wife—Miss Sybil Conway, the actress. She has appeared on your side."

"Ah, yes. Is she with you?"

"She is not. We had a slight disagreement about two months ago, and she left me and came over to San Remo, on the Italian Riviera. She is there now. Our tour touches there, and I am hoping to see her, smooth over our difficulties, and persuade her to go the rest of the way round the world with me."

"I see," Duff nodded. The New Yorker had taken out a cigarette, and was holding a lighter to it. His hand trembled violently. Looking up, he saw the detective staring at him.

"This affair has been a great shock to me," he explained. "I got to know Mr. Drake on the boat, and I liked him. Then, too, I am not in the best of health. That is why I came on this tour. After my wife left me, I had a nervous breakdown, and my doctor suggested travel."

"I'm sorry," said Duff. "But it's rather odd, isn't it, Mr. Honywood, that a man who has just had a nervous breakdown should be such—a sound sleeper?"

Honywood appeared startled. "I—I have never had any trouble that way," he replied.

"You're very fortunate," Duff told him. "I am meeting all the members of your party on the ground floor." He explained this again, and sent the New Yorker below to await him. When the man was out of hearing Duff turned to Hayley.

"What do you make of that, old chap?" he inquired.

"In a frightful funk, wasn't he?"

"I don't believe I ever saw a man in a worse," Duff agreed. "He knows a lot more than he's telling, and he's a badly rattled lad. But confound it, that's not evidence. Slowly, old man—we must go slowly—but we mustn't forget Mr. Honywood. He knew when the murder took place, he knew that the door was fastened on both sides. And he has been suffering from a nervous breakdown—we'll have to admit he looks it—yet he sleeps as soundly as a child. Yes, we must keep Mr. Honywood in mind."

Kent came in again, this time accompanied by an old servant who was built along the general lines of Mr. Pickwick.

"This is Eben, our night-watchman," the manager explained. "You'll want to hear his story, Inspector?"

"At once," Duff answered. "What have you to tell, Eben?"

"It's this way, sir," the old man began. "I make my rounds of the house every hour, on the hour, punching the clocks. When I came on to this floor last night, on my two o'clock round, I saw a gentleman standing before one of the doors."

"Which door?"

"I'm a bit confused about it, sir, but I think it was number 27."

"Twenty-seven. That's the Spicer woman's room. Go on."

"Well, sir, when he heard me, he turned quickly and came towards where I was standing, at the head of the stairs. 'Good evening,' he said. 'I'm afraid I'm on the wrong floor. My room is below.' He had the air of a gentleman, a guest, so I let him pass. I fancy I should have questioned him, sir, but here at Broome's we have never had any queer doings—up to now—so I didn't think of it."

"You saw his face?"

"Quite clearly, sir. The light was burning in the corridor. I saw him, and I can identify him if he is still about."

"Good." Duff rose. "We'll have you look over the members of Doctor Lofton's party immediately."

"One moment, sir. I had another little adventure."

"Oh, you did? What was that?"

"On my four o'clock round, when I reached this floor, the light was no longer burning. Everything was black darkness. 'Burnt out,' I thought, and I reached for my electric torch. Suddenly, as I put my hand to my pocket, I was conscious of someone standing at my side. Just felt him there, sir, breathing hard in the quiet night. I got the torch out and flashed it on. I saw the person was wearing grey clothes, sir—and then the torch was knocked from my hand. We struggled here, at the top of the stairs—but I'm not so young as I once was. I did get hold of the pocket of his coat—the right-hand pocket—trying to capture him and he trying to break away. I heard the cloth tear a bit. Then he struck me and I fell. I was out for a second, and when I knew where I was again, he had gone."

"But you are certain that he wore a grey suit? And that you tore the right-hand pocket of his coat?"

"I'd swear to those two points, sir."

"Did you get any idea at this time that you were dealing with the same man you had encountered on your two o'clock round?"

"I couldn't be sure of that, sir. The second one seemed a bit heavier. But that might have been my imagination, as it were."

"What did you do next?"

"I went downstairs and told the night porter. Together we searched the entire house as thoroughly as we could without disturbing any of the guests. We found no one. We debated about the police—but this is a very respectable and famous hotel, sir, and it seemed best——"

"Quite right, too," the manager put in.

"It seemed best to keep out of the daily press, if possible. So we did nothing more then, but of course I reported both incidents to Mr. Kent when he arrived this morning."

"You've been with Broome's a long time, Eben?" Duff inquired.

"Forty-eight years, sir. I came here as a boy of fourteen."

"A splendid record," the inspector said. "Will you please go now and wait in Mr. Kent's office. I shall want you later on."

"With pleasure, sir," the watchman replied, and went out.

Duff turned to Hayley. "I'm going down to meet that round the world crowd," he remarked. "If you don't mind a suggestion, old chap, you might get a few of your men in from the station and, while I'm holding these people downstairs, have a look at their rooms. Mr. Kent will no doubt be happy to act as your guide."

"I should hardly put it that way," said Kent gloomily. "However, if it must be done——"

"I'm afraid it must. A torn bit of watch-chain— a grey coat with the pocket ripped—it's hardly likely you'll succeed, Hayley. But of course we dare not overlook anything." He turned to the finger-print expert and the photographer, who were still on the scene. "You lads finished yet?"

"Just about, sir," the finger-print man answered.

"Wait for me here, both of you, and clear up all odds and ends," Duff directed. He went with Hayley and Kent into the hall. Then he stood, looking about him. "Just four rooms on this corridor," he remarked. "Rooms 27, 28 and 29, occupied by Mrs. Spicer, poor Drake and Honywood. Can you tell me who has room 30—the only one remaining? The one next to Honywood?"

"That is occupied by a Mr. Patrick Tait," Kent replied. "Another member of the Lofton party. A man of about sixty, very distinguished-looking—for an American. I believe he has been a well-known criminal lawyer in the States. Unfortunately he suffers from a weak heart, and so he is accompanied by a travelling companion—a young man in the early twenties. But you'll see Mr. Tait below, no doubt— and his companion too."

Duff went alone to the first floor. Doctor Lofton was pacing anxiously up and down before a door. Beyond, Duff caught a glimpse of a little group of people waiting amid faded red-plush splendour.

"Ah, Inspector," the doctor greeted him. "I haven't been able to round up the entire party as yet. Five or six are still missing, but as it's nearly ten, they should be in soon. Here is one of them now."

A portly, dignified man came down the corridor from the Clarges Street entrance. His great shock of snow-white hair made him appear quite distinguished —for an American.

"Mr. Tait," said Lofton, "meet Inspector Duff, of Scotland Yard."

The old man held out his hand. "How do you do, sir?" He had a deep booming voice. "What is this I hear? A murder? Incredible. Quite incredible. Who—may I ask—who is dead?"

"Just step inside, Mr. Tait," Duff answered. "You'll know the details in a moment. A rather distressing affair——"

"It is, indeed." Tait turned and with a firm step crossed the threshold of the room. For a moment he stood, looking about the group inside. Then he gave a strangled little cry, and pitched forward on to the floor.

Duff was the first to reach him. He turned the old man over, and with deep concern noted his face. It was as blank as that of the dead man in room 28.

CHAPTER IV

DUFF OVERLOOKS A CLUE

THE next instant a young man was at Duff's side, a good-looking American with frank eyes, now somewhat startled. Removing a small, pearl-like object from a bottle, he crushed it in his handkerchief, and held the latter beneath the nose of Mr. Patrick Tait.

"Amyl nitrite," he explained, glancing up at the inspector. "It will bring him around in a moment, I imagine. It's what he told me to do if he had one of these attacks."

"Ah, yes. You are Mr. Tait's travelling companion?"

"I am. My name's Mark Kennaway. Mr. Tait is subject to this sort of thing, and that is why he employed me to come with him."

Presently the man on the floor stirred and opened his eyes. He was breathing heavily and his face was whiter than his shock of snowy hair.

Duff had noted a door on the opposite side of the room and, crossing to it, he discovered that it led to a smaller apartment, among the furnishings of which was a broad and comfortable couch. "Best get him in here, Mr. Kennaway," he remarked. "He's still too shaky to go upstairs." Without another word, he picked the old man up in his arms and carried him to the couch. "You stay here with him," Duff suggested. "I'll talk to you both a little later." Returning to the larger room, he closed the door behind him.

For a moment he stood looking about the main lounge of Broome's Hotel. Plenty of red plush and walnut had been the scheme of the original decorator, and it had remained undisturbed through the years. There was a bookcase with a few volumes, a pile of provincial papers on a table, on the walls a number of sporting prints, their once white mounts yellowed by time.

The group of very modern people who sat now in this musty room were regarding Inspector Duff with serious and, it seemed to him, rather anxious eyes. Outside the sun had at last broken through the fog, and a strong light entered through the many-paned windows, illuminating these faces that were to be the chief study of the detective for a long time to come.

He turned to Lofton. "Some of your party are still missing?"

"Yes—five. Not counting the two in the next room—and of course, Mrs. Potter."

"No matter," shrugged Duff. "We may as well get started." He drew a small table into the middle of the floor, and sitting down beside it, took out his note-book. "I presume everyone here knows what has happened. I refer to the murder of Mr. Drake in room 28 last night." No one spoke, and Duff continued. "Allow me to introduce myself. I am Inspector Duff, of Scotland Yard. I may say, first of all, that this entire group, and all the other members of your party, must remain together here at Broome's Hotel until released by the authorities at the Yard."

A little man, with gold-rimmed eyeglasses, leaped to his feet. "Look here, sir," he cried in a high shrill voice, "I propose to leave the party immediately. I am not accustomed to being mixed up with murder. In Pittsfield, Massachusetts, where I come from——"

"Ah, yes," said Duff coldly. "Thank you. I scarcely knew where to begin. We will start with you." He took out a fountain pen. "Your name, please?"

"My name is Norman Fenwick." He pronounced it Fennick.

"Spell the last name, if you will."

"F-e-n-w-i-c-k. It's an English name, you know."

"Are you English?"

"English descent, yes. My ancestors came to Massachusetts in 1650. During the Revolution they were all loyal to the mother country."

"That," smiled Duff grimly, "was some time ago. It will hardly enter into the present case." He stared with some distaste at the little man who was so obviously eager to curry favour with the British. "Are you travelling alone?"

"No, I'm not. My sister is with me." He indicated a colourless, grey-haired woman. "Miss Laura Fenwick."

Duff wrote again. "Now tell me, do either of you know anything about last night's affair?"

Mr. Fenwick bristled. "Just what do you mean by that, sir?"

"Come, come," the inspector protested. "I've a bit of a job here and no time to waste. Did you hear anything, see anything, or even sense anything that might have some bearing on the case?"

"Nothing, sir, and I can answer for my sister."

"Have you been out of the hotel this morning? Yes? Where?"

"We went for a stroll through the West End. A last look at London. We are both quite fond of the city. That's only natural, since we are of British origin——"

"Yes, yes. Pardon me. I must get on——"

"But one moment, Inspector. We desire to leave this party at once. At once, sir. I will not associate——"

"I have told you what you must do. That matter is settled."

"Very well, sir. I shall interview our ambassador. He's an old friend of my uncle's——"

"Interview him by all means," snapped Duff. "Who is next? Miss Pamela, we have had our chat. And Mrs. Spicer—I have seen you before. That gentleman next to you——"

The man answered for himself. "I am Stuart Vivian, of Del Monte, California." He was bronzed, lean, and would have been handsome had it not been for a deep scar across the right side of his forehead. "I must say that I'm quite in sympathy with Mr. Fenwick. Why should we be put under restraint in this affair? Myself, I was a complete stranger to the murdered man—I'd never even spoken to him. I don't know any of these others, either."

"With one exception," Duff reminded him.

"Ah—er—yes. With one exception."

"You took Mrs. Spicer to the theatre last evening?"

"I did. I knew her before we came on this tour."

"You planned the tour together?"

"A ridiculous question," the woman flared.

"Aren't you rather overstepping the bounds?" cried Vivian angrily. "It was quite a coincidence. I hadn't seen Mrs. Spicer for a year, and imagine my surprise to come on to New York and find her a member of the same party. Naturally there was no reason why we shouldn't go on."

"Naturally," answered Duff amiably. "You know nothing about Mr. Drake's murder?"

"How could I?"

"Have you been out of the hotel this morning?"

"Certainly. I took a stroll—wanted to buy some shirts at the Burlington Arcade."

"Make any other purchases?"

"I did not."

"What is your business, Mr. Vivian?"

"I have none. Play a bit of polo now and then."

"Got that scar on the polo field, no doubt?"

"I did. Had a nasty spill a few years back."

Duff looked about the circle. "Mr. Honywood, just one more question for you."

Honywood's hand trembled as he removed the cigarette from his mouth. "Yes, Inspector?"

"Have you been out of the hotel this morning?"

"No, I—I haven't. After breakfast I came in here and looked over some old copies of the *New York Tribune.*"

"Thank you. That gentleman next to you?" Duff's gaze was on a middle-aged man with a long, hawk-like nose and strikingly small eyes. Though he was dressed well enough and seemed completely at ease, there was that about him which suggested he was somewhat out of place in this gathering.

"Captain Ronald Keane," he said.

"A military man?" Duff inquired.

"Why—er—yes——"

"I should say he is a military man," Pamela Potter put in. She glanced at Duff. "Captain Keane told me he was once in the British army, and had seen service in India and South Africa."

Duff turned to the captain. "Is that true?"

"Well——" Keane hesitated. "No, not precisely. I may have been—romancing a bit. You see—on board a ship—a pretty girl——"

"I understand," nodded the detective. "In such a situation one tries to impress, regardless of the truth.

It has been done before.   Were you ever in any army,
Captain Keane?"

Again Keane hesitated.   But the Scotland Yard
man was in too close touch with records to make
further lying on this point advisable.   "Sorry," he
said.   "I—er—this title is really honorary.   It means
—er—little or nothing."

"What is your business?"

"I haven't any at present.   I've been—an engineer."

"How did you happen to come on this tour?"

"Why—for pleasure, of course."

"I trust you are not disappointed.   What do you
know about last night's affair?"

"Absolutely nothing."

"I presume that you, too, have been out for a stroll
this morning?"

"Yes, I have.   I cashed a cheque at the American
Express Office."

"You were supposed to carry only Nomad
cheques," put in Doctor Lofton, his business sense
coming to the fore.

"I had a few of the others," Keane replied.   "Is
there any law against that?"

"The matter was mentioned in our agreement——"
began Lofton, but Duff cut him off.

"There remains only the gentleman in the corner,"
said the detective.   He nodded toward a tall man in
a tweed suit.   This member of the party had a heavy
walking stick, and one leg was stiff in front of him.
"What is your name, sir?" Duff added.

"John Ross," the other replied.   "I'm a lumber
man from Tacoma, Washington.   Been looking forward to this trip for years, but I never dreamed it
would be anything like this.   My life's an open book,
Inspector.   Give the word, and I'll read aloud any
page you select."

"A Scot, I believe?" Duff suggested.

"Does the burr still linger?" Ross smiled. "It shouldn't—Lord knows I've been in America long enough. I see you're looking at my foot, and since we're all explaining our scars and our weaknesses, I'll tell you that when I was down in the redwoods some months ago, I was foolish enough to let a tree fall on my right leg. Broke a lot of bones, and they haven't knitted as they should."

"That's a pity. Know anything about this murder?"

"Not a thing, Inspector. Sorry I can't help you. Nice old fellow, this Drake. I got pretty well acquainted with him on the ship—he and I both had rather good stomachs. I liked him a lot."

"I imagine that you, too——"

Ross nodded. "Yes—I went for a walk this morning. Fog and all. Interesting little town you've got here, Inspector. Ought to be out on the Pacific Coast."

"Wish we could bring the coast here," Duff replied. "Climate especially."

Ross sat up with interest. "You've been there, Inspector?"

"Briefly—a few years ago."

"What did you think of us?" the lumber man demanded.

Duff laughed and shook his head. "Ask me some other time," he said. "I've more pressing matters to occupy me now." He stood up. "You will all wait here just for a moment," he added, and went out.

Fenwick went over to Doctor Lofton. "See here— you've got to give us our money back on this tour," he began, glaring through his thick glasses.

"Why so?" inquired Lofton suavely.

"Do you suppose we're going on after this?"

"The tour is going on," Lofton told him. "Whether you go or not rests with you. I have been making this trip for many years, and death is not altogether an unknown occurrence among the members of my parties. That it happens to be a murder in this case in no way alters my plans. We shall be delayed for a time in London, but that is, of course, an act of God. Read your contract with me, Mr. Fenwick. Not responsible for acts of God. I shall get the party around the world in due course, and if you choose to drop out, there will be no rebate."

"An outrage," Fenwick cried. He turned to the others. "We'll get together. We'll take it up with the Embassy." But no one seemed to be in a mood to match his.

Duff returned, and with him came Eben, the night-watchman.

"Ladies and gentlemen," the inspector began, "I have asked this man to look you over and see if he can identify a certain person who, at two o'clock last night, was a trifle confused as to the whereabouts of his room. A person who, in point of fact, was wandering about the floor on which the murder took place."

He turned to Eben, who was grimly studying the faces of the men in that old-fashioned room. The servant stared at Lofton, then at Honywood, at Ross, the lumber man, and at Vivian, the polo player. He gave the weak face of Fenwick but a fleeting glance.

"That's him," said Eben firmly, pointing at Captain Ronald Keane.

Keane sat up. "What do you mean?"

"I mean it's you I met on my two o'clock round. You told me you'd got on to that floor by mistake, thinking it was your own."

"Is this true?" Duff asked sternly.

"Why——" Keane looked anxiously about him.

"Why, yes—I was up there. You see, I couldn't sleep, and I wanted a book to read."

"That's pretty old—that wanted-a-book-to-read stuff," the detective reminded him.

"I fancy it is," returned Keane with a sudden show of spirit. "But it happens occasionally—among literate people I mean. I knew Tait had a lot of books —that young fellow reads to him until late at night. I found it out on the boat. I knew, too, that he was on the third floor, though I wasn't sure of the room. I just thought I'd go up there and listen outside the doors, and if I heard anyone reading, I'd go in and borrow something. Well, I didn't hear a thing, so I decided it was too late. When I met this watchman here, I was on my way back to the floor below."

"Why the statement about being confused as to the location of your room?" Duff wanted to know.

"Well, I couldn't very well take up the subject of my literary needs with a servant. He wouldn't have been interested. I just said the first thing that came into my head."

"Rather a habit with you, I judge," Duff remarked. He stood for a moment staring at Keane. A mean face, a face that he somehow didn't care for at all, and yet he had to admit that this explanation sounded plausible enough. But he resolved to keep an eye on this man. A sly, wary sort, and the truth was not in him.

"Very good," the detective said. "Thank you, Eben. You may go now." He thought of Hayley, still searching above. "You will all remain here until I release you," he added, and ignoring a chorus of protest, walked briskly over and stepped into the smaller room.

As he closed the connecting door behind him, he saw Patrick Tait sitting erect on the couch, a glass of

spirits in his hand. Kennaway was hovering solicitously about.

"Ah, Mr. Tait," Duff remarked. "I am happy to
see you are better."

The old man nodded his head. "Nothing," he said.
"Nothing at all." The booming voice was a feeble
murmur now. "I am subject to these spells—that is
why I have this boy with me. He will take good care
of me, I'm sure. A little too much excitement,
perhaps. Murder, you know—I hardly bargained
for that."

"No, of course not," the inspector agreed, and sat
down. "If you're quite well enough now, sir——"

"Just a moment." Tait held up his hand. "You
will pardon my curiosity, I'm sure. But I still don't
know who was killed, Mr. Duff."

The detective gave him a searching look. "You're
sure you are strong enough——"

"Nonsense," Tait answered. "It means nothing
to me, one way or the other. To whom did this
appalling thing happen?"

"It happened to Mr. Hugh Morris Drake, of
Detroit," said Duff.

Tait bowed his head, and was silent for a moment.
"I knew him, very slightly, for many years," he
remarked at last. "A man of unsullied past,
Inspector, and with the most humanitarian impulses.
Why should anyone want to remove him? You are
faced by an interesting problem."

"And a difficult one," Duff added. "I should like
to discuss it with you for a moment. You occupy, I
believe, room 30, which is near the spot where the
unfortunate affair occurred. At what time did you
retire for the night?"

Tait looked at the boy. "About twelve, wasn't it,
Mark?"

Kennaway nodded. "Or a few minutes after, perhaps. You see, Inspector, I go to Mr. Tait's room every evening and read him to sleep. Last night I began to read at ten, and at a few minutes past twelve he was sleeping soundly. So I slipped out, and went to my own room on the second floor."

"What do you read, mostly?" asked Duff, interested.

"Mystery stories," Kennaway smiled.

"To a man with a bad heart? I should think the excitement——"

"Bah," put in Tait. "There's little enough excitement in the things. I have been a criminal lawyer for many years back home, and as far as the word murder goes——" He stopped suddenly.

"You were about to say," suggested Duff gently, "that murder is not, where you are concerned, an exciting topic."

"What if I were?" demanded Tait, rather warmly.

"I was only wondering," continued Duff, "why this particular murder brought on such a serious spell this morning?"

"Oh, well—meeting it in one's own life is quite different from reading about it in books. Or even from talking about it in a Court."

"Quite, quite," agreed Duff. He was silent, drumming with his fingers on the arm of his chair. Suddenly he turned, and with the speed and precision of a machine-gun began to fire questions at the lawyer.

"You heard nothing on that third floor last night?"

"Nothing."

"No outcry? No call for help?"

"Nothing, I tell you."

"No scream from an old man brutally attacked?"

"I have told you, sir——"

"I am asking you, Mr. Tait. I meet you in the

hall, and you appear to be strong and well. You have heard rumours of a murder, but you do not know who was killed. You walk with a firm step to the door of the room. You glance around the faces inside, and in another moment you are on the floor, in what seems a mortal attack——"

"They come like that——"

"Do they? Or did you see someone in that room——"

"No! No!"

"Some face, perhaps——"

"I tell you, no!"

The old man's eyes were blazing, the hand that held the glass trembled. Kennaway came forward.

"Inspector, I beg your pardon," he said quietly. "You are going too far. This man is ill——"

"I know," admitted Duff softly. "I'm sorry. I was wrong, and I apologize. I forgot, you see—I have my job to do, and I forgot." He arose. "None the less, Mr. Tait," he added, "I think that some surprising situation dawned upon you as you stood in that doorway this morning, and I intend to find out what it was."

"It is your privilege to think anything you please, sir," replied the old man, and as Duff went out he carried a picture of the great criminal lawyer, grey of face and breathing heavily, sitting on a Victorian sofa and defying Scotland Yard.

Hayley was waiting in the lobby. "Been through the rooms of every man in the party," he reported. "No fragment of watch-chain. No grey coat with a torn pocket. Nothing."

"Of course not," Duff replied. "Practically every mother's son of 'em has been out of the hotel this morning, and naturally any evidence like that went with them."

"I really must get back to my duties at Vine Street," Hayley went on. "You'll drop in after you've finished, old man?"

Duff nodded. "Go along. What was it that street musician was playing? *There's a Long, Long Trail A-Winding*. It's true, Hayley. Damned true."

"I'm very much afraid it is," the other answered. "See you at the station."

As Duff turned, his worried frown disappeared. Pamela Potter was beckoning to him from the room doorway. He went over to her at once.

"I was wondering, Inspector," she said, "if you want to see mother now, I believe I can arrange it."

"Good," he answered. "I'll go up with you in a moment." He stepped inside the room, and with one final warning against leaving Broome's Hotel for the present, he dismissed the assembled crowd. "I shall want to see the five remaining members of your party," he said to Lofton.

"Of course. The moment they come in, I'll let you know," Lofton agreed. He went on down the lobby, with Fenwick still arguing at his heels.

At the door of the suite occupied by Pamela Potter and her mother, Duff waited while the girl went inside. After several moments, during which he heard the sounds of a discussion going on beyond the door, the young woman returned and admitted him.

The shades were all drawn in the sitting-room where he now found himself. Gradually accustoming his eyes to the gloom, he perceived, on a *chaise longue* in the darkest corner, the figure of a woman. He stepped nearer.

"This is Inspector Duff, Mother," said Pamela Potter.

"Oh, yes," answered the woman faintly.

"Mrs. Potter," remarked the detective, feeling rather ill at ease, "I am extremely sorry to trouble you. But it cannot be avoided."

"I fancy not," she replied. "Won't you be seated? You won't mind the curtains being down, I hope. I'm afraid I'm not looking my best after this terrible shock."

"I have already talked with your daughter," continued Duff, moving a chair as close to the couch as he dared, "so I shan't be here more than a moment. If there is anything you can tell me about this affair, I assure you that it is very important you should do so. Your knowledge of the past is, of course, a trifle more extensive than that of Miss Pamela. Had your father any enemy?"

"Poor father," the woman said. "Pamela, the smelling salts." The girl produced a green bottle. "He was a saint, Mr.—er—what did you say his name was, my dear?"

"Mr. Duff, Mother."

"My father was a saint on earth if ever there was one. Not an enemy in the world. Really, I never heard of anything so senseless in all my life."

"But there must be sense in it somewhere, Mrs. Potter. It is for us to find out. Something in your father's past——" Duff paused, and took from his pocket a wash-leather bag. "I wonder if we might have that curtain up just a little way?" he added to the girl.

"Certainly," she said, and raised it.

"I'm sure I look a fright," protested the woman.

Duff held out the bag. "See, Madam—we found this on the bed beside your father."

"What in the world is it?"

"A simple little bag, Mrs. Potter, of wash-leather —chamois, I believe you call it." He poured some of the contents into the palm of his hand. "It was filled with a hundred or more pebbles, or small stones. Do they mean anything to you?"

"Certainly not. What do they mean to you?"

"Nothing, unfortunately. But—think, please, Mrs. Potter. Your father was never, for example, engaged in mining?"

"If he was, I never heard of it."

"These pebbles could have no connection with motor-cars?"

"How could they? Pamela—this—pillow——"

"I'll fix it, Mother."

Duff sighed, and returned the bag to his pocket. "You did not mingle, on the boat, with the other members of the travel party?"

"I never left my cabin," the woman said. "Pamela here was constantly wandering about. Talking with all sorts of people, when she should have been with me."

The detective took out the fragment of watch-chain, with the key attached. He handed it to the girl. "You did not, I suppose, happen to notice that chain on anyone with whom you talked?"

She examined it, and shook her head. "No. Who looks at a man's watch-chain?"

"The key means nothing to you?"

"Not a thing. I'm sorry."

"Please show it to your mother. Have you ever seen that chain or key before, Madam?"

The woman shrugged. "No, I haven't. The world is full of keys. You'll never get anywhere that way."

Duff restored this clue to his pocket and stood up. "That is all, I fancy," he remarked.

"The whole affair is utterly senseless, I tell you," the woman said complainingly. "There is no meaning to it. I hope you get to the bottom of it, but I don't believe you ever will."

"I shall try, at any rate," Duff assured her. And he went out, conscious of having met a vain and very shallow woman. The girl followed him into the hall.

"I thought it would be better for you to see mother," she said. "So you might understand that I happen to be spokesman for the family, sort of in charge, if you care to put it that way. Poor mother has never been strong."

"I understand," Duff answered. "I shall try not to trouble her again. It's you and I together, Miss Pamela."

"For grandfather's sake," she nodded gravely.

Duff returned to room 28. His two assistants were waiting, their paraphernalia packed.

"All finished, Mr. Duff," the finger-print man told him. "And very little, I fear, sir. This, however, is rather odd." He handed to the inspector the ear-phone of the dead man.

Duff took it. "What about this?"

"Not a print on it," the other said. "Not even that of the man on the bed. Wiped clean."

Duff stared at the instrument. "Wiped clean, eh? I wonder now. If the old gentleman and his ear-phone were in some other part of the hotel—if he was killed there, and then moved back here—and the ear-phone was carried back too——"

"I'm afraid I don't follow you, sir," the assistant remarked.

Duff smiled. "I was only thinking aloud. Come on, boys. We must be getting along." He returned the ear-phone to the table.

Though he did not suspect it at the moment, he had just held in his hand the key to his mystery. It had been Hugh Morris Drake's deafness that led to his murder in Broome's Hotel.

CHAPTER V

LUCHEON AT THE MONICO

WHEN they reached the ground floor, Duff directed his two assistants to return to the Yard at once with their findings, and then send the chauffeur back with the green car to await his own departure from Broome's. He began a round of the corridors, and came presently upon Doctor Lofton, who still had an upset and worried air.

"The other five members of the party are here," the doctor announced. "I've got them waiting in that same room. I hope you can see them now, as they are rather restless."

"At once," answered Duff amiably, and together with Lofton, entered the familiar room.

"You people know what has happened," the conductor said. "This is Inspector Duff, of Scotland Yard. He wants to talk with you. Inspector, Mr. and Mrs. Elmer Benbow, Mr. and Mrs. Max Minchin and Mrs. Latimer Luce."

The inspector stood regarding this oddly assorted group. Funny lot, these Americans, he was thinking: all types, all races, all classes of society, travelling together in apparent peace and amity. Well, that was the melting-pot for you. He was reaching for his note-book when the man named Elmer Benbow rushed up and pumped enthusiastically at his hand.

"Pleased to meet you, Inspector," he cried. "Say, this will be something to tell when we get back to

Akron. Mixed up in a murder—Scotland Yard and all that—just like I've been reading about in your English mystery novels. I read a lot of 'em. My wife tells me they won't improve my mind, but when I get home from the factory every night, I'm just about done up, and I don't want any of the heavy stuff——"

"Really?" broke in Duff. "Now, just a moment, Mr. Benbow." Benbow waited, his flow of talk momentarily checked. He was a plump, genial soul; the naïve, unsophisticated sort the British so love to think of as a typical American. In his hand he carried a motion picture camera. "What was the name of that place you expect to return to one day?" Duff asked.

"Akron. You've heard of Akron, haven't you? Akron, Ohio."

"I have now," Duff smiled. "On a pleasure trip, I presume?"

"Sure. Been talking about it for years. Business wasn't so good this winter, and my partner he says to me: 'Elmer, why don't you dig down into the old sock and take that trip around the world you've been boring me with for the past five years? That is,' he says, 'if there's anything in the sock after this Wall Street crash.' Well, there was plenty, for I'm no speculator. Good safe investment—that's my motto. I wasn't afraid to spend the money, because I knew that business was fundamentally sound and would turn the corner in time. I look for a return to normalcy—Harding came from Ohio, too—about the time we get back to Akron. You take the rediscount rate——"

Duff glanced at his watch. "I got you here, Mr. Benbow, to ask if you could throw any light on that unfortunate affair in room 28?"

"Unfortunate is right," Benbow replied. "You said it. As nice an old gentleman as you'd want to meet. One of the big men of the country, rich as all get out, and somebody goes and murders him. I tell you, it's a slap at American institutions——"

"You know nothing about it?"

"I didn't do it, if that's what you mean. We make too many tyres in Akron to go round killing off our best customers, the automobile men. No sir, this is all a big mystery to Nettie and me. You've met the wife?"

The detective bowed in the direction of Mrs. Benbow, a handsome, well-dressed woman who, not being needed at the factory, had evidently had more time for the refinements of life than had her husband.

"A great pleasure," he said. "I take it that you have been out this morning for a walk about London?"

Mr. Benbow held up the camera. "Wanted to get a few more shots on the good old film," he explained. "But say—the fog was terrible. I don't know how some of these pictures will turn out. It's my hobby, you might say. When I get back from this tour I expect to have enough movies to make a fool of contract bridge at our house for months to come. And that will be O.K. with me."

"So you spent the morning taking pictures?"

"I sure did. The sun came out a while ago, and then I really went to it. Nettie, she says to me: 'Elmer, we'll be late for that train,' so I finally tore myself away. I was out of film by that time, anyhow."

Duff sat studying his notes. "This Akron," he remarked. "Is it near a town called"—he flipped the pages of his note-book—"is it near Canton, Ohio?"

"Just a few miles between 'em," Benbow answered. "McKinley came from Canton, you know. Mother of presidents—that's what we call Ohio."

"Indeed," murmured Duff. He turned to Mrs. Latimer Luce, a keen-eyed old woman of indefinite age and cultivated bearing. "Mrs. Luce, have you anything to tell me about this murder?"

"I'm sorry, Inspector," she replied, "but I can tell you nothing." Her voice was low and pleasing. "I've been travelling most of my life, but this is a new experience."

"Where is your home?"

"Well—Pasadena, California—if I have one. I keep a house there, but I'm never in it. I'm always on the go. At my age, it gives me something to think about. New scenes, new faces. I'm so shocked over this Drake affair. A charming man."

"You've been out of the hotel this morning?"

"Yes—I breakfasted with an old friend in Curzon Street. An Englishwoman I knew when I lived in Shanghai, some twenty years ago."

Duff's eyes were on Mr. Max Minchin, and they lighted with interest. Mr. Minchin was a dark, stocky man with close-cropped hair and a protruding lower lip. He had shown no such enthusiasm as had Mr. Benbow at meeting a man from Scotland Yard. In fact, his manner was sullen, almost hostile.

"Where is your home, Mr. Minchin?" Duff inquired.

"What's that got to do with the case?" Minchin inquired. With one hairy hand he fingered a big diamond in his tie.

"Oh, tell him, Maxy," said his wife, who overflowed a red plush chair. "It ain't nothing to be ashamed of, I guess." She looked at Duff. "We're from Chicago," she explained.

"Well, Chicago it is," her husband remarked harshly. "And what of it, hey?"

"Have you any information about this murder?"

"I ain't no dick," said Maxy. "Do I look it? Dig up your own info. Me—I got nothing to say. My lawyers—well, they ain't here. I ain't talking. See what I mean?"

Duff glanced at Doctor Lofton. Some queer characters had certainly crept into Lofton's Round the World Tour this year. The doctor looked the other way obviously embarrassed.

Mrs. Minchin also appeared rather uncomfortable. "Come on, Maxy," she protested. "There's no use nursing a grouch. Nobody's accusing you."

"Patrol your own beat," he said. "I'll handle this."

"What have you been doing this morning?" Duff inquired.

"Buying," answered Minchin tersely.

"Look at that sparkler." Sadie held out a fat hand. "I seen it in a window, and I says to Maxy— if you want me to remember London, that's what I remember it by. And he come across, Maxy did. A free spender—ask the boys in Chicago——"

Duff sighed, and stood up. "I won't detain you any longer," he remarked to the little group. He explained again that no one must leave Broome's Hotel, and the five went out. Lofton turned to him.

"What's to be the outcome of this, Mr. Duff?" he wanted to know. "My tour is on schedule, of course, and a delay is going to tangle things frightfully. Boats, you understand. Boats all along the line, Naples, Port Said, Calcutta, Singapore. Have you any information that will entitle you to hold any of my party here? If so, hold them, and let the rest of us go on."

A puzzled frown was on Duff's usually serene face. "I'll be honest with you," he said. "I've never encountered a situation like this before. For the moment, I'm not quite certain about my future course of action. I must consult my superiors at the Yard. There'll be a coroner's inquest in the morning, which will no doubt be adjourned for a few weeks."

"A few weeks!" cried Lofton, in dismay.

"I'm sorry. I'll work as fast as I can, but I may tell you that until I've solved this thing, I'll be very reluctant to see your tour resume."

Lofton shrugged. "We'll see about that," he remarked.

"No doubt," Duff answered, and they parted.

Mark Kennaway was waiting in the hallway. "May I see you a moment, Inspector?" he said. They sat down on a near-by bench.

"You have information?" the detective inquired rather wearily.

"Of a sort—yes. It probably means nothing. But when I left Mr. Tait last night and went down to the second floor, I saw a man lurking about in the shadows opposite the lift."

"What man?"

"Oh, don't expect any big surprise, Inspector. It was no one but our old friend, Captain Keane."

"Ah, yes. Hoping to borrow a book, perhaps."

"Might have been. The night lift man is a great reader. I've caught him at it. But his library is not extensive."

Duff studied the young man's face. He rather liked Kennaway. "Tell me," he said, "how long have you known Mr. Tait?"

"Only since we started on this tour. You see, I'd just left Harvard Law School last June, and there didn't seem to be any great public clamour for my services. A friend told me about this job. I wanted to travel, and it seemed like a good chance to pick up pointers on the law—from a man like Tait."

"Picking any up?"

"No. He doesn't talk much. He demands a lot of attention, and if he's going to have many more attacks like that this morning, I may wish I was back in Boston."

"That was your first experience with one of Mr. Tait's attacks?"

"Yes—he's seemed perfectly all right up to now."

Duff leaned back on the hard bench, and began to fill his pipe. "How about giving me a few of your impressions about this crowd?" he suggested.

"Well, I'm not sure that I'm a particularly bright-eyed boy," Kennaway smiled. "I got to know a few of them on the boat. Variety seems to be the key-note of the expedition."

"Take Keane, for example."

"A four-flusher—and a snooper, too. I can't figure out where he got the cash for this. It's an expensive tour, you know."

"Was the dead man—Drake—in evidence on the boat?"

"Very much so. A harmless old gentleman. Sociably inclined, too, which made it a little hard for the rest of us. His deafness, you understand. However, I used to be a cheer leader at college, so I didn't mind."

"What do you think of Lofton?"

"He's a rather remote sort of person. An educated man—he knows his stuff. You should have heard his little talk on the Tower of London. He's worried and distrait most of the time. No wonder, With this outfit on his hands."

"And Honywood?" Duff lighted his pipe.

"Never saw him on the boat, until the last morning. I don't believe he ever left his cabin."

"He told me he got to know Mr. Drake quite well during the crossing."

"He was kidding you. I stood between them when we were drawing up to the pier at Southampton, and introduced them. I'm certain they'd never spoken to each other before."

"That's interesting," said Duff thoughtfully. "Did you take a good look at Honywood this morning?"

"I did," nodded Kennaway. "Like a man who'd seen a ghost, wasn't he? I was struck by it. Not well, I thought. But Lofton tells me these tours of his are very popular with the sick and the aged. I'm expecting to have a merry time of it."

"Miss Potter's a very charming girl," Duff suggested.

"So she is—and this is where she gets off. That would happen to me. It's the famous Kennaway luck."

"How about this fellow Minchin?"

The young man's face lighted. "Ah—the life of the party. Oozes money at every pore. He gave three champagne suppers on the way over. Nobody came but the Benbows, Keane and myself—and old Mrs. Luce. She's a good sport—never misses anything, she tells me. That is, we all went to the first soirée. After that, it was just Keane, and some terrible passengers Maxy picked up in the smoking-room."

"Party was too gay, eh?"

"Oh, not that. But after a good look at Maxy —well, even champagne can't atone for some hosts."

Duff laughed. "Thanks for the tip about Keane," he said, rising.

"Don't imagine it means anything," Kennaway answered. "Personally, I don't like to tell tales. But poor old Drake was so nice to everybody. Well —see you later, I imagine."

"You can't help yourself," Duff told him.

After a few words with the managing director of the hotel, the detective went out to the street. The little green car was waiting. As he was about to step into it, a cheery voice sounded behind him.

"Say, listen, Inspector. Just turn around and face me, will you?" Duff turned. Mr. Elmer Benbow was on the sidewalk, smiling broadly, his motion picture camera levelled and ready for action.

"Atta-boy," he cried. "Now, if you'll just take off the benny—the hat, you know—the light isn't so good——"

Cursing inwardly, Duff did as directed. The man from Akron held the machine before his eyes, and was turning a small crank.

"Let's have the little old smile—great—just for the folks back in Akron, you understand—now, move about a little—one hand on the door of the car—I guess this won't give them a kick back home—famous Scotland Yard inspector leaving Broome's Hotel in London, England, after investigating mysterious murder in round-the-world party—now, get into the car—that's the stuff—drive off—thanks!"

"Ass!" muttered Duff to his chauffeur. "Go around to Vine Street, please."

In a few moments they drew up before the police station that is hidden away in the heart of the West End, on a street so brief and unimportant it is unknown to most Londoners. Duff dismissed the car, and went inside. Hayley was in his room.

"Finished, old man?" he inquired.

Duff gave him a weary look. "I'll never be finished," he remarked. "Not with this case." He glanced at his watch. "It's getting on to twelve. Will you come have a spot of lunch with me, old chap?"

Hayley was willing, and presently they were seated at a table in the Monico Grill. After they had ordered, Duff sat for some moments staring into space.

"Cheerio!" said his friend at last.

"Cheerio, my hat!" Duff answered. "Was there ever a case like this before?"

"Why the gloom?" Hayley wanted to know. "A simple little matter of murder."

"The crime itself—yes, that's simple enough," Duff agreed. "And under ordinary conditions, no doubt eventually solved. But consider this, if you will." He took out his note-book. "I have here the names of some fifteen or more people, and among them is probably that of the man I want. So far, so good. But these people are travelling. Where? Around the world, if you please. All my neat list of suspects, in one compact party, and unless something unexpected happens at once, that party will be moving along. Paris, Naples, Port Said, Calcutta, Singapore—Lofton just told me all about it. Moving along, farther and farther away from the scene of the crime."

"But you can hold them here."

"Can I? I'm glad you think so. I don't. I can hold the murderer here, the moment I have sufficient evidence of his guilt. But I'll have to get that immediately, or there will be international complications—the American consulate—perhaps the Ambassador himself—a summons for me from the

Home Office. On what grounds do you hold these people? Where is your evidence that one of them committed the crime? I tell you, Hayley, there's no precedent for this situation. Such a thing has never happened before. And now that it's decided to happen at last, I'm the lucky lad it has happened to. Before I forget it, I must thank you for that."

Hayley laughed. "You were longing for another puzzle last night," he said.

Duff shook his head. "The calm man is the happy man," he murmured, as his roast beef and bottle of stout were put before him.

"You got nothing from your examination of the party?" Hayley asked.

"Not a thing that's definite. Nothing that links any one of them with the crime, even remotely. A few faint suspicions—yes. A few odd incidents. But nothing that I could hold anybody on—nothing that would convince the American Embassy—or even my own superintendent."

"There's an unholy lot of writing in that book of yours," commented the Vine Street man. "Why not run over the list you talked with? You might get a flash—who knows?"

Duff took up the note-book. "You were with me when I interviewed the first of them. Miss Pamela Potter, a pretty American girl, determined to find out who killed her grandfather. Our friend Doctor Lofton, who had a bit of a row with the old man last evening, and with whose strap the murder was committed. Mrs. Spicer, clever, quick, and not to be trapped by unexpected questions. Mr. Hony-wood——"

"Ah, yes, Honywood," put in Hayley. "From a look at his face, he's my choice."

"That's the stuff to give a jury!" replied Duff sarcastically. "He looked guilty. I think he did, myself, but what of it? Does that get me anywhere?"

"You talked with the others downstairs?"

"I did. I met the man in room 30—a Mr. Patrick Tait." He told of Tait's heart attack at the door of the room. Hayley looked grave.

"What do you make of that?" he inquired.

"I suspect he was startled by something—or someone—he saw in that room. But he's a famous criminal lawyer on the other side—probably a past master of the art of cross-examination. Get something out of him that he doesn't want to tell, and you're a wonder. On the other hand, he may have nothing to tell. His attacks, he assured me, come with just that suddenness."

"None the less, like Honywood, he should be kept in mind."

"Yes, he should. And there is one other." He explained about Captain Ronald Keane. "Up to something last night—heaven knows what. A fox in trousers, if I ever met one. Sly—and a self-confessed liar."

"And the others?"

Duff shook his head. "Nothing there, so far. A nice young chap who is Tait's companion. A polo player with a scar—a Mr. Vivian. Seems somehow connected with Mrs. Irene Spicer. A lame man named Ross, in the lumber trade on the West Coast. A brother and sister named Fenwick—the former a pompous little nobody who has been frightened to death, and seems determined to leave the tour."

"Oh, he does, does he?"

"Yes, but don't be deceived. It means nothing. He hasn't nerve enough to kill a rabbit. There are just four, Hayley—four to be watched. Honywood, Tait, Lofton and Keane."

"Then you didn't see the remaining members of the party?"

"Oh, yes I did. But they don't matter. A Mr. and Mrs. Benbow from a town called Akron—he runs a factory and is quite insane about a motion picture camera he carries with him. Going to look at his tour around the world when he gets home, and not before. But stop a bit—he told me Akron was near Canton, Ohio."

"Ah, yes—the address on the key?"

"Quite so. But he wasn't in this, I'm sure—he's not the type. Then there was a Mrs. Luce, an elderly woman who's been everywhere. An inevitable feature, I fancy, of all tours like Lofton's. And a pair from Chicago—quite terrible people, really—a Mr. and Mrs. Max Minchin——"

Hayley dropped his fork. "Minchin?" he repeated.

"Yes, that was the name. What about it?"

"Nothing, old chap, except that you have evidently overlooked a small item sent out from the Yard several days ago. This man Minchin, it seems, is one of Chicago's leading racketeers, who has recently been persuaded to interrupt—perhaps only temporarily—a charming career of violence and crime."

"That's interesting," nodded Duff.

"Yes, isn't it? In the course of his activities he has been forced to remove from this world, either personally or through his lieutenants, a number of business rivals—'to put them on the spot,' I believe the phrase goes. Recently, for some reason, he was moved to abdicate his throne and depart. The New York police suggested we keep a tender eye on him as he passes through. There are certain friends of his over here who, it is felt, might attempt to pay off old scores. Maxy Minchin, one of Chicago's first citizens."

Duff was thinking deeply. "I shall have another chat with him after lunch," he said. "Poor old Drake's body wasn't riddled with machine-gun bullets —but then, I fancy the atmosphere of Broome's might have its chastening effect even on a Maxy Minchin. Yes—I shall have a chat with the lad directly."

CHAPTER VI

ELEVEN O'CLOCK FROM VICTORIA

WHEN they had finished luncheon, Duff went with Hayley back to the Vine Street station. Together they unearthed a dusty and forgotten atlas of the world, and Duff turned at once to the map of the United States.

"Good lord," he exclaimed, "what a country! Too big for comfort, Hayley, if you ask me. Ah— I've found Chicago. Max Minchin's city. Now, where the deuce is Detroit?"

Hayley bent over his shoulder, and in a moment laid a finger on the Michigan city. "There you are," he remarked. "No distance at all, in a country the size of that. Well?"

Duff leaned back in his chair. "I wonder," he said slowly. "The two cities are close together, and that's a fact. Was there some connection between the Chicago gangster and the Detroit millionaire? Drake was an eminently respectable man—but you never can tell. Liquor, you know, Hayley—liquor comes over the border at Detroit. I learned that when I visited the States. And liquor has been, no doubt, at least a side-line with Mr. Minchin. Was there some feud—some ancient grudge? How could the pebbles figure in it? They may have been picked up from a lake shore. Oh, it all sounds devilish fantastic, I know—but in America, anything is possible. This angle will bear looking into, old chap."

With Hayley's encouragement, Duff set out for Broome's Hotel to look into it. Mr. Max Minchin sent down word that he would receive the inspector in his suite. The detective found the celebrated racketeer in shirt sleeves and slippers. His hair was rumpled, and he explained that he had been taking his afternoon siesta.

"Keeps me fresh—see what I mean?" he remarked. His manner was more friendly than it had been earlier in the day.

"I'm sorry to disturb you," Duff said. "But there are one or two matters——"

"I get you. The third degree for Maxy, hey?"

"Something which is not practised over here," Duff told him.

"Yeah?" remarked Maxy, shrugging. "Well, if it ain't, that's another thing you got on us Americans. Oh, we think we're on the up and up in our country, but I guess we got a few things to learn. Well, what's the dope, Officer? Make it snappy. We was just talking about going to a pitcher."

"There was a murder in this hotel last night," the detective began.

Maxy smiled. "And who do you think I am? Some hick that just got in from Cicero? I know there was a murder."

"From information received, I believe that murder is one of your avocations, Mr. Minchin."

"Try that again."

"One of your pastimes, if I may put it that way."

"Oh, I get you. Well, maybe I have had to rub out a few guys now and then. But they had it coming, get me? And them things don't concern you. They happened in the good old U.S.A."

"I know that. But now that there has been a killing in your immediate vicinity, I am—er—forced to——"

"You gotta prowl around me a little, hey? Well, go ahead. But you're wasting your breath."

"Had you ever met Mr. Drake before you took this journey?"

"Naw, I useta hear about him in Detroit—I went over there now and then. But I never had the pleasure of his acquaintance. I talked with him on the boat—a nice old guy. If you think I put that necktie on him, you're all wet."

"Kindest man in the world, Maxy is," his wife interposed. She was slowly unpacking a suit-case. "Maybe he has had to pass the word that put a few gorillas on the spot in his day, but they wasn't fit to live. He's out of the racket now, ain't you, Maxy?"

"Yeah—I'm out," her husband agreed. "Can you beat it, Officer? Here I am, retired from business, trying to get away from it all, just taking a pleasure trip like any other gentleman. And right off the bat a bird is bumped off almost in my lap, you might say." He sighed. "It just seems a guy can't get away from business, no matter where he goes," he added gloomily.

"At what time did you retire last night?" Duff inquired.

"When did we go to bed? Well—we went to a show. Real actors, get me? But slow—boy, I couldn't keep awake. When I take a chance and go to a theatre, I want action. This bunch was dead in their tracks. But we didn't have nothing else on, so we stuck it out. Come back here about eleven-thirty, and hit the hay at twelve. I don't know what happened in this hotel after that."

"Out of the racket, like he told you," added Sadie Minchin. "He got out for little Maxy's sake. That's our boy. He's at a military school, and doing fine. Just seemed to take naturally to guns."

Despite the fact that he was getting nowhere, Duff laughed. "I'm sorry to have troubled you," he said, rising. "But it's my duty to explore every path, you know."

"Sure," agreed Maxy affably. He stood up too. "You got your racket, just like I got mine—or did have. And say—listen. If I can help you any way, just hoist the signal. I can work with the bulls, or against 'em. This time I'm willing to work with 'em, get me? There don't seem no sense to this kick-off, and I ain't for that sort of thing when it don't mean nothing. Yes, sir." He patted Duff's broad back. "You want a hand on this, you call on Maxy Minchin."

Duff said good-bye, and went out into the corridor. He was not precisely thrilled over this offer of assistance from Mr. Minchin, but he reflected that indeed he seemed to need help from some quarter.

On the ground floor he encountered Doctor Lofton. With the conductor was a strikingly elegant young man, who carried a walking-stick and wore a gardenia in the buttonhole of his perfectly-fitting coat.

"Oh, Mr. Duff," Lofton greeted him. "Just the man we want to see. This is Mr. Gillow, an under-secretary at the American Embassy. He has called about last night's affair. Inspector Duff, of Scotland Yard."

Mr. Gillow was one of those youthful exquisites who are the pride of the embassies. They usually sleep all day, then change from pyjamas to evening clothes and dance all night for their country. He gave Duff a haughty nod.

"When is the inquest, Inspector?" he inquired.

"To-morrow at ten, I believe," Duff replied.

"Ah, yes. And if nothing new is disclosed at that time, I presume the doctor may continue his tour as planned?"

"I don't know about that," muttered the detective.

"Really? You have some evidence then, that will enable you to hold the doctor here?"

"Well—not precisely."

"You can hold some of his party, perhaps?"

"I shall hold them all."

Mr. Gillow lifted his eyebrows. "On what grounds?"

"Well—I—I——" For once the capable Duff was at a loss.

Mr. Gillow gave him a pitying smile. "Really, my dear fellow, you're being rather absurd," he remarked. "You can't do that sort of thing in England, and you know it. Unless you have more evidence after the inquest than you have now, your hands are tied. Doctor Lofton and I have been over the entire case."

"Someone in that party killed Hugh Drake," protested Duff stubbornly.

"Yes? And where is your proof? What was the motive behind the killing? You may be right, and on the other hand you may be talking nonsense. Perhaps some hotel prowler——"

"With a platinum watch-chain," Duff suggested.

"Someone who had no connection with the party —just as probable, my dear sir. Even more so, I should say. Evidence—you must have evidence, as you well know. Otherwise I am sorry to tell you that Doctor Lofton and his group will continue their tour at once."

"We'll see about that," Duff answered grimly. He left Mr. Gillow's presence with ill-concealed annoyance. He did not approve of elegant young men, and he disliked this one all the more because he foresaw that unless light broke quickly, Mr. Gillow's prediction would undoubtedly come true.

The inquest on the following morning revealed nothing that was not already known. The hotel servants and the members of the Lofton party repeated all they had told Duff on the previous day. The little bag of stones roused considerable interest, but since no explanation of it was available, the interest quickly died. There was obviously no evidence sufficient to hold anyone on, and the inquest was adjourned for three weeks. Duff saw Mr. Gillow smiling at him from across the room.

For the next few days Duff worked like a madman. Had someone in that travel party purchased a watch-chain to replace the one torn in the struggle at Broome's? He visited every jeweller's shop in the West End, and many in the City. Had the grey suit with a torn pocket been disposed of through a pawnshop or a second-hand clothier's? These, too, were thoroughly combed. Or had the suit been made up into a bundle and carelessly tossed away? Every lost package that turned up in that great city was personally examined by Duff. Nothing came of his efforts. His face grew stern, his eyes weary. Rumblings from the region above him warned him that his time was short, that Lofton was preparing to move on.

Mrs. Potter and her daughter were planning to sail for home on Friday, just one week after the morning when Drake's body was discovered in that room at Broome's. On Thursday evening Duff had a final talk with the two women. The mother seemed more helpless and lost than ever; the girl was silent and thoughtful. With a feeling of chagrin such as he had never known before, the inspector bade them good-bye.

When, after a fruitless day of it, he came back to his office at the Yard late on Friday afternoon, he was startled to find Pamela Potter waiting for him. With her was Mrs. Latimer Luce.

"Hello," Duff cried. "Thought you'd sailed, Miss Potter?"

She shook her head. "I couldn't. With everything unsolved—up in the air—no answer to our question. No—I engaged a maid for mother, and sent her home without me. I'm going on with the tour."

The detective had heard that American girls did pretty much as they pleased, but he was none the less surprised. "And what did your mother say to that?" he inquired.

"Oh—she was horrified, of course. But I'm sorry to tell you I've horrified her so often, she's rather used to it now. Mrs. Luce here agreed to take up the old-fashioned rôle of chaperon—you've met Mrs. Luce?"

"Of course," Duff nodded. "I beg your pardon, Madam. I was so taken back at seeing Miss Pamela——"

"I understand," smiled the old lady. "The girl's got spirit, hasn't she? Well, I like spirit. Always did. Her mother and I happened to have mutual friends, so I helped put it over. Why not? Naturally the child is curious. So am I. Give five thousand dollars right now to know who killed Hugh Drake, and why."

"Two questions that are not going to be so easy to answer," Duff told her.

"No, I judge not. Sorry for you. Hard case. I

don't know whether you're aware of it or not, but Lofton's round-the-world party is moving on next Monday morning."

Duff's heart sank. "I expected it," he said. "And I can assure you that it's a bit of bad news for me."

"Cheer up," the old lady answered. "Nothing's as bad as it seems to be—I know. I've tested that out pretty well in the past seventy-two years. Pamela and I will go along—with eyes and ears open. Wide open—eh, my dear?"

The girl nodded. "We must get to the bottom of this. I shan't rest until we do."

"Bravo!" Duff said. "I'll appoint you both to my staff. The entire party's going, I presume?"

"Every last one of them," Mrs. Luce replied. "We had a meeting at the hotel this morning. That little Fenwick creature tried to start a mutiny, but it failed. It ought to fail. Never had any use for anyone who can't see a thing through. Speaking for myself, I'd go on if they'd all been murdered but me."

"So Fenwick kicked up a row?" Duff reflected aloud. "I should have been invited to that meeting."

"Lofton didn't want you," the woman told him. "Funny man, Lofton, I can't understand him. And I don't like men I can't understand. Well, anyhow, Fenwick tried to wreck the tour, but when he saw he was alone, he let the rest shame him out of it. So we're all going on—just one great big happy family —and a murderer right in the middle of it, or I miss my guess."

Duff smiled at her. "You don't usually miss your guess, I fancy," he said.

"Not as a rule. And I'm not missing it this time, am I?"

"I'm inclined to think you're not," he assured her.

She stood up. "Well, I've been travelling all my life. Getting a little sick of it, but this is like a tonic. I expect to enjoy Doctor Lofton's tour to the hilt—oh, I'm sorry, my dear."

"It's quite all right," smiled Pamela Potter, rising too. "I'm not going along as a skeleton at the feast. I'm going along to help solve a mystery if I can, and I mean to be cheerful despite the nature of that mystery."

Duff regarded her with keen approval. "You're a sportsman, Miss Potter," he remarked. "It's put new heart in me to know that you are continuing with the tour. I shall see you both before you leave on Monday—and I'll be in touch with you after that too, no doubt."

When the two women had gone, the inspector found a memorandum on his desk, requesting him to see his superior at once. He went to the superintendent's office, knowing in advance the reason for the summons.

"It couldn't be avoided, Mr. Duff," the superintendent said. "The American Ambassador himself took an interest in the matter. We have been forced to grant that party permission to go on. Don't look so disappointed, my boy. There are, you know, such things as treaties of extradition."

Duff shook his head. "The case that isn't solved promptly is likely to go unsolved," he remarked.

"An exploded theory. Look over the records of the Yard. Think of the months spent on many important cases. For example—the Crippen affair."

"All the same, sir, it's hard to stand aside and watch that crowd wander off heaven knows where."

"I appreciate your position, my boy. You wouldn't care to hold this fellow Keane? We might arrange for a warrant."

"There'd be nothing in that, sir, I'm sure. I'd

rather have Honywood, or even Tait. But of course
I have nothing to take them on."

"How about Mr. Max Minchin?"

"Poor chap. Trying to put all this sort of thing
behind him."

The superintendent shrugged. "Well, there you
are. You will, of course, secure from the conductor a
complete itinerary of the tour, with the understanding
that he must notify you at once of any change. Also,
he must let you know immediately if any members of
the party drop out en route."

"Of course, sir," nodded Duff. "A fat lot of good
that will do," he reflected.

"For the present, you had better pursue your
inquiries in London," his superior continued. "If
they come to nothing, we shall send a man to keep an
eye on the party—someone who is unknown to them.
I'm afraid that bars you, Mr. Duff."

"I know it does, sir," the inspector replied.

He went back to his desk, baffled and in despair.
But he did not let his state of mind interfere with his
activities, which were many and varied. All through
Saturday, and even under the handicap of Sunday,
when all shops were closed, he searched and questioned
and studied his problem. Hayley lent his staff and
his cheery comment. It was all to no avail. The
murder in Broome's Hotel remained as far from
solution as it had been on the foggy morning when
the little green car first drew up before that respectable
door.

On Monday morning, Duff went to Victoria Station
on as odd a mission as a Scotland Yard detective had
ever been called upon to perform. He was there to
say good-bye to a round-the-world party, to shake
hands with them all and wish them a pleasant journey.
And among the hands he must shake, he was quite

certain in his mind, was one of the pair that had strangled Hugh Morris Drake in Broome's Hotel on the early morning of February seventh.

As he came on to the platform beside the eleven o'clock train for Dover, Doctor Lofton greeted him cordially. There was elation in the conductor's bearing; he was like a schoolboy off on a long vacation. He gripped Duff warmly by the hand.

"Sorry we must tear ourselves away," he remarked, with what was for him a near approach to levity. "But a tour is a tour, you know. You have our schedule, and any time you care to join us, we'll make you welcome. Eh, Mr. Benbow?"

Duff had heard a grinding sound at his back, and turned to find Benbow busy with his eternal camera. The man from Akron shifted it quickly to his left hand, and gave Duff his right.

"Sorry you fell down on the case," he said, with amiable tactlessness. "Never knew a Scotland Yard man to do that—in the books. But this isn't a book, and I guess things are different in real life, eh?"

"I think it's a bit early to give up hope," Duff replied. "By the way, Mr. Benbow——" He took a key and three links of a chain from his pocket. "Have you seen this before?"

"Saw it at the inquest—but from a distance," Benbow told him. He took the key and examined it. "Do you know what I think this is, Inspector?"

"I should be happy to learn."

"Well, it's a key to a safety-deposit box in some American bank," the man from Akron explained. "The only kind of key, except for luggage, that a fellow would be likely to carry on a tour like this. A bank over on our side usually gives a depositor two keys, so maybe there's a duplicate floating about somewhere."

Duff took the clue and studied it with new interest. "And this name—the Dietrich Safe and Lock Company, Canton, Ohio—that ought to mean the bank is somewhere in your neighbourhood?"

"No, not at all. It's a big concern. They sell lock-boxes and keys all over the States. Might be San Francisco, or Boston, or New York—anywhere. But if I were you, I'd think about that key."

"I shall," Duff told him. "Of course, it may have been placed in the dead man's hand to mislead me."

Benbow was busy with his camera, and looked up quickly. "Never thought of that," he admitted.

His wife came up. "Oh, for pity's sake, Elmer," she said. "Put that camera away. You're getting on my nerves."

"Why?" he answered plaintively. "There's nothing I have to look at here, is there? I thought it was just a railroad station. Or is it a ruined castle or a museum, or something? I'm getting so I don't know one from the other."

Patrick Tait and his young companion strolled up. The old man appeared to be in glowing health, his step was firm, his cheeks ruddy. Somehow, a bit of Lofton's elation seemed to be reflected in his face.

"Well, Inspector," he remarked, "this is good-bye, I imagine. Sorry you haven't had better luck. But of course you won't give up."

"Hardly," Duff returned, looking him steadily in the eye. "It's not our habit, at the Yard."

Tait met the gaze for a moment, then his eyes wandered up and down the platform. "Ah, yes," he murmured. "That's what I've always understood."

The detective turned to Kennaway. "Miss Potter is going with you, after all," he said.

Kennaway laughed. "So I hear. More of the

famous Kennaway luck. We have all kinds—good
and bad."

The detective crossed the platform to where Mrs.
Spicer and Stuart Vivian were standing. Vivian's
good-bye was cool and unfriendly, and the woman was
not very cordial either. A lack of cordiality, however,
was not evident in the farewell of Captain Ronald
Keane, who stood near by. He rather overdid the
handshaking, Duff thought. So did John Ross, the
lame man, but in the latter instance Duff did not so
much mind the enthusiasm.

"Hope to see you on the Pacific coast some day,"
Ross told him.

"Perhaps," nodded the inspector.

"A little more interest, please," smiled the other.
"I certainly would like to introduce you to our redwoods. Finest trees in the world."

Honywood appeared on the platform. "It isn't
every party that is seen off by a Scotland Yard
inspector," he said. His tone attempted lightness,
but there was an odd look in his eyes, and the hand
he gave to Duff was damp and clammy.

The detective had a few final words with Mrs. Luce
and Pamela Potter, and then with the Minchins. He
looked at his watch, and walked over to Lofton.
"Three minutes," he remarked. "Where are the
Fenwicks?"

The doctor looked uneasily down the platform. "I
don't know. They agreed to be here."

A minute passed. All save Lofton were now aboard
the train. Suddenly, at the far end of the station, the
Fenwicks appeared, running. They arrived quite out
of breath.

"Hello," said Duff. "Afraid you weren't coming."

"Oh—we're—coming," panted Fenwick. His sister
climbed aboard. "Going a little way, anyhow. But

if there's any more funny business, we leave the party"—he snapped his fingers—"like that."

"There will be no more funny business," Lofton assured him firmly.

"I'm glad you're going along," Fenwick said to Duff.

"But I'm not," the detective smiled.

"What—not going?" The little man stared at Duff, open-mouthed. "You mean you're dropping the whole matter?" Doors were slamming all along the platform.

"Get in, Mr. Fenwick," Lofton cried, and half lifted him aboard. "Good-bye, Inspector."

The train began to move. For as long as he could see it, Duff stood there on the platform staring after it. Someone in that party—that party moving on to Paris—to Italy—to Egypt—to India—to the ends of the earth——

The detective turned away with a sigh. For one imaginative moment he wished he might be aboard the express, invisible, watching the expressions of those various faces that interested him so much.

If he had been there, he might have come upon Walter Honywood, alone in a compartment, his face pressed close to the window as he watched the drab backyards of London drift by. His lips were parted, his eyes staring, and little beads of moisture were on his forehead.

The door of the compartment opened—almost noiselessly, but not quite. Just enough sound so that Honywood turned in a flash, and on his face was a surprising look of terror. "Oh, hello," he said.

"Hello," returned Fenwick. He advanced into the compartment, followed by his silent colourless sister. "May we come in here? We were late—all the seats taken——"

Honywood wet his lips with his tongue. "Come in, by all means," he said.

The Fenwicks sat down. The unlovely side of the great grey city continued to glide by the windows.

"Well," remarked Fenwick at last, "we're leaving London. Thank God for that."

"Yes, we're leaving London," Honywood repeated. He took out a handkerchief and mopped his brow. The look of terror was gradually fading from his face.

CHAPTER VII

AN ADMIRER OF SCOTLAND YARD

ON the following Thursday night, Inspector Duff again walked into Hayley's room at the Vine Street station. The divisional inspector took one look at his old friend, and smiled sympathetically.

"I don't need to ask," he remarked.

Duff took off coat and hat and tossed them on to a chair, then slumped into another beside Hayley's desk.

"Do I show it as plainly as that?" he said. "Well, it's true, old chap. Not a thing, Hayley, not a blessed thing. I've hung round Broome's Hotel until I'm beginning to feel a hundred years old myself. I've scoured the shops until my feet ache. A clever lad, the murderer of Hugh Morris Drake. The trail is cold."

"You're about done up," Hayley told him. "Relax a bit, my boy, and try some entirely different method of approach."

"I'm thinking of taking a new tack," Duff nodded. "There's this key we removed from the dead man's hand." He repeated to his friend what Benbow had told him about its probable nature. "There was, very likely, a duplicate, and the murderer may have that with him now. I might follow up the party, and search the luggage of everyone in it. But they know who I am—the difficulties would be enormous. Even if we sent someone unknown to them, his task would be a tremendous one. I might go to the States, and visit the home town of every man in the party, seeking to ascertain if any one of them has a safety box at his bank numbered 3260. Difficulties there, too. But I talked it over with the chief this afternoon, and he favours it."

"Then you'll be leaving soon for America?" Hayley inquired.

"I may. We'll decide to-morrow. But good lord —what a job that looks."

"I know," Hayley nodded. "But it seems to me the wise course. If the murderer did have a duplicate key, he has long since thrown it away."

Duff shook his head. "Not at all," he objected. "I don't believe he has. To do so would be to arrive back at his bank and report the loss of both keys. That would be inviting a dangerous amount of attention to an affair he no doubt wants kept very dark. No, I am certain—if he is the man I think he is—that he will hold on to the duplicate through thick and thin. But he will hide it, Hayley. It's a small object and can be cleverly concealed. So cleverly, perhaps, that a search for it on our part would be hopeless. The chief is right—the American journey is clearly indicated—though I dread the whole idea. However, I've reached the end of my string here, and I'm damned if I'll give up."

"It wouldn't be like you if you did," Hayley replied. "Take heart, old man. I never knew a case to get on your nerves before. Why worry— you're certain to win out in the end. What was it Inspector Chan said? Success will always walk smiling at your side. He sensed it, and according to him, the Chinese are psychic people."

A slow smile spread over Duff's face. "Good old Charlie. I wish I had him with me on this case." He stopped. "I noticed Honolulu on the itinerary of the tour," he added thoughtfully. "However, that's a long time yet. And much may happen before Doctor Lofton's none too select group comes into Honolulu harbour." He rose with a sudden air of determination.

"Going already?" Hayley asked.

"Yes. Much as I enjoy your society, old chap, it just flashed into my mind that I'm getting nowhere sitting here. Perseverance—that was Chan's method. Patience, hard work and perseverance. I'm going to make one more stab at Broome's Hotel. There may be something there—something I haven't got—and if there is, I'm going to get it or die in the attempt."

"Spoken like your old self," his friend answered. "Go to it, and the best of luck."

Once again Inspector Duff was walking down Piccadilly. The cold drizzle of the afternoon had turned into a fitful snowfall. Just enough to make his footing on the pavement uncertain, to penetrate down his collar and annoy him. Under his breath he cursed the English climate.

The night porter was on duty at the desk just inside the Half Moon Street entrance of Broome's Hotel. He put aside his evening paper and regarded the inspector benevolently over his spectacles.

"Good evening, sir," he said. "My word—is it snowing?"

"It's trying to," Duff answered. "Look here, you and I haven't seen much of each other. You recall the night when the American was killed in room 28?"

"I am not likely to forget it, sir. A most disturbing occurrence. In all my years at Broome's——"

"Yes, yes, of course. Have you thought much about that night lately? Have you recalled any incident about which you haven't told me?"

"There was one thing, sir. I meant to speak to

you about it if I saw you again. I'm afraid that so far there has been no mention of the cablegram."

"What cablegram?"

"The one that came in about ten o'clock, sir. Addressed to Mr. Hugh Morris Drake."

"There was a cablegram addressed to Mr. Drake? Who received it?"

"I did, sir."

"And who took it up to his room?"

"Martin, the floor waiter. He was just going off for the night, and none of the bell-boys was available. So I asked Martin if he would kindly take it up to Mr. Drake——"

"Where is Martin now?"

"I don't know, sir. Perhaps he is still at supper in the servants' dining-room. I can send a messenger, if you wish——"

But Duff had already beckoned to a venerable bell-boy who was resting comfortably on a bench farther down the hall. "Quick," he cried. He handed the old man a shilling. "Get Martin, the floor waiter, for me before he leaves the hotel. Try the servants' dining-room."

The old man disappeared with surprising speed, and Duff again addressed the night porter. "I should have heard of this before," he said sternly.

"Do you really think it's important, sir?" inquired the porter blandly.

"Everything is important in a matter of this sort."

"Ah, sir, you've had so much more experience with such matters than we have. I was naturally a bit upset and——"

The detective turned away, for Martin had arrived. His jaws were still moving, so suddenly had he left the table. "You want——" He swallowed. "You want me, sir?"

"I do." Duff was all action now; his words crisp and clear. "About ten o'clock on the night Mr. Hugh Morris Drake was murdered in room 28, you delivered a cablegram to his room?"

He stopped, surprised. For the usually ruddy Martin had gone white and seemed about to collapse on the spot.

"I did, sir," he managed to say.

"You took it up, I presume, and knocked at Mr. Drake's door? Then what happened?"

"Why—why, Mr. Drake, sir, he came to the door and took the envelope. He thanked me, and gave me a tip. A generous one. Then I came away."

"That is all?"

"Yes, sir. Yes, sir. Quite all."

Duff seized the young man rather roughly by the arm. He meant it to be rough—all the authority of Scotland Yard behind it. The waiter cringed.

"Come with me," Duff said. He pushed the servant along to the manager's office, deserted and in semi-darkness. Thrusting Martin into a chair, he fumbled for the switch of the lamp on the manager's desk, and turned it on. Moving the lamp so that the full glare of it fell on the servant, he slammed shut the door and sat down in a chair facing the young man.

"You're lying, Martin," he began. "And by heaven, I'm in no mood to stand it. I've dilly-dallied over this case as long as I mean to. You're lying— a blind man would know it. But you've finished now. The truth from you, my boy, or by gad——"

"Yes, sir," muttered the waiter. He whimpered a little. "I'm sorry, sir. My wife has been telling me I ought to give you—the whole story. She's been nagging me. 'Tell him,' she says. But I—I didn't know what to do. You see, I'd taken the hundred pounds."

"What hundred pounds?"

"The hundred pounds Mr. Honywood gave me, sir."

"Honywood gave you money? What for?"

"You won't send me to prison, Inspector——"

"I'll lock you up in a minute if you don't talk, and talk fast."

"I know I've done wrong, sir—but a hundred pounds is a lot of money. And when I accepted it, I didn't know anything about the murder."

"Why did Honywood give you a hundred pounds? Stop a bit. Take it from the beginning. The truth, or I'll arrest you at once. You went upstairs with that cablegram for Mr. Drake. You knocked on the door of room 28. Then what?"

"The door opened, sir."

"Yes, of course. Who opened it? Drake?"

"No, sir."

"What! Who, then?"

"Mr. Honywood opened it, sir. The gentleman who had room 29."

"So Honywood opened Drake's door? What did he say?"

"I gave him the envelope. 'It's for Mr. Drake,' I told him. He looked at it. 'Oh, yes,' he said, and handed it back. 'You will find Mr. Drake in room 29, Martin. We have changed rooms for the night.'"

Duff's heart leaped at the words. A feeling of exultation, so long in coming, swept over him. "Yes," he remarked. "Then what?"

"I knocked on the door of room 29—Mr. Honywood's room—and after a time Mr. Drake came to the door. He was wearing his pyjamas, sir. He took the cablegram, thanked me, and gave me a tip. So I came away."

"And the hundred pounds?"

"At seven in the morning when I went on duty, Mr. Honywood rang for me. He was back in room 29 again, sir. He asked me not to say anything about the change of rooms the night before. And he handed me two fifty-pound notes. Fair took my breath away, he did. So I promised—gave him my word. At a quarter before eight, I found Mr. Drake murdered in room 28. I was frightened, and no mistake. I—it seemed I couldn't think, sir—I was that frightened. I met Mr. Honywood in the hall. 'I have your word,' he reminded me. 'I swear I had nothing to do with the murder. You stick to your promise, Martin, and you won't regret it.'"

"So you stuck to your promise," said Duff accusingly.

"I'm—I'm sorry, sir. No one asked me about the cablegram. If they had, things might have been different. I was afraid, sir—it seemed best just to keep mum. When I got home, my wife said I'd done wrong. She's been begging me to tell."

"You follow her advice in the future," Duff advised. "You've disgraced Broome's Hotel."

Martin's face paled again. "Don't say that, sir. What are you going to do to me?"

Duff rose. In spite of all the delay this weak young man had caused him, he found it difficult to view the matter as sternly as he should. This was the sort of news he had been waiting for, praying for, and now that it had come, his heart was light and he was extremely happy.

"I have no time for you," he said. "What you have told me here you are not to repeat unless I ask you to do so. Is that understood?"

"Perfectly, sir."

"You are not to leave your present position or home without advising me of your whereabouts. With these restrictions, things go on as usual. Tell your wife she was right, and give her my compliments."

He left the waiter wilted and perspiring in the manager's office, and walked with jaunty air to the street. Pleasant, a bit of snow after so much rain. Just what London needed. Pretty good climate, the English. The very sort to keep a man on his toes, full of vim and energy. Martin's story, it will be seen, had completely altered Inspector Duff's outlook on life.

He walked along, considering what the waiter had told him. "Mr. Drake is in room 29, Martin. We have changed rooms for the night." In that case, Drake must have been murdered in room 29. But in the morning, he was back in his own bed in room 28. Well, it all fitted in with what Duff had thought at the time. "Something tells me that Hugh Morris Drake was murdered elsewhere," he had said. That something had been right. Duff had been right. Not such a fool, if you came right down to it. The inspector's spirits soared.

Back in his own bed in the morning. Who had put him there? Honywood, of course. Who had murdered him? Who but Honywood?

But stop a bit. If Honywood intended murder, why the change in rooms? A ruse, perhaps, to get the door open between them and free access to the person of Hugh Morris Drake. Yet he had already stolen the housekeeper's key. Such a ruse was hardly necessary. And if he was intending murder, would he have calmly involved himself by telling Martin of the change of rooms?

No, he wouldn't. Duff came down a bit from the clouds. The matter didn't work out quite so neatly as he had thought it would. Puzzles still. But one thing was certain, Honywood was mixed up in it

somehow.   Martin's story would bring the New York
millionaire back from the Continent in a hurry.
And once they had him again at the Yard, the skein
would begin to unravel.

Duff went back and tried again.   It didn't appear
likely that Honywood had intended murder when he
changed rooms with Hugh Morris Drake, and then
told Martin what had been done.   No—the resolution
must come later.   Perhaps that cablegram——

Going to the near-by cable office, the detective
found it about to close for the night.   After a show
of authority he was handed a copy of the message
Drake had received on the evening of February 6.
It was merely a business communication.   "Directors
voted price increase in effect July first hope you
approve."   The cablegram was not the answer,
evidently.   But Duff blessed that cablegram none
the less.

Taking a taxi to the Yard, he called the home of
his superior.   That gentleman, torn away from a
game of bridge, was inclined at first to be short and
crisp.   But as Duff's story unrolled, he began to
share the excitement of his subordinate.

"Where is the travel party now?" he inquired.

"According to the schedule, sir, they are leaving
Paris for Nice to-night.   They will be in Nice for
three days."

"Good.   You will take the regular Riviera Express
from Victoria in the morning.   Nothing to be gained
by starting sooner.   That will bring you into Nice
early on Saturday.   I shall see you to-morrow before
you leave.   Congratulations, my boy.   We appear to
be getting somewhere at last."

And the superintendent went back to play four
hearts, doubled.

After a happy chat with Hayley over the telephone,

Duff went to his rooms and packed a bag. At eight in the morning he was in the superintendent's office. His superior took a package of bank-notes from the safe, where money was kept for just such occasions, and handed it over.

"You have your seat booked, I presume?"

"Yes, sir. I fixed that on my way here."

"Have the French police hold Honywood for us in Nice until I can get the necessary papers. I'm taking the matter up with the Home Office at once. Good-bye, Mr. Duff, and the best of luck."

Action was what Duff had wanted, and he rode down to Dover in high spirits. The channel crossing was rough, but that meant nothing to him. By evening they were on the outskirts of Paris, and the train began its slow journey round the ceinture, with many interminable stops. Duff was relieved when they finally reached the Gare de Lyon, and the road to the Riviera stretched straight before them.

As he sat enjoying an excellent dinner, and watching the last walls of Paris disappear into the dusk, he thought deeply about Mr. Walter Honywood. No wonder the man had been in such a funk the morning after the murder. If only, Duff reflected, he might have arrested him then, saved himself this long journey. But things were going to come out all right in the end. Silly to worry—they usually did. Soon he would be coming back along this same route, and Honywood would be with him. Perhaps the man's confession would be in the detective's pocket. Not a strong character, Honywood. Not the sort to hold out in the face of all Duff knew now.

The next morning, at a little before ten, Duff's taxi drew up before the gateway leading to the Hôtel Excelsior Grand in Nice. This was the name of the hostelry he had found on the detailed itinerary left with him by Lofton. The Excelsior Grand was an enormous rambling affair, set high on a hill over-looking the city and the aquamarine sea, in the midst of extensive grounds. Duff noted orange and olive trees, with here and there a tall cypress, gloomy even under the gracious Riviera sun. The taxi man sounded his asthmatic horn, and after some delay a bell-boy appeared and took the detective's bag. Duff followed the servant up the gravel walk that led to the hotel's side entrance. Giant palms were overhead, and bordering the walk were beds of fragrant Parma violets.

The first person the inspector saw when he entered the hotel lobby was the bearded Doctor Lofton. The second person he noted gave him a distinct shock. This was a Frenchman, also bearded, and as resplen-dent in gold lace and gorgeous uniform as the doorman of a Ritz hotel. The two men were in close converse, their beards almost touching, and Lofton looked worried. He glanced up and saw Duff.

"Ah, Inspector," he remarked, and a shadow crossed his face. "You made quick time. I scarcely expected you so soon."

"You expected me?" Duff returned, puzzled.

"Naturally. If you please, Monsieur le Com-missaire. May I present Inspector Duff, of Scotland Yard, Monsieur Henrique?" He turned to Duff. "This gentleman, as you have no doubt gathered from his uniform, is the local commissary of police."

The Frenchman rushed over to Duff and grasped his hand. "I am so happy for this meeting. Me, I am a fond admirer of Scotland Yard. I beg of you that you will not judge harshly in this case, Monsieur Duff. Consider if you will the stupidity with which we have been faced. Is the body left as it fell? No. Is the pistol permitted to lie in peace where it was?

Not for a moment. All—all have touched it—the concierge, two bell-boys, a clerk—five or six people. With what result? In the matter of finger-prints we are helpless. Is it possible that you can picture such stupidity——"

"One moment, please," Duff broke in. "A body? A pistol?" He turned to Lofton. "Tell me what has happened."

"You don't know?" Lofton asked.

"Of course not."

"But I thought—however, it is too soon. I understand now. You were already on your way. Well, Inspector, you arrive most opportunely. Poor Walter Honywood killed himself in the grounds of this hotel last night."

For a moment Duff said nothing. Walter Honywood had killed himself—while Scotland Yard moved forward to take him. A guilty conscience, no doubt. Killed Drake, and then himself. The case was over. But Duff felt no elation; he felt instead an unpleasant sensation of being let down. This was too easy. Too easy altogether.

"But did Monsieur Honywood finish himself?" the commissary was saying. "Alas, Inspector Duff, we cannot be certain. The finger-prints on the pistol —destroyed by the stupidity of the hotel employees, as I have related to you. True—it lay by his side, as though fallen from a dying hand. No one was seen near that vicinity. But even so, I welcome eagerly the opinion of a man from Scotland Yard."

"You have found no note of farewell? No message of any sort?"

"Alas, no. Last night we searched his apartment. To-day I am here to repeat the process. I should be overjoyed if you would be kind enough to join me."

"I'll be with you in a moment," Duff said, with an air of dismissal.

The commissary bowed and retired.

Duff turned at once to Doctor Lofton. "Please tell me all you know about this," he directed. They sat down together on a sofa.

"I gave the party only three days in Paris," Lofton began. "Trying to make up for the time lost in London, you see. We arrived here yesterday morning. In the afternoon Honywood decided to drive over to Monte Carlo. He invited Mrs. Luce and Miss Pamela Potter to go with him. At six o'clock last evening I was here in the lobby talking with Fenwick —the prize pest of the tour, between you and me —when I saw Mrs. Luce and the girl enter that side door over there. I asked them about their drive, and they said they'd enjoyed it immensely. Honywood, they told me, was out at the gate paying off the driver of the car—he would be in in a moment. They went on upstairs. Fenwick continued to pester me. There was the sound of a sharp report from outside, but I paid no attention. I thought it the exhaust of a car, or possibly a bursting tyre—you know how they drive over here. In another moment Mrs. Luce came rushing from the lift. She's the calmest of women ordinarily, and I was struck by her appearance. She seemed to be in a state of high excitement——"

"One moment," Duff put in. "Have you told any of this to the commissary of police?"

"No. I thought it better to save it for you."

"Good. Go on. Mrs. Luce was upset——"

"Extremely so. She hurried up to me. 'Has Mr. Honywood come in yet?' she demanded. I stared at her. 'Mrs. Luce—what has happened?' I cried. 'A great deal has happened.' she replied.

'I must see Mr. Honywood at once. What can be keeping him?' The memory of that sharp report— like a shot, I realized it now—came back to me. I rushed out, followed by Mrs. Luce. We found the gardens in darkness, dusk had fallen, these economical French had not yet lighted the lamps. About half-way down the walk we came upon Walter Honywood, lying partly on the walk, partly on the floral border. He was shot unerringly through the heart, the pistol lay at his side, near his right hand.'

"Suicide?" said Duff, giving the doctor a searching look.

"I believe so."

"You want to believe so."

"Naturally. It would be better——" Lofton stopped. Mrs. Luce was standing just back of the sofa.

"Suicide, your grandmother," she remarked briskly. "Good morning, Inspector Duff. You're wanted here. Murder again."

"Murder?" Duff repeated.

"Absolutely," returned the old lady. "I'll tell you in a moment why I think so. Oh, you needn't look so shocked, Doctor Lofton. Another member of your party has been killed, and what worries me is, will there be enough of us to supply the demand? It's still quite some distance around the world."

CHAPTER VIII

FOG ON THE RIVIERA

LOFTON was standing, and he began to pace nervously back and forth over a patch of bright sunlight that lay on the Persian rug. He was chewing savagely at the ends of his moustache, a habit he had when perturbed. Mrs. Luce wished he wouldn't do it.

"I can't believe it," the conductor cried. "It's incredible. One murder in the party I might admit —but not two. Unless someone is trying to wreck my business. Someone with a grudge against me."

"It seems more likely," the old lady said dryly, "that someone has a grudge against the members of your party. As for your believing that this second affair is murder too, listen to what I have to say, and then tell me what you think." She sat down on the sofa. "Come," she went on, "draw up that chair and stop pacing. You remind me of a lion I used to see at the Hamburg Zoo—I got to know him quite well—but no matter. Inspector Duff, won't you sit here beside me? I think you will both find my story interesting."

Duff meekly took his place, and Lofton also obeyed orders. Somehow, this was the type of woman who doesn't have to speak twice.

"Mr. Honywood, Miss Pamela and I drove to Monte Carlo yesterday afternoon," Mrs. Luce continued. "Perhaps you already know that, Inspector. Mr. Honywood has been rather distraught and worried on this tour, but during our jaunt over to

Monaco he seemed to relax—he was quite charming, really. More, I imagine, like his real self. He was not contemplating suicide—I am confident of that. There was a man once at the hill station of Darjeeling, in India—it happened I was the last person to see him alive—but I needn't go into it. Mr. Honywood was light-hearted, almost gay. He returned here at dusk last night still in that mood. We left him out at the gate paying off the driver of the car and, coming in, went to our rooms."

"I saw you," Lofton reminded her.

"Yes, of course. Well, as I was unlocking my door, it came over me in a flash that the lock had been tampered with. Once, in Melbourne, Australia, my hotel room was entered—I'd had experience, you see. The doors here have shrunk, the cracks are wide, and I saw about the lock the marks of some sharp instrument, probably a knife. A simple matter to force the spring. I went inside and turned on the light. Instantly my impressions were verified. My room was in the utmost confusion, it had been searched from top to bottom. My trunk was broken open, and in a moment I made sure that what I had feared had happened. A document that had been entrusted to my keeping was missing."

"What sort of document?" Duff inquired with interest.

"We must go back to London, and the period following the murder of Hugh Drake. On the Saturday afternoon just two days before our departure from your city, Mr. Duff, I had a message from Mr. Walter Honywood asking me to meet him at once in the lounge of Broome's Hotel. I was puzzled, of course, but I did as he asked. He came into the room in what seemed a very perturbed state of mind. 'Mrs. Luce,' he said without preamble, 'I know you are a woman of wide experience and great discretion. Though I have no right to do so, I am going to ask a favour of you.' He took a long white envelope from his pocket. 'I wish you to take charge of this envelope for me. Keep it well guarded, and if anything should happen to me on this tour, please open it and read the contents at once.' "

"And that is the document which was stolen?" Duff demanded.

"Let's not get ahead of our story," the old lady replied. "Naturally I was somewhat taken aback. I hadn't said two words to him thus far on the tour. 'Mr. Honywood,' I inquired, 'what is in this envelope?' He looked at me in a queer way. 'Nothing,' he replied. 'Nothing save a list of instructions as to what must be done in case I—in case I am not here any more.' 'Certainly Doctor Lofton is the person with whom this should be left,' I told him. 'No,' he said. 'Doctor Lofton is decidedly not the person to hold that envelope.'

"Well, I just sat there, wondering. I asked him what he thought was going to happen to him. He murmured something about being ill—one never could tell, he said. He looked so spent, so utterly weary, I felt sorry for him. We were all rather on edge. I knew that Mr. Honywood was supposed to be suffering from a nervous breakdown, and I told myself that this was perhaps the whim of a sick and troubled mind. It seemed to me a small thing he was asking, and I told him I would take the envelope. He appeared to be delighted. 'It's so good of you,' he said. 'I would keep it locked up, if I were you. We had better not leave this room together. I will wait here until you have gone. And if you don't mind, I suggest we keep as far apart as possible when we are with the other members of the tour.'

"All that was rather queer, too. But I had an engagement with some friends in Belgravia that afternoon, and I was already late. I patted the poor man on the back, told him not to worry, and hurried out. When I got to my room, I glanced at the envelope. On it was written in small script: 'To be opened in case of my death. Walter Honywood.' I hastily locked it in my trunk, and went out."

"You should have communicated with me at once," Duff reproved her.

"Should I? I couldn't decide. As I say, I thought it the notion of a sick mind, and of no importance. And I was very busy those last few days in London. It wasn't until I got on the train for Dover on Monday morning that I really began to think about Mr. Honywood and the document he had given into my care. For the first time I wondered if it could have had any connection with the murder of Hugh Drake. When I walked on to the deck of the channel boat at Dover, I determined to find out.

"I saw Mr. Honywood leaning against the starboard rail, and I went over and joined him. He seemed very reluctant to have me do so. All the while we talked he kept glancing up and down the deck with a sort of hunted and terrified look in his eyes. I was quite uncomfortable about the whole affair by this time. 'Mr. Honywood,' I said, 'I have been thinking about that envelope you left with me. I feel the moment has arrived for a frank talk between us. Tell me—have you any reason to believe your life is in danger?'

"He started at that, and gave me a searching look. 'Why—no,' he stammered. 'Not at all. No more than anyone's life is in danger in this uncertain world.' His reply didn't satisfy me. I decided to put into words a thought that had come to me in the

train. 'If you should meet the same fate as Hugh
Morris Drake,' I said, 'would the name of your
assailant be found inside that envelope?'

"It seemed for a moment that he wasn't going to
answer me. Then he turned, and his eyes were so
sad that again I pitied him. 'My dear lady,' he
remarked, 'why should you think I would put such
a burden on you? That envelope contains just what
I said it did—instructions to be carried out in case
of my death.' 'If that is true,' I answered, 'why
wasn't it left with Doctor Lofton? Why must I
guard it so carefully? Why do you object to our
being soon together?' He nodded. 'Those are fair
questions,' he admitted, 'and I'm frightfully sorry I
can't answer them. But I give you my word, Mrs.
Luce—I am not letting you in for anything. Please
—I beg of you—hold that envelope just a little longer,
and say nothing. The matter will soon be settled.
And now—if you don't mind'—he was still looking
up and down in that frightened, anxious way—'I
don't feel very well and I am going inside to lie
down.' Before I could say another word, he had
gone.

"Well, I went on to Paris, still worried. I'm
sorry to say I didn't believe what the poor man had
told me. I thought that with my usual perspicacity
I had hit upon the true situation. I was certain that
Walter Honywood expected to be murdered, just as
Hugh Morris Drake was murdered, and by the same
person. And I was almost as certain that he had
written the name of that person in the letter he left
with me. That would make me a sort of accomplice
in the Drake murder or something like it. I had no
fear on that score. Once, in Japan, where I lived
three years, I protected—oh, well, I had right on my
side, there's nothing more to be said. But in this

case I didn't want to protect anybody. I wanted the man who had killed Drake discovered and punished. I was upset—and I'm not often upset. I didn't know what to do."

"There was just one thing to do," remarked Duff sternly. "And I am disappointed in you that you didn't do it. You had my address——"

"Yes, I know. But I'm not accustomed to calling in some mere man to help me solve my difficulties. There was one other thing to do, and I'm disappointed in you that you haven't thought of it. Have you never heard of the old trick of opening an envelope by the use of steam?"

"You steamed open that envelope?" Duff cried.

"I did, and I make no apologies. All's fair in love and murder. That night in Paris I released the flap, and took out the sheet of paper the envelope contained."

"And what was on it?" Duff asked eagerly.

"Just what poor Mr. Honywood had told me was on it. A brief note that ran something like this:

"'DEAR MRS. LUCE,—I am so sorry to have troubled you. Will you be kind enough to ask Doctor Lofton to communicate at once with my wife, Miss Sybil Conway? She is at the Palace Hotel, San Remo, Italy.'"

"Meaning precisely nothing," Duff sighed.

"Precisely," agreed Mrs. Luce. "I felt rather small when I read it. And puzzled. I had never been so puzzled in all my seventy-two years. Why couldn't he have left that message with the doctor? There was no need of it in the first place. Doctor Lofton knew the name and whereabouts of Mr. Hony-wood's wife. A number of us did—he had mentioned her several times, and said that she was in San Remo. Yet here he had written this unnecessary bit of

information on a slip of paper and given it to me,
intimating that I must guard it with my life."

Duff stared thoughtfully into space. "I don't get
it," he admitted.

"Nor I," said Mrs. Luce. "But can you wonder I
believe Mr. Honywood was murdered? I am sure he
saw it coming—the look in his eyes. And the
murderer thought it necessary to get possession of
that slip of paper in my trunk before going on with
his plans. Why? Heaven knows. Who told him
there was such a paper? Did Walter Honywood?
It's all too obscure for me. You must unravel it,
Mr. Duff. I hand the whole matter over to you."

"Thanks," answered Duff. He turned to Doctor
Lofton. "Is it true you already knew that Honywood's wife was in San Remo?"

"I certainly did," Lofton replied. "Honywood
told me so himself. He asked me to stop over there
a day, at the Palace Hotel, in the hope that he might
persuade her to join our tour."

Duff frowned. "The fog increases," he sighed.
" You've notified the lady, I presume?"

"Yes, I called her on the telephone last night, and
when she heard my news, I believe she fainted. At
least, it sounded that way—I heard her fall, and I
lost the connection. This morning her maid tele-
phoned me and said that Mrs. Honywood—or Sybil
Conway, as she calls herself—was unable to come to
Nice, and that she wanted me to bring her husband's
body to San Remo."

Duff considered. "I must have a talk with the lady
at my earliest. Well, Doctor, now that we have heard
Mrs. Luce's story, what have you to say about Honywood's death?"

"What should I say? I must admit that it begins
to look like something more than a simple case of

suicide. As a matter of fact, I shall have to tell you
that my own room was searched repeatedly while we
were in Paris. Yes, it was probably murder, Inspector
—but can you think of any good reason why anyone
save the three of us here should know it? If the
French police find it out—well, you understand what
red tape is over here, Mr. Duff."

"There's a lot in what you say, Doctor," Duff
agreed. "I must admit I wouldn't care to have the
Paris Sûreté enter the case now—much as I respect
their intelligence and their record. No, it's my job,
and I want to do it."

"Precisely," said Lofton, with evident relief.
"Consider this, too. Shall we tell the remaining
members of the party what we suspect? They're a
bit on edge already. Fenwick has tried to stir up
mutiny before, and this would certainly start him off
again. Suppose the party broke up and scattered to
the four winds? Would that help your investigation?
Or would you prefer that we stick together until your
case is solved?"

Duff smiled grimly. "You put it all most logically
and convincingly, Doctor. If you'll get your party
together, I'll have another chat with them, and then
I'll see what I can do with that commissary of police.
I don't believe he'll prove difficult."

Lofton departed, and Duff stood staring after him.
He looked down at Mrs. Luce.

"Honywood thought Lofton was decidedly not the
person to hold the envelope," he remarked.

She nodded vigorously. "He was very firm on
that point," she said.

Pamela Potter and Mark Kennaway had entered
the side door of the hotel. Duff nodded and waved
to them. They came over at once.

"Why, it's Inspector Duff," the girl cried, with

every evidence of pleasure. "How nice to see you again."

"Hello, Miss Pamela," the detective said. "And Mr. Kennaway. Been out for a stroll?"

"Yes," answered the girl. "We managed to evade the eagle-eyed chaperon and took a walk along the beach. It was heavenly—at least I thought it was. But I'm given to understand that the air is nowhere near so invigorating as on the North Shore, in Massachusetts."

Kennaway shrugged. "I'm afraid I'm in wrong," he remarked. "I ventured to say a good word for my native state, and I hear that in Detroit it isn't even regarded as a good market for automobiles. And how could we sink lower than that? However, I do approve of Nice——"

"Fine," laughed the girl. "They won't have to tear it down just yet. Why—what's wrong with Mr. Tait?"

The famous lawyer was approaching rapidly, his face a purplish red that boded ill for a man with a heart like his.

"Where the devil—oh, hello, Mr. Duff," he began. "Where the devil have you been, Kennaway?"

The young man flushed at his tone. "I have been for a walk with Miss Pamela," he said in a low voice.

"Oh, you have, have you?" Tait went on. "Leaving me to shift for myself. Did you think of that? To tie my own necktie." He indicated the polka-dot bow he affected. "Look at the damn' thing. I never could tie them."

"I wasn't aware," Kennaway said, his voice rising, "that I was engaged as a valet."

"You know perfectly well what you were engaged for. To be my companion. If Miss Potter wants a companion, let her hire one——"

"That is a service," began the young man hotly, "for which some people do not have to——"

"Just a moment." Pamela Potter stepped forward with a conciliating smile. "Do let me fix that tie, Mr. Tait. There. That's better. Go look in a mirror and see."

Tait softened a bit—he couldn't very well help it. But he continued to glare at the boy. Then he started to walk away.

"Pardon me, Mr. Tait," Duff said. "The members of Doctor Lofton's party are asked to meet in the salon over there——"

Tait wheeled. "What for? More of your damned silly investigation, eh? You may waste the time of the others, but not mine, sir, not mine. You're a fumbler, Inspector, an incompetent fumbler—I saw that in London. Where did you get there? Nowhere. To hell with your meetings." He took a few steps then turned and came back. His face was contrite. "I beg your pardon, Inspector. I'm sorry. It's my blood pressure—my nerves are all shot to pieces. I really didn't mean what I said."

"Very good," Duff answered quietly. "I quite understand. In that room across the way, please."

"I will wait there," Tait replied humbly. "Are you coming, Mark?"

The young man hesitated a second, then shrugged his shoulders and followed. Mrs. Luce and the girl accompanied him. Duff went to the desk of the hotel to register at last. He arranged with a bell-boy to take his bag upstairs. As he turned away, he encountered Mr. and Mrs. Elmer Benbow.

"Rather expected to see you," Benbow said, after a genial greeting. "But you got here sooner than I thought you would. Too bad about Honywood, isn't it?"

"A great pity," Duff agreed. "What do you think of that affair?"

"Don't know what to think," Benbow told him. "But—well, I guess I'd better tell him, Nettie."

"Of course you'd better tell him," Mrs. Benbow advised.

"I don't know whether it has anything to do with all this or not," Benbow continued. "But one night Nettie and I went to one of those hot shows in Paris— boy, did I need my smoked glasses?—and when we got back to the hotel, our room was a wreck. Every bit of baggage ripped open and searched, but not a thing taken. I didn't know what to make of it. Wasn't Scotland Yard, was it?"

Duff smiled. "Hardly. Scotland Yard is not so clumsy as that, Mr. Benbow. So your room was searched. Tell me—have you been seeing much of Mr. Honywood since you left London?"

"Well, yes—we have. His room was near ours, in Paris. I went around a little with him there. He knew the town like I know Akron. Say—do you believe he killed himself?"

"It looks that way," Duff replied. "Will you wait for me over there, please?"

"Sure," Benbow answered, and he and his wife walked to the room Duff had indicated.

The detective followed. As he crossed the threshold, the Minchins appeared in his path. Maxy gave him a friendly greeting.

"Well, another guy has been put on the spot," the racketeer remarked, in a hoarse whisper. "Looks like there was something doing in this mob. What do you make of it, Officer?"

"What do you?" Duff inquired.

"Too deep for this baby," Maxy assured him. "No, I don't get it. But that guy Honywood didn't

rub himself out, you can gamble your roll on that.   I
been watching.   I see other birds get the news their
number was up, and believe me, he had it.   You could
tell it from his eyes.   Looked like he was praying
to know which way the hot lead was coming from."

"Mr. Minchin," Duff said.   "I'm going to ask a
favour of you.   When we discuss the affair here this
morning, will you be good enough to keep that
opinion to yourself?"

"I'm wise," Minchin replied.   "It's just like I
told you—I trail along with the bulls this time.
Sealed like a coffin—that's my lips."

Lofton arrived at that moment with Mrs. Spicer
and Stuart Vivian.   While they were finding chairs,
Ross came limping in.   He was followed by Keane,
whose sly little eyes travelled everywhere about the
room before he sat down.

"All here but the Fenwicks," Lofton remarked to
Duff.   "They seem to be out, and I didn't make
much effort to find them.   If we can get everything
settled before that little fool shows up, so much the
better."

Duff nodded, and faced the group.   "Here I am
again," he began grimly.   "I want to say a few
words to you about your future plans, in view of
last night's unhappy affair.   I refer to the suicide
of Mr. Walter Honywood."

"Suicide?" inquired Mrs. Spicer languidly.   She
looked very smart in a white frock, with a trim
little hat pulled far down over her brilliant eyes.

"Suicide is what I said," Duff went on.   "Has
any one of you anything to tell me about the unfortunate occurrence?"

No one spoke.   "Very good," Duff continued.   "In
that case we will——"

"Just a moment," Vivian broke in.   The scar on

his forehead stood out with appalling clarity in that
bright room. "Merely a little incident, Inspector.
It may mean nothing. But Mr. Honywood and I
came down here in the same sleeping compartment.
I'd got to know him rather well in Paris—I liked
him. We went to the dining-car together for dinner.
When we returned to our compartment, both of my
bags had been broken into and obviously searched.
Nothing belonging to Honywood had been touched.
It seemed a bit odd—and odder still when I looked
at his face, after I had made my discovery. He was
deathly pale, and trembling like a leaf. I asked
him what was wrong, but he turned my questions
aside. None the less, he was obviously alarmed—if
that is a strong enough word."

"Thanks," Duff said. "Interesting, but it doesn't
upset the suicide theory."

"You think, then, he committed suicide?" Vivian
asked, with just a faint note of incredulity.

"That is what the French police believe, and I am
inclined to agree with them," Duff told him. "Mr.
Honywood had suffered a nervous breakdown. His
wife, of whom he appeared very fond, was estranged
from him. The stage was all set for a tragedy of
that sort."

"Perhaps it was," Vivian replied, but there was a
question in the words.

"You have had a most distressing tour so far,"
Duff continued. "But I am inclined to think your
troubles are now over. It is possible the secret of
Mr. Drake's—er—accident has died with Honywood.
I may tell you that certain of my discoveries in
London would indicate that it has. Better let them
think so, anyhow. It might put the murderer off
his guard. I should like to see you, as soon as the
police investigation here is finished, resume your tour.

I feel sure that it will be without unpleasant incident from here on. Is there any reason why you shouldn't?"

"None whatever," said Mrs. Luce promptly. "I'll go on as long as there's a tour."

"That's the way we feel, lady," Maxy Minchin added.

"I knew you would," Mrs. Luce assured him.

"Well, I don't see any reason for stopping," Captain Keane announced.

"I couldn't go back to Akron without the pictures I promised 'em," Benbow remarked. "I'd be the laughing stock of the town. Around the world—that was my order, and when I turn in an order, I want to see it filled."

"Mr. Ross?" Duff inquired.

The lumber man smiled. "By all means," he said, "let's go on with the tour. It's taken me a long time to get started, and I'd hate to drop it now."

"Mrs. Spicer?"

That lady took out a long holder, and inserted a cigarette. "I'm no quitter," she remarked. "Who's got a match?"

Vivian leaped into action. It was evident he would follow where she led.

"Who began all this, anyhow?" Tait wanted to know. His temper appeared still uncertain. "No one has ever talked of stopping, except that little idiot Fenwick. Do I have to apologize? No—he isn't here, is he?"

"Good," Doctor Lofton said. "We shall leave here whenever the commissary of police gives the word. I'll let you know the time of the train later. Our next stop will be San Remo, over the border in Italy."

Amid a buzz of comment, the meeting broke up. Duff followed Mrs. Luce from the room. He stopped her beside the sofa where they had talked before.

"By the way," he remarked, "when you came back

last night, and entered the lobby with Miss Pamela, I
believe Lofton was here talking with Fenwick?"

"He was—yes."

"When you hurried down again, after discovering
the theft of that envelope, was Fenwick still with the
doctor?"

"He was not. Doctor Lofton was alone."

"Lofton had asked you about Honywood when
you came in?"

"Yes. He inquired about Mr. Honywood in a
rather anxious way."

"Be careful. I don't want editorial opinions, Mrs.
Luce. I want facts. So far as you know, Lofton
and Fenwick may have separated the moment you
went up in the lift to your room?"

"Yes. And Doctor Lofton may have rushed
outside and fired that——"

"Never mind."

"But I don't like the man either," protested the
old lady.

"What do you mean by that word either?" Duff
inquired. "I don't have likes and dislikes, Mrs.
Luce. I can't afford to, in my business."

"Oh, I guess you're human, like the rest of us,"
said Mrs. Luce, and went on her way.

Lofton came up. "Thank you, Inspector," he
remarked. "You settled our future plans in short
order. If you can have an equal success with the
commissary of police, all will be well."

"I fancy it will. By the way, Doctor Lofton—
last night, when you heard that shot outside, were
you still talking with Fenwick?"

"Yes, of course. I couldn't shake the man."

"Do you think he also heard the sound of the shot
being fired?"

"I imagine he did. He started a bit."

"Ah, yes. Then you and he both have a very good alibi."

Lofton smiled in a somewhat strained way. "I guess we have. Unfortunately, however, Mr. Fenwick is not here to verify what I say."

"What do you mean, he's not here?" Duff cried.

"I didn't tell you in the room," Lofton answered, "but this note has been found, pinned to the pillowcase in Fenwick's room. You'll notice it is addressed to me." He handed it over. Duff read:

"DEAR DOCTOR LOFTON,—I warned you that if there was any more funny business, we'd quit. Well, there has been more funny business, and we're off. I've arranged it with the concierge, and we're pulling out in a car at midnight. You can't stop us, and you know it. You have my Pittsfield address, and I shall expect to find a rebate on the price of the tour waiting for me there when I get back. That means you had better get it off at once.

"NORMAN FENWICK."

"Leaving at midnight," mused Duff. "I wonder which way they went."

"The hotel people tell me Fenwick was asking about the boats from Genoa to New York."

"Genoa, eh? Then they went east along the Riviera. They're over the border by now."

Lofton nodded. "Undoubtedly. Over the border in Italy."

"You appear rather pleased, Doctor Lofton," Duff remarked.

"I'm delighted," the doctor returned. "Why should I try to conceal it? In fifteen years of touring, I never met a worse pest than Fenwick. I'm glad he's gone."

"Even though your alibi went with him?" Duff suggested.

Lofton smiled. "Why should I need an alibi?" he inquired blandly.

CHAPTER IX

DUSK AT SAN REMO

LOFTON stepped over to the desk, leaving the detective to ponder this somewhat disconcerting news. Two of his travelling group of suspects had broken away from the fold. Nothing had been discovered that connected the Fenwicks with the London murder in any way—or with that of Honywood either. None the less, Duff felt that every member of the Lofton party was under suspicion until the problem was solved, and the Fenwicks were not immune. The man did not look like a murderer, but experience had taught the inspector that few murderers do. He was exceedingly annoyed by the high-handed conduct of the pompous little chap from Pittsfield. Yet what could he do about it? He had no authority to dictate the actions of anyone in that party save Honywood—and Honywood was dead.

A commotion about the lift attracted his attention and the next moment the resplendent commissary of police was marching towards him. How well that dazzling uniform fitted into the colourful background of the Riviera.

"Ah, Inspector, you do not arrive above," the commissary cried. "I wait, but you do not appear."

Duff shook his head. "There was no need, Monsieur le Commissaire. I know only too well the keen eyes of the French police. May I congratulate

you on your conduct of this case? I have investigated, and I am struck by the intelligence you have
shown."

"That is so kind of you to say," the commissary
beamed. "Me, I have learned much that I know
from a study of Scotland Yard methods." His chest
expanded. "Yes, I believe what you say is correct
—I have done well here under the conditions. But
what conditions! Impossible even for the most
brilliant mind. The stupidity of the servants—
Monsieur, I could easily weep. Footprints trampled
upon, finger-prints destroyed. What is it there
remains I can do?"

"Fortunately, there is nothing more you need to
do," Duff assured him. "It is a case of suicide,
Commissary. I can guarantee that."

The Frenchman's face lighted with relief. "It is
a thing I am most 'appy to hear. A woman—she is
in it, of course?"

Duff smiled. "Yes," he said, taking his cue
neatly. "The dead man's wife. He loved her
passionately, and she deserted him. Heart-broken
he tried to go on alone. It was no use. Even here
in your charming and cheerful city, he perceived it
was no use. Hence the pistol, the body on the walk."

The commissary shook his head. "Ah, the woman,
Monsieur. Always the woman! What suffering,
what sorrow, is she not responsible for? Yet—could
we do without her?"

"Hardly," ventured Duff.

"Never!" cried the commissary, with vehemence.
"I shudder to think——" He paused. "But I fear
we get beside the point. The Doctor Lofton tells
me why you are here, Inspector. I accept your
word of the suicide. Who should know better than
you? So I will report it, and the affair closes itself."

"Very good," Duff nodded. "Then I take it that the party may continue its tour at once?"

The commissary hesitated. After all, one must not treat the affair too lightly. "Not quite so fast, Monsieur, if you please," he said. "I go now to the room of the Juge d'Instruction. With him rests the final decision. Presently I shall call you with the telephone and inform you what that is. The arrangement is satisfactory, Inspector?"

"Oh, quite," Duff answered. "Once more, my heartiest congratulations."

"You say too much, Monsieur."

"Not at all. I have been impressed—deeply impressed."

"How can I thank you? How indicate my pleasure at this meeting?"

"Do not attempt it, Monsieur."

"Again I accept your advice. Bon jour, Inspector."

"Bon jour," repeated Duff, with a Yorkshire accent.

The glittering commissary strode away.

Lofton came up to Duff at once. "Well?" he inquired.

The detective shrugged. "It will be all right, I fancy. The commissary was glad to be convinced. But he has to report the matter to the examining magistrate before a final decision can be made. I am to await a telephone call. I hope it comes soon, as I am eager to put through one myself for San Remo the moment I know what our plans are to be."

"I shall be somewhere in the hotel," Lofton told him. "Naturally I want to hear about it as soon as you get the call. There's a train de luxe at four-thirty this afternoon, and I hope very much we can be on it."

An hour passed before the word came through from the commissary that they could go on whenever they pleased. Duff hastily scribbled a note for Lofton, gave it to a bell-boy, and then stepped up to the desk.

"Please get me the Palace Hotel at San Remo on the telephone," he said. "I wish to speak with Mrs. Walter Honywood—or Miss Sybil Conway, as she sometimes calls herself."

This, it appeared, was viewed by the staff as a considerable undertaking. An excited discussion took place behind the scenes. Duff sat down in a near-by chair and waited. After many minutes a bell-boy came to him breathless with news. "A lady in San Remo has the wire," he said.

The detective hastened into the booth that was pointed out to him. "Are you there?" he cried. His deep distrust of Continental telephones moved him to shout at the top of his voice.

An answering voice, faint, far-away, but musical, sounded in his ear. "Did someone wish to speak to Miss Conway?"

"Yes—I did. Inspector Duff, of Scotland Yard."

"I cannot hear you. Inspector what?"

"Duff. Duff."

"Perhaps you speak a little too loudly. I still can't hear you."

Duff was perspiring freely, and he suddenly realized that he had been bellowing. He spoke in a lower tone, and more distinctly.

"I am Inspector Duff, of Scotland Yard. It has been my duty to investigate the murder of Mr. Hugh Drake, of the Lofton travel party, in London. I am now in Nice, where I have happened upon the unfortunate death of your husband, Mr. Walter Honywood."

"Yes." The voice was very faint.

"Madam, I am deeply sorry."

"Thank you. What did you wish to say to me?"

"I am wondering if you know anything that may throw light on his death?"

"Doctor Lofton told me it was suicide."

"It was not suicide, Madam." Duff's voice was now very low. "Your husband was murdered. Are you still there?"

"I am here." Very faintly.

"I feel certain the murder has some connection with that of Mr. Drake in London," Duff went on.

There was a pause. "I can assure you that it has, Inspector," said the woman.

"What's that?" Duff cried.

"I am telling you that the two are connected. They are, in a manner of speaking, the same murder."

"Good lord," the detective gasped. "What do you mean by that?"

"I will explain when I see you. The story is a long one. You will come to San Remo with the Lofton party?"

"I certainly will. We are leaving here at four-thirty this afternoon, and should reach your hotel about two hours later."

"Very well. The matter can wait until then. Mr. Honywood wanted the whole affair kept quiet for my sake. I imagine he feared it would hurt my career in the theatre, and that I'd be distressed on that account. But I have made up my mind. I mean to see justice done, at any cost to myself. You see—I know who murdered my husband."

Again Duff gasped.

"You know who——"

"I do, indeed."

"Then, for God's sake, Madam, don't let's take any chances. Tell me now—at once."

"I can only tell you that it was a man who is travelling with the Lofton party around the world."

"But his name—his name!"

"I do not know what he calls himself now. Years ago, when we met him in—in a far country, his name was Jim Everhard. Now he is travelling with the Lofton party, but under another name."

"Who told you this?"

"My husband wrote it to me."

"But he did not write you the name?"

"No."

"Did this same man kill Hugh Morris Drake?" Duff held his breath. It was Drake's murderer he had to find.

"Yes, he did."

"Your husband told you that, too?"

"Yes—it is all in the letter, which I shall give you to-night."

"But this man—who is he—that is what I must discover, Madam. You say you met him years ago. Will you recognize him if you meet him again?"

"I shall recognize him instantly."

Duff took out a handkerchief and mopped his brow. This was magnificent.

"Madam, are you still there? Mrs. Honywood?"

"I am still here."

"What you have told me is—very satisfactory." Duff was always given to understatement. "I shall arrive at your hotel at about half-past six this evening. I am not certain of the exact moment. With me will be the entire Lofton party." A thought of Fenwick flashed through his mind, but he dismissed it. "There must be no accident. I beseech you to stay in your rooms until I communicate with you again. I shall arrange for you to see every member of the party, preferably from a point where you yourself will remain unseen. When you have made your identification, the rest will lie with me. Everything will be made as easy for you as possible."

"You are very kind. I shall do my duty. I have made up my mind. At any cost to myself—and the cost will not be inconsiderable—I shall help you to bring Walter's murderer to justice. You may rely on me."

"I am relying on you, and I am eternally grateful. Until to-night, then, Mrs. Honywood."

"Until to-night. I shall be awaiting your call in my rooms."

As Duff left the booth, he was startled to find Doctor Lofton standing just beside it.

"I got your message," Lofton remarked. "We're booked for the four-thirty express. There's a ticket for you, if you want it."

"Of course I want it," Duff answered. "I'll pay you for it later."

"No hurry." Lofton started to walk away, then paused. "Ah—er—you have talked with Mrs. Honywood?"

"I just finished."

"Could she tell you anything?"

"Nothing," Duff replied.

"What a pity," Lofton said casually, and moved on towards the lift.

Duff went to his room as near to elation as he ever got. A difficult case—one of the most difficult he had ever been called upon to face—and another seven hours would solve it. As he sat in the dining-room at luncheon, he made a cautious study of the men in Lofton's travel party. Which one? Which one could smile and smile, and be a villain still? Lofton himself? Lofton was travelling with the party. With, the woman had said, not in. Was that significant? Possibly. Tait, who had experienced that terrific heart attack just as he entered the room at Broome's Hotel? Not out of it, not by a long shot.

A man could have a weak heart, and still gather the strength to strangle another man of Drake's advanced age. And Tait had about him the look of far countries. Kennaway? A mere boy. Benbow? Duff shook his head. Ross or Vivian or Keane? All possible. Maxy Minchin? He hardly seemed to fit into the setting, but the affair was quite in his line. Fenwick? The detective's heart sank. Suppose it were Fenwick—well, what of it? He'd go after him, even to the ends of the earth—to Pittsfield, Massachusetts, wherever that was—he'd go after Fenwick and bring him back.

At four-thirty that afternoon they were all aboard the train de luxe, bound for San Remo. Duff had confided in no one, so he alone knew what was waiting ahead. He went from one compartment to another, making sure once more—though he had counted them at the station—that no one was missing. After chatting with a number of the others, he entered the compartment occupied by Tait and Kennaway.

"Well, Mr. Tait," he began amiably, dropping into a seat, "I trust that for your sake the exciting part of your tour around the world is now ended."

Tait gave him an unfriendly look. "You needn't worry about me," he said.

"How can I help it?" Duff smiled. He sat for a moment in silence, staring out at the passing scene. Wooded hills and richly cultivated plains swept by, a tiny seaport with a chapel, a ruined castle. Beyond the blue and sparkling Mediterranean. "Rather pretty country along here," the detective ventured.

"Looks like the movies," growled Tait, and picked up a copy of the *New York Herald's* Paris edition.

Duff turned to the young man. "First trip abroad?" he inquired.

Kennaway shook his head. "No, I used to come over in college vacations. Had a grand time in those days—I didn't know my luck." He looked at the old man and sighed. "Nothing to worry me—nothing on my mind but my hair."

"This is different," Duff suggested.

"I'll sign a statement to that effect any time," smiled the boy.

Duff turned back to the old man with an air of determination. "As I was saying, Mr. Tait," he remarked loudly, "how can I help worrying about you? I saw one of your attacks, you may recall, and my word—I thought you were gone, I did indeed."

"I wasn't gone," Tait snapped. "Even you must have noticed that."

"Even I?" Duff raised his eyebrows. "Quite true. I'm not much of a detective, am I? So many points I haven't solved. For example, I don't yet know what you saw inside Broome's sitting-room that brought on such a severe heart attack."

"I saw nothing, I tell you—nothing."

"I've forgotten," the inspector went on blandly. "Have I asked you this before? On the night Hugh Morris Drake was murdered, did you hear no sound —no cry—you know what I mean?"

"How should I? Honywood's room was between mine and Drake's."

"Ah, yes. So it was. But you see, Mr. Tait"— the detective's eyes were keen on the old man's face —"Drake was murdered in Honywood's room."

"What's that?" Kennaway cried. Tait said nothing, but the inspector thought his face had grown a trifle paler.

"You understood what I said, Mr. Tait? Drake was murdered in Honywood's room."

The old man tossed down his newspaper. "Perhaps you're a better detective than I thought you," he remarked. "So you've found that out, have you?"

"I have. And under the circumstances, don't you want to alter your story a bit?"

Tait nodded. "I'll tell you just what happened," he said. "I presume you won't believe it, but that won't matter a damn. Early on the morning of February 7, I was awakened by the sounds of some sort of struggle going on in the room next to mine at Broome's Hotel. Honywood's room, it was. The struggle was extremely brief, and by the time I was fully awake, all indication of it had ceased. I debated with myself what I should do. I'd been trying for some months to rest, and the thought of becoming involved in a matter that did not concern me was very distasteful. No thought of murder, of course, came into my mind. Some sort of trouble— yes—I sensed that. But everything was quiet by that time, and I determined to go back to sleep and forget it.

"In the morning I rose at an early hour and decided to breakfast outside. After I'd had my coffee—it's forbidden but, dammit, no man can live for ever—I went for a walk in St. James's Park. When I arrived back at Broome's I met a servant at the Clarges Street entrance who told me that an American had been murdered upstairs. He didn't know the name, but it came to me suddenly that I knew it. Honywood! That struggle! I had heard Honywood murdered and had made no move to help him, to apprehend his assailant.

"I had already had one great shock, you see, when I came to you at the door. I stepped across the threshold, certain that Honywood was dead upstairs. He was the first person I saw. That shock, added

to the previous one, was too much. My heart went
back on me."

"I see," nodded Duff. "But you told me nothing
of the struggle in Honywood's room. Was that sporting of you?"

"Probably not. But when I saw you again, I was
weak and ill. My one thought was to keep out of the
thing if I could. You had your job—you could do it.
All I wanted was peace. That's my story. Believe
it or not, as you like."

Duff smiled. "I am rather inclined to believe it,
Mr. Tait. Subject, of course, to what the future may
reveal."

Tait's look softened. "By Jove," he remarked,
"you *are* a better detective than I thought you were."

"Thank you very much," answered Duff. "I
believe we are already at San Remo."

As the hotel bus rolled through the streets of the
town in the dusk, Doctor Lofton spoke a few words
to his charges. "We're leaving here to-morrow
noon," he announced. "None of you will unpack any
more than is absolutely necessary. You understand
that we must go on to Genoa at the earliest possible
moment."

Presently they drew up before the entrance of the
Palace Hotel. Duff secured a room on the first floor,
at the head of the stairs leading up from the lobby.
There was a lift of the Continental type not far from
his door, he noted, as he made a study of his surroundings. Though not a man given to moments of excitement, his heart was beating at a quite surprising rate.
The Palace was a comparatively small establishment,
not one of the huge show places of the town, but even
so there was an air of spaciousness and comfort about
it. Dinner, the detective discovered, was only half an
hour away. About the lobby and the corridors hung

that atmosphere of quiet characteristic of a resort hotel when the guests are dressing for the evening.

Duff had ascertained at the desk that Miss Sybil Conway—it was under that name she had registered —was on the fourth floor. His room, he was glad to discover, was equipped with a telephone. He called Miss Conway's apartment, and in another moment the low musical voice, which must have been so pleasing in the theatre, was answering him.

"Inspector Duff, of Scotland Yard." He half-whispered it.

"I'm so glad. The wait has been terrible. I—I am ready to go through with it."

"Good. We must meet at once. The members of the party are all in their rooms, but they will reappear in the lobby presently for dinner. While we are waiting for them, you and I will have a chat."

"Of course. I shall bring you a letter my husband wrote me from London. It will explain many things. And after that——"

"After that, you and I will watch the members of Doctor Lofton's travel party go in to dinner. I have selected our hiding-place, behind a cluster of palms. For our chat, I have planned it this way. There is a small deserted public room just beside my room on the first floor. You understand what I mean by the first floor—the one above the lobby—I believe you would call it the second in America. The door of the little place can be locked from the inside. I suggest we meet there. Is your apartment near the lift?"

"A few steps only."

"Splendid. You will come down in the lift—— Stop a bit. I have thought of a better way. I will come and fetch you. Number 40, I believe—your room?"

"Number 40, yes. I shall be waiting."

Duff went immediately into the hall. He was pleased to see that the corridor was in semi-darkness, illuminated only by such light as came up from below along the open elevator shaft. He pressed the lift button. Occasional visits to modest hotels in Paris had made him familiar with the whims of the automatic Continental elevator. The cage rose slowly and majestically—thank heaven, for once it was not out of order. He got in, and pressed another button, this time for the fourth floor.

He knocked at the door of number 40, and it was opened by a tall graceful woman. A blaze of light at her back left her face in shadow, but he knew at once that she was beautiful. Her hair was gold, like her gown, and her voice, heard now over no telephone wire, thrilled even the stolid inspector.

"Mr. Duff—I'm so glad." She was a little breathless. "Here—this is my husband's letter."

He took it and put it in his pocket. "Thanks a thousand times," he said. "Will you come with me? The lift is waiting."

He ushered her into the narrow cage, then followed and pushed the button for the first floor. Slowly, hesitantly, the unsteady car began its descent.

"I have been ill," Sybil Conway told him. "I am finding it difficult to go on with this. But I must— I must——"

"Hush!" admonished the detective. "Not now, please." They were slipping past the third floor. "In a moment, you must tell me everything——"

He stopped in horror. From slightly above his head came the sharp explosion of a shot. A small object hurtled through the air and fell at his feet. The woman's face appalled him. He caught her in his arms, for he had seen, on the bodice of her gold silk gown, a spreading. dull red stain.

"It's all over," Sybil Conway whispered. Duff could not speak. He reached out one hand and fought savagely with the locked door of the lift. The imperturbable invention of the French moved resolutely on. A great bitterness was in the detective's heart.

This was a situation that would haunt Inspector Duff to the end of his career. He had seen a woman murdered at his side, had held her dying in his arms, locked with her in a little cage, the door of which would open all in good time. He looked aloft into the darkness and knew that it was no use. When the lift released him, he would be too late.

It released him at the first floor. Doors were opening, half-clothed guests were peering out. He carried Sybil Conway to a sofa. She was dead, he knew. Running back to the lift, he picked up an object that was lying there. A small bag of wash leather—he did not need to open it. He knew what it contained. Pebbles gathered from some beach—a hundred silly, meaningless little stones.

CHAPTER X

THE DEAFNESS OF MR. DRAKE

As Duff left the elevator he closed the door behind him, and almost instantly the bell rang and the cage began to ascend. He stood for a moment watching it slowly rising, the only spot of light in that dark scene. Too late he noted what a target was presented by anyone who stood on the unprotected platform. Like most foreign lifts it moved along a shaft which was, save for a sparse iron grill work, open on all sides. The platform was surrounded by a similar grill, no higher than the average passenger's shoulder. What a shining mark that gold silk gown, how simple to kneel on the floor of the hallway and fire through the grill from above, just as the lift and its human freight passed slowly out of sight. It seemed so obvious now that it had happened, but it was one of those things that no honest man, lacking in imagination, would ever see in advance. As he turned away, the inspector was muttering savagely beneath his breath. In his heart was an unwilling respect for his antagonist.

The owner-manager of the Palace was puffing up the stairs. He was a man of enormous girth, innumerable yards of black frock coat encircled him. Mountains of spaghetti must have existed, ere he could be. After him came his clerk, also in a frock coat, but thin and with a chronically anxious look. The hallway was filled with excited guests.

Quickly the detective led the two men into the ante-room, and locked the door. They stood staring at the sofa and its pathetic burden.

As briefly as possible, Duff presented the situation.

"Murdered in the lift? Who would do that?" The eyes widened in the owner's fat face.

"Who, indeed?" replied Duff crisply. "I was with her at the time——"

"Ah, you were? Then you will remain here and talk with the police when they arrive."

"Of course I will. I am Inspector Duff, of Scotland Yard, and this dead woman was to have been an important witness in the matter of a murder which took place in London."

"It becomes clearer," the big man nodded. "The poor, poor lady. But such things, you must know, are bad for my hotel. There is a doctor who lives here." He turned to his clerk. "Vito—you will fetch him at once. Though it is, I fear, too late."

He waddled to the door, unlocked it, and stood there facing the guests. As a screen, he was efficient.

"A small accident," he announced. "It concerns none of you. You will return to your rooms, if you please." Reluctantly the group melted away. As Vito was hurrying by him, the proprietor laid a hand on the clerk's arm. "Call also the City Guards. Not, you understand, the Carabinieri." He glanced at Duff. "They would bring Il Duce himself into the affair," he shrugged.

The clerk dashed down the stairs. Inspector Duff started to leave the room, but the fat man blocked his way. "Where do you go, Signore?" he demanded.

"I want to make an investigation," the detective explained. "I tell you I am from Scotland Yard. How many guests are at present in the hotel?"

"Last night there slept here one hundred and twenty," the owner answered. "It is the season's high point. Quite filled, Signore."

"One hundred and twenty," Duff repeated grimly. A bit of work for the City Guards. A bit of work even for him, who knew that of this great group, only the members of the Lofton party need be considered.

With some difficulty he edged by the owner, and went aloft by way of the stairs. The third-floor hallway was silent and deserted; he found no sign of any sort about the lift shaft. If ever there was a murder without a clue, he reflected, this was no doubt one. Dejectedly he went on up and knocked at the door of room 40.

A white-faced maid opened to him. Briefly he related what had happened. The woman seemed quite overcome.

"She feared this, sir. All afternoon she has been worried. 'If anything happens to me, Tina,' she said, over and over, and she gave me directions what I must do."

"What was that?"

"I was to take her body back to the States, sir. And that of poor Mr. Honywood as well. There are cables I must send, too. To friends in New York."

"And relatives, perhaps?"

"I never heard her speak of any relatives, sir. Nor Mr. Honywood, either. They seemed quite alone."

"Really? Later, you must give me a list of those to whom you are cabling. Now you had better go down to the room on the first floor. Tell the manager who you are. They will no doubt bring your mistress back here presently. I will stop in the rooms a moment."

"You are Inspector Duff?"

"I am."

"My poor mistress spoke of you. Many times in the past few hours."

The maid disappeared, and Duff passed through a small entrance hall into a pleasant sitting-room. The letter Sybil Conway had given him burned in his pocket, demanding to be read, but first he wanted to search these rooms. In a moment the Italian police would arrive and he would be too late. He went to work with speed and system. Letters from American friends—not many—telling nothing. Drawer after drawer—the open trunks—he hurried on. At last he was conscious, as he bent over a bag in Sybil Conway's bedroom, that someone was watching from the doorway. He swung about. A major of the City Guards was standing there, an expression of surprise and displeasure on his dark face.

"You search the rooms, Signore?" he inquired.

"Let me introduce myself," said Duff hastily. "I am Inspector Duff, of Scotland Yard. The British consul will vouch for me."

"From Scotland Yard?" The policeman was impressed. "I begin to understand. It was you who was with the lady when she was killed?"

"Yes," nodded Duff uncomfortably. "I did find myself in that unpleasant position. If you'll sit down——"

"I prefer to stand."

Naturally, in that uniform, Duff thought. "As you please," he went on. "I want to tell you something of this affair." As briefly as he could, he outlined the case on which he was engaged, and explained Sybil Conway's rôle in it. Not sure as yet just how much he wanted the Italian police to know, he was none too explicit. Especially was he careful to say nothing of Lofton's Round the World Tour.

The Italian listened with unruffled calm. When

Duff had finished, he nodded slowly. "Thank you very much. I assume you will not leave San Remo without communicating with me?"

"Well, hardly." Duff smiled grimly, thinking of the innumerable times he had made a similar remark to other men.

"What did you find in your search of these rooms, Inspector?"

"Nothing," said the Scotland Yard man quickly. "Not a thing." His heart beat a little faster. Suppose this policeman, annoyed at his interference, ordered him searched, found Honywood's letter?

For a moment they stared at each other. It was an international crisis. But Duff's appearance of stolid respectability won out.

The Italian bowed. "I shall have the honour of meeting you later," he said. It was a dismissal.

Much relieved, Duff hastened to his room. Without delay he meant to read the letter Sybil Conway had handed him a few moments before her death. He locked his door, drew a chair up beneath a feeble light, and took out the already opened envelope. It bore in the upper left corner the crest of Broome's Hotel, London, and it was postmarked February 15. Eight days after the murder of Hugh Drake, the detective reflected, and only a short time before the Lofton party started for the Continent.

He removed the bulky contents of the envelope. Walter Honywood wrote an unusually small hand, but even so this message to his wife covered many pages. With eager anticipation, Duff began to read:

"DEAREST SYBIL,—You will see from the letter-head that I have now reached London on that tour around the world which, as I wrote you from New York, the doctors advised. It was to have been a rest for me, a release, a period of relaxation. Instead it has turned into the most terrible nightmare imaginable. Jim Everhard is also with the tour!

"I found this out on the morning of February 7, a little more than a week ago. Found it out under the most frightful circumstances. Under circumstances so bizarre, so horrible—but wait.

"When I went aboard the boat in New York, even the names of the other members of the party were unknown to me. I had not so much as met the conductor. We were called together on the deck for a moment before sailing, and I shook hands with all of them. I did not recognize Jim Everhard. Why should I? I saw him, you will remember, only the once and the light was poor—a dim oil lamp in that little sitting-room of yours. So many years ago. Yes, I shook hands with them all—with Jim Everhard—the man who had sworn to kill me—and to kill you, too. And I never suspected—never dreamed——

"Well, we sailed. It proved a rough passage, and I did not leave my cabin, except for a few brief strolls on the deck after dark, until the morning we reached Southampton. We came on here to London, and still I had no inkling. There was much sightseeing during the first few days, but I kept out of it. That was not what I had come abroad for—and London was an old story, anyhow.

"On the night of February 6 I was sitting in the lounge of Broome's Hotel when another member of the party came in. A fine old fellow from Detroit, named Hugh Morris Drake, the kindest man alive, and very deaf. We got into conversation. I told him about my illness, and added that I had got very little sleep for the past few nights, owing to the fact that someone was reading aloud in the room on one side of me until a late hour. I said I was reluctant to go upstairs to bed, because I knew I could not rest.

"At that the dear old chap had an idea. He pointed out that, owing to his deafness, the sort of thing that was troubling me would mean nothing to him, and he offered to change rooms with me for the night. It developed that he had the room on the other side of me, so it seemed a simple matter to arrange. I accepted Mr. Drake's offer gratefully. We went upstairs. It was agreed we would leave all our possessions just as they

were, unlock the door between the rooms, and merely
change beds. I closed the connecting door between us
and retired—in Mr. Drake's bed.

"The doctor had given me a package of sleeping
powders to use as a last resort, and as an added guarantee
of sleep I had taken one of those. In the unaccustomed
silence, and with the aid of the powder, I slept as I
hadn't slept for months. But I was awake at six-thirty,
and inasmuch as Mr. Drake had told me he wanted to
rise early—we were expecting to leave for Paris that
morning—I went into the other room.

"I entered and looked about me. His clothes were
on a chair, his ear-phone on a table; all the doors and
windows were closed. I went over to the bed to wake
him. He had been strangled with a luggage strap. He
was dead.

"At first I didn't understand—early morning, only
half awake—you see how it was. Then on the bed, I
saw a little wash-leather bag. You remember, my dear?
One of those bags we gave Jim Everhard—there were
two, weren't there? Am I wrong, or were there two
wash-leather bags, with the pebbles inside?

"I sat down and thought the matter out. It was
simple enough. Jim Everhard was somewhere in
Broome's Hotel. He had located me with the tour—
he had made up his mind to carry out his old threat at
last—he had stolen into my room to strangle me in
the night and return the bag of stones. Into my room!
But it wasn't my room that night. Hugh Morris Drake
was in my bed in that dark corner where the light of
the street lamps never penetrated. And Hugh Morris
Drake had died; died because of his kindness to me;
died—if you like irony—because he was deaf.

"It was horrible. But I knew I must pull myself
together. There was nothing I could do for Drake. I
would gladly have given my life to prevent what had
happened—too late now. I must get through the thing
somehow—I wanted to see you again—to hear your
voice—I love you, my dear. I loved you from the
moment I saw you. If I hadn't, all this would never
have been. But I don't regret it. I never shall.

"I decided that I couldn't leave poor Drake there in
my bed, among my things. How explain that? So I
carried him to his own room and put him in his bed,

There was the bag of stones. I didn't want that. I didn't know what to do with it. It would mean nothing to anyone—save to Jim Everhard—and to us. I tossed it down on the bed beside Mr. Drake. I almost smiled as I did so—smiled at the thought of Everhard carrying it all those years, and leaving it at last in the wrong place, wreaking his vengeance on the wrong man.—Of course, he still has that other bag.

"I unlocked my door into the hall, then slipped back into Drake's bedroom and locked the door between the rooms on his side. The ear-phone caught my attention; I had been forced to move it, so I wiped it clean of finger-prints. Lucky I thought of that. Then I went from his room into the hall, and so to my own room again. You can rest assured that no one saw me. But I remembered a waiter who had brought up a cable for Drake the night before and who knew about the change of rooms. As soon as he came on duty, I rang for him and bribed him. It was easy. Then I sat down to wait for the breakfast hour—another day. My meeting with Jim Everhard.

"I saw him. I knew him this time—the eyes—there is something about a man's eyes that never changes through the years. I was sitting in a room of the hotel waiting for the Scotland Yard inspector, and I looked up. He was standing there. Jim Everhard, with another name now. And travelling with the party, too.

"While the Scotland Yard man was asking questions, I tried to think what I had better do. I couldn't very well drop out of the party—I was already in a bad position. My nerves—I hadn't stood the questioning very well. If I dropped out, they might arrest me at once. The whole unhappy story might be revealed. No, for the present I must go on, travel side by side with a man who was no doubt now more determined than ever to kill me—who had, in fact, already killed me, after a manner of speaking.

"I decided that it must be done. For a week I slept every night with a bureau against my door—or tried to sleep. Gradually I evolved a scheme for my protection. I would go to Everhard, tell him I had left in a safe place a sealed envelope, to be opened in case anything happened to me. In that envelope, I would give him to understand was written his name—the name of my murderer, if murder had occurred. That, I thought, would stay his hand, for a time at least.

"I prepared such an envelope. But in the brief note inside I did not mention Everhard's name. Even if it happens—even if he gets me in the end—the old story must not come out. The old scandal. It would ruin your fine career, my dear. I couldn't have that. I have been so proud of you.

"I left the envelope only this afternoon with a member of the party I am certain no one would ever suspect of having it. A few moments ago I saw Jim Everhard in the lobby. I went and sat beside him, and in the most casual way, as though I were discussing the weather, I told him what I had done. He didn't speak. He just sat there looking at me. I told him of the envelope, with his name inside. The last part wasn't true, of course, but I think my plan will serve its purpose.

"So I am coming on with the party, as far as Nice. I am sure he will do nothing before we reach there. The whole affair appears to have shaken him badly— as well it might. The first night our party is in Nice, I propose to slip away in a car in the dark, to come to San Remo and get you. Scotland Yard has given up the chase for the moment, and I doubt if they could stop me in any case. We shall hide until the threat has passed. I am taking it for granted that in the face of this unexpected danger, our differences are buried.

"No, my dear—I am not going to tell you the name under which Jim Everhard travels with our party. You were always so impulsive, so quick to act. I am afraid if you knew it, and something happened to me, you could not remain silent. You would throw away your splendid career with one grand gesture, expose the whole situation—and no doubt live to regret bitterly what you had done. If something should happen to me, for God's sake get out of the path of the Lofton party at once. Disappear from San Remo—your own safety must be your first thought. Motor to Genoa and take the first boat for New York. For my sake—I beseech you. Don't spoil the remaining years of your life—what good would it do? Let the dead past bury its dead.

"But nothing will happen to me. You have only to keep calm, as I am doing. My hand is quite steady as I write this. Everything will come right in the end, I am sure. I shall wire you the date; be ready for me when I come. We'll go away for a second honeymoon. Everhard and the events of the long ago will fade back into the shadows where they have remained so many years.

"With all my love, for ever,
"WALTER."

Gravely Inspector Duff folded the letter and put it back into its envelope. An acute feeling of helplessness stole over him. Again he had been so close to knowing, again the hotly desired knowledge had been snatched away at the last moment. The news that the murder of Hugh Morris Drake had been pure accident did not greatly surprise him. He had suspected as much these past few days. But accident or not, its perpetrator must be seized and brought to justice. And all through this letter the name of that perpetrator—now a triple murderer—had seemed on the very point of Honywood's pen. Then—nothing. What name? Tait—Kennaway—Vivian? Lofton or Ross? Minchin, Benbow or Keane? Or perhaps even Fenwick. But no, Fenwick was no longer with the party. He could hardly have been concerned in this murder to-night.

Well, he would know in the end, Duff thought. Know, or after that scene in the lift feel eternally disgraced. With his lips set in a firm line that betokened determination, he locked the letter securely away in his bag, and went downstairs.

Doctor Lofton was the only person in the lobby at the moment. He came to Duff at once, and the inspector was struck by his appearance. His face was white beneath his beard, his eyes staring.

"My God, what's this?" he demanded.

"Honywood's wife," answered Duff calmly. "Murdered by my side in the lift. Just as she was about to point out to me the killer of Drake and of Honywood. Point him out to me—in your party."

"In my party," Lofton repeated. "Yes, I believe it now. All along I've been telling myself—it couldn't be true." He shrugged his shoulders despairingly. "Why go on?" he added. "This is the end."

Duff gripped him firmly by the arm. People were coming out of the dining-room, and the detective led the way to a far corner.

"Of course you're going on," he insisted. "My word—you won't be the one to fail me, I hope. Listen to me—it wasn't a member of your party who was killed this time—you need tell your crowd little or nothing about the affair. I'm keeping you entirely out of the local investigation. Your people will perhaps be questioned—but along with all the other guests in the house. There isn't a chance these Italian police will get anywhere. Better men than they would be stumped. In a day or two you'll go on— go on as though nothing had happened. Do you hear me?"

"I hear you. But so much *has* happened."

"Only a few of us know how much. You will go on, and the murderer in your party will begin to think himself safe. He has finished his work now. Resume your tour, and leave the rest to me—and the Yard. Do you understand that?"

Lofton nodded. "I understand. I'll go, if you say so. But this last affair seemed almost too much. I was badly shaken for a moment."

"Naturally you were," answered Duff, and left him. As he sat down to dinner at a table just inside the dining-room door, the detective was thinking hard. For the first time, Lofton spoke of giving up the tour. At this moment—when the killer's work was finished.

The inspector was busy with an excellent soup, when

Pamela Potter came in. She stopped beside his table.

"By the way," she said, "I've news for you. Mr. Kennaway and I went for a stroll soon after we got here—Mr. Tait was taking a nap. Just as we were leaving the hotel, a car drew up and waited. Something told me to stop a minute—just to see who it was waiting for."

"Ah, yes," smiled Duff. "And whom was it waiting for?"

"I get you," she nodded. "But there are finer things in life than who and whom—don't you think so, too? The car was waiting for some old friends of ours. They came hurriedly out of this very hotel, with all their baggage. The Fenwicks, I mean."

Duff's bushy eyebrows rose. "The Fenwicks?"

"None other. They seemed surprised to see Mr. Kennaway and me. Said they thought we weren't due here until to-morrow. I explained that the schedule had undergone one of its usual changes."

"What time was this?" the inspector inquired.

"A few minutes past seven. I know, because it was just seven when Mr. Kennaway and I met in the lobby."

"A few minutes past seven," Duff repeated thoughtfully.

The girl went on to join Mrs. Luce at a distant table, and Duff sat down again to his soup. It had been just six-forty-five, he reflected, when that shot was fired into the lift.

CHAPTER XI

THE GENOA EXPRESS

ALL through the entrée—and it was really a pity, for a mind divided cannot truly appreciate a chef's masterpiece of the evening—Duff debated with himself over the Fenwicks. Should he look up that Italian policeman and suggest that the pair be apprehended and brought back to San Remo? The matter could be easily accomplished—but what then? There was absolutely no evidence against Norman Fenwick. To call attention to him would be to involve the Lofton travel party—a thing which Duff certainly didn't want to do. No, he determined over the inevitable roast chicken, he would make no mention to the Italian police of that somewhat precipitate departure.

When he saw the major of the City Guards again, Duff was glad he had decided not to complicate that gentleman's troubled existence with Fenwicks. Though the Italian had seemed serene enough during the interview in Miss Conway's suite, such a state of mind had evidently not long endured. As he got farther along with the case, the poor man had begun to realize the true nature of the situation which faced him, and now he was temperamental and Latin in the extreme. A murder without a clue, without a fingerprint or a footprint, with no weapon to be examined, no witness save Duff, who was from Scotland Yard and so, obviously, above suspicion. A hundred and twenty guests and thirty-nine servants in the house when the shot was fired. It was no wonder that the distracted policeman raged about, asking useless questions, and gradually drifted into a state of nervous excitement that led him into a long passionate argument about the case, in which his opponent was a small and emotional bell-boy who knew nothing whatever about it.

At ten o'clock that night Duff came upon Pamela Potter and Kennaway seated in wicker chairs on the hotel terrace. "Heavenly spot for a chat," the detective remarked, sitting down beside them.

"Yes, isn't it?" said Kennaway. "Note the over-size moon, and the scent of orange blossoms drifting up from the grounds. We were just wondering if these were included in the rate, or if they'd be among the extras on our bills. Lofton's contract, you know. Not responsible for personal expenses such as mineral waters, wines and laundry. Moonlight and orange blossoms usually turn out to be rated a personal expense."

"I'm sorry to interrupt your romantic speculations," Duff smiled. "Miss Potter has told me that the two of you took a stroll just before dinner?"

Kennaway nodded. "We were trying to build up an appetite," he explained. "After you've been on a tour of this kind for a while, life seems just one long table d'hôte."

"When you told Mr. Tait you were going out did he offer any opposition to the plan?"

"No, he didn't. As a matter of fact, he acted rather in favour of it. He said he didn't care to dine before eight, as he was very tired, and wanted to lie down for a while before eating. Our rooms are quite small, and possibly he figured I might disturb him if I stuck around."

"On what floor are your rooms?"

"On the third floor."

"Are you near the lift?"

"Just opposite it."

"Ah, yes. At six-forty-five this evening, I believe you had not yet left the hotel. Did you hear the sound of a shot about that time?"

"I did."

"Where were you at the moment?"

"I was down in the lobby, waiting for Miss Potter. We weren't supposed to meet until seven, but Mr. Tait had sort of shooed me out."

"Who else was in the lobby? Any other member of the party?"

"No. Just myself and a few servants. I heard the shot, but I didn't realize what it was right away. You see, it came from the elevator shaft. Having ridden on the elevator, I wasn't surprised. I was expecting to see it blow up in a cloud of red smoke at any moment."

"Then when the shot was fired, Mr. Tait was alone in your suite?"

"Undoubtedly. Alone, and probably sound asleep."

"Probably," nodded Duff.

At that instant, Tait appeared on the terrace. He stood there straight and tall, a handsome figure in evening dress under the Riviera moon. Duff had been thinking of him as an old man, but it suddenly occurred to the inspector that Tait was not so old as he seemed—illness, anxiety, in his face perhaps, but not age.

"I thought I'd find you here," the lawyer remarked to Kennaway.

"Sit down, Mr. Tait," Duff suggested. "We've been admiring the view."

"I'm fed up with views," Tait snapped. "Wish

I was back in New York. Active all my life, and this loafing is hell." Duff wondered. Was Tait thinking of dropping out of the party too? "Come on, Mark, let's go upstairs," the lawyer went on. "I want to get to bed. You won't have to read to me very long to-night."

"Still mystery stories?" the detective inquired.

"Not a chance," Tait answered. "There's enough murder in real life without reading about it in books. We've taken up the Russians now. It was Mark's idea. He thought he was clever, but I'm on to him. I have to listen or go to sleep, so naturally I go to sleep. That gives him more time for the ladies." He turned and walked towards the lighted french window through which he had come. "Are you ready, Mark?" he said, over his shoulder.

Kennaway rose reluctantly. "When duty calls with clarion voice, the youth replies, I come," he remarked. "Sorry, Miss Potter. Mark Kennaway swinging off. If the orange blossoms are an extra, you'll have to bear the expense alone from now on."

"Nice chap, isn't he?" Duff inquired, as the young man disappeared.

"Very nice," answered the girl. "At times. To-night was one of the times."

"What do you mean, at times?" the detective inquired.

"Oh, he has his moments. At others, he looks at me as much as to say, how in the world did I ever come to speak to this person from the crude Middle West? It's Boston, you know. But there—you wouldn't understand."

"I'm afraid not," Duff replied. "Tell me—how are the members of the travel party taking our latest murder?"

"Calmly enough, I believe. I've always heard that one gets used to anything in time. I presume we'll be held here for a while?"

"It's hard to say," Duff told her. "A murder investigation in Italy, you know, is likely to be a complicated affair. There are three branches of the police, the City Guards, the Carabinieri and the Municipal Force. The last are concerned only with minor crimes, but often the other two branches are called upon simultaneously to investigate a murder, and the result is a very pretty little row between them. So far, only the City Guards have come into this case, and I am hoping the Carabinieri stay out. If they do, I don't anticipate much difficulty. I believe I can convince that worried major that this is my affair, and that he mustn't trouble, really."

The girl leaned suddenly closer. "Tell me something, please?" she said gravely. "Is the murderer the same person every time? My grandfather, poor Mr. Honywood, and now Mrs. Honywood? All killed by the same man?"

Duff nodded slowly. "Undoubtedly, Miss Pamela. The same man."

"Who?" Her voice was low, tense. "Who?"

The detective smiled. "All in good time, we know," he replied. "I am quoting an old friend—a Chinese whom I want you to meet when you reach Honolulu. At present moment we are faced by stone wall. We swing about, seeking new path. Still quoting my friend." The girl did not speak. After a brief silence Duff continued. "I looked you up to-night because I have something to tell you, Miss Pamela. A part of our mystery at least has been solved. I have in my bag a letter which fully explains how your grandfather happened to be involved in this affair."

The girl leaped to her feet. "You have! I must see it."

"Of course." Duff also rose. "If you will come up with me I will give it to you. Take it to your own room and read it. I should like to have it back in the morning."

Without a word, she went with him into the brightly lighted lobby. They moved towards the lift. Duff regarded the little cage with marked distaste. "I'm on the first floor," he suggested hopefully.

"Then we won't bother with that thing," said the girl. "Let's walk."

She waited in his doorway while he brought the letter. He was frantically searching his mind for words of preparation and of sympathy, but none came to him. Words were not his forte. All he could say was: "At what hour shall we meet to-morrow?"

"At eight o'clock," the girl answered. "In the lobby." Seizing the thick envelope eagerly, she hurried away.

Duff returned downstairs, where he had another chat with the baffled major of the City Guards. Subtly he planted in that official's mind the uselessness of further investigation. This particular murder, he pointed out, looked to be solution-proof, but fortunately it happened to be one of a series, and since the first had taken place in London, the whole matter was up to Scotland Yard. He intimated that the Yard stood ready to relieve the Italian police of a difficult and thankless task.

The major intimated that the Italian police stood ready to be relieved. When they parted, the local man seemed to be in a much happier frame of mind.

The next day proved to be the type which the Riviera does so well—deep blue sky, sparkling sea, and sunlight like a gold piece just from the mint. At eight o'clock, as they had planned, Duff met Pamela Potter in the lobby. The beauty of the morning was seemingly lost on the girl. Her violet eyes were clouded with the evidence of recent tears. She handed the letter back to Duff.

"I wanted to prepare you," he told her. "But I didn't know how. My methods are rather clumsy— I'm so sorry."

"Not at all," she answered in a low voice. "You took the very best course. Poor grandfather—dead for no reason whatever. Dead because he did another man a kindness."

"Who could ask a better epitaph?" the detective said gently.

Pamela Potter looked at him, and her fine eyes flashed. "Well, this doesn't end the matter with me," she cried. "I want that man—that man who killed him. I shan't rest until he's been found."

"Nor I," Duff replied. He thought of the lift. "No, by gad—nor I. I mean to run down Jim Everhard if it's the last act of my life. Have you any idea——"

She shook her head. "I lay awake nearly all night, thinking. Who of the men in our party? They all seem incapable of such a thing—even Maxy Minchin. Who—who? Mr. Vivian—he appears to be interested only in Mrs. Spicer. Captain Keane—such a sneaky air—I don't like him, but that's not enough, of course. Mr. Tait—he's very disagreeable at times. But then, the poor man is ill. Mr. Ross—there's not a thing to connect him with all this. As for Mr. Benbow, I'm sure he'd never do anything he couldn't photograph and show the boys back in Akron. There's Doctor Lofton left. And that foolish little Fenwick man. But it would be absurd to think that he——"

"Nothing is absurd in this business," Duff broke in. "And by the way—you've forgotten one member of the party."

"Really?" She appeared surprised. "Who? Or should it be whom? I know how fussy you are about grammar."

"I was referring to Mark Kennaway."

She smiled. "Oh, don't be ridiculous."

"I never overlook anyone myself," he remarked. "And since I am about to take you in as my partner——"

"What do you mean by that?"

"I mean that I shall probably leave the party for a time. I don't expect any more—er—accidents, and there is little I could accomplish if I came along. As I told you last night, I am faced with stone wall, and I must swing about, seeking another path. Sooner or later I shall no doubt join you again. In the meantime, I should like to have you act as my representative. Please make a study of the men in this group, and write me occasionally from the various ports where your tour touches. Just tell me how things are going. If you come across anything that looks like a clue, let me have it. You know—nice gossipy letters—you're very good at that sort of thing, I'm sure. And a cable if anything important turns up—New Scotland Yard, London, will reach me. Will you do that?"

"Of course," the girl nodded. "I'm writing to some twenty boys already. The more the merrier."

"I'm flattered to be included on the list," Duff replied. "Thank you so much."

Mrs. Luce came up. "Oh, there you are, Pamela," she said. "I'm glad to see you in such safe company. Oh, don't look at me like that, Inspector. Where matters of the heart are concerned, I presume you're just as dangerous as any man. There—I've probably made you very happy by saying that."

Duff laughed. "Gorgeous morning, isn't it?" he inquired.

"Is it?" she answered. "I'm from southern California myself, and I'm not impressed."

"I hope you slept well, my dear," the girl remarked pleasantly.

"I always sleep well—provided I change bedrooms often enough. Even a murder doesn't disturb me. I remember once at Maiden's Hotel, in Delhi—of course, he was only a bus boy—the victim, I mean. But I must save that for my reminiscences. What have you made of last night's affair, Inspector?"

"Nothing, as usual," Duff replied grimly.

"Well, I'm not surprised. You're no superman, and this friend of ours with the urge to kill begins to look like one. Clever, certainly. One reassuring thing—he's starting to operate outside the party. There may be enough of us to last him, after all. Are you breakfasting, Pamela?"

"I'm famished," said the girl, and followed Mrs. Luce into the dining-room.

By noon it was apparent that the Italian authorities would attempt to hold none of the travellers in the hotel. The tourist business was no mean industry along the Riviera di Ponente, and not to be disturbed to satisfy a policeman's whim. Bags were piled up at the door of the hotel, and a number of guests departed. The word went around among the Lofton party that they were to take the two o'clock express for Genoa. All of them were eager to be off. Lofton himself had recovered from his despairing mood of the night before; he was everywhere at once, spreading information and advice.

As for the major of the City Guards, his spirits had

risen noticeably.   After a talk with his associates, and a telegram to Rome, it had been decided to hand the whole matter over to Scotland Yard, which left the major nothing to do but wear his uniform and impress the ladies.   At both of these tasks he excelled, and he knew it.

Again, as on that morning in London, Inspector Duff found himself in the odd position of saying goodbye to a group of people among whom was undoubtedly the quarry he so much wanted to capture.   Of seeing them off on a long journey—Naples, Alexandria, Bombay, the far ports of the Orient.   But by this time he was resigned to any turn which fate might take.   With a cheery air he went with them to the station on the west bay, just outside the new town.

They gathered on the platform to await the train. Benbow with his camera, Sadie Minchin loaded down with recent purchases in the jewellery line.   "Maybe Maxy won't have to come across when he meets a customs man," she predicted proudly.

Suddenly Mrs. Spicer gave a little cry.   "Good heavens—I never realized it before," she exclaimed.

"What is the trouble?" Doctor Lofton asked solicitously.

"There are thirteen of us," she replied, with a stricken look.

Maxy Minchin patted her on the back.   "Don't mean a thing, lady," he assured her.

Doctor Lofton smiled wearily.   "There are only twelve in the party now," he told her.   "I'm not in it, really, you know."

"Oh, yes, you are," the woman persisted.   "And you're the thirteenth."

"Nonsense, Irene," Stuart Vivian said.   "Surely you're not superstitious?"

"Why not? Everybody is."

"Only the ignorant," he replied. "Oh—I'm sorry——"

He was sorry a bit too late. The woman had given him a look. Even those at whom it was not directed were startled to see it. There was a dangerous fire in her green eyes.

"I'm superstitious too," Mrs. Luce put in diplomatically. "Not about thirteen, though. That's always been lucky for me. But when it comes to a black cat—one crossed before my rickshaw on the Bubbling Well Road in Shanghai ten years ago, and half an hour later an automobile struck us. I pulled through all right, but I always blamed the cat. Thirteen, as I was saying, Mrs. Spicer——" But that lady had walked haughtily away.

The express thundered in, crowded as usual, and there began a hurried search for seats in the first-class compartments. Duff helped Mrs. Luce and Pamela Potter to find places. Once more he spoke to the girl about the letters.

"Don't worry," she smiled. "I'm positively garrulous with a fountain pen."

The detective leaped back to the platform. Doors were slamming shut, one by one the Lofton travel party was disappearing from his ken. He noted Benbow, his camera hanging from a black strap across his shoulder, climbing into a compartment from which his wife had beckoned; noted Ross with his Malacca stick helped aboard by a porter, caught a last knowing smile from Captain Keane. The final face he saw was that of Patrick Tait, the lined, worried face of a man old before his time, white as death now in the dazzling Riviera sunshine.

"Well, that's that," shrugged Duff, and returned to the hotel to inquire about London trains.

The next morning but one he sat in the superintendent's office at Scotland Yard. His face was very red
and he was perspiring freely, for he had just related
the latter part of his story—the disturbing incident
of the·murder in the lift. His superior looked at
him in a kindly way.

"Don't take it too hard, my boy. It might have
happened to any of us."

"I shall take it just this hard, sir," Duff replied.
"I shall go on searching for Jim Everhard until I
find him. It may take months, but I mean to have
him in the end."

"Naturally," the superintendent nodded. "I know
how you feel. And every facility of the Yard will be
put at your disposal. But don't forget this. Evidence
in the matter of the killing of Honywood and his wife
is of no value to us. Those cases could never be tried
in London. No—it is the murder of Hugh Morris
Drake that alone concerns us. We must capture
Everhard and bring him here to answer for that, and
our proofs must be unanswerable."

"I understand that, sir. It was why I didn't
linger on in Nice or San Remo."

"Have you mapped out any future course of
action?"

"No, I haven't. I thought I would consult with
you about that."

"Precisely." The superintendent nodded his complete approval. "Will you please leave with me all
your notes on the case? I shall look them over
during the day. If you will come in at five this
afternoon, we will decide at that time what we had
better do. And once more—don't worry about that
affair in the lift. Think of it only as a stronger
incentive to get your man."

"Thank you, sir."

Feeling much better than when he had entered the room, Duff left it. A good egg, his superior.

He lunched with Hayley, who was even more sympathetic than the superintendent. At five that afternoon he returned to his superior's office.

"Hello," that gentleman said. "Sit down, please. I've read your notes. A puzzle, of course. But I was struck by one thing. No doubt you were, too."

"What was that?"

"This man Tait, Mr. Duff."

"Ah, yes—Tait."

"Rather queer, my boy, rather queer. His story may be absolutely true, but doubts crept into my mind as I read. He thought Honywood had been murdered, he entered that room and saw Honywood alive, and the shock nearly finished him. Why should he take it so hard? Honywood and he were, it seems, practically strangers. Why should the matter have been such a shock, unless——" The superintendent paused.

"I quite understand, sir," Duff said. "Unless he supposed Honywood dead because he thought he himself had strangled the man in the night. Unless —in other words—Tait is Jim Everhard."

"Precisely," nodded the superintendent. "It is a matter to think about. Now, with regard to the future. As far as the travel party is concerned I believe, Mr. Duff, that for the time being your usefulness in that quarter is ended." The inspector's face fell. "Don't misunderstand me, my boy. I merely feel that you are too well known among them to accomplish anything there. I have looked over the itinerary Lofton gave you. After Egypt, I note four boat trips—on a P. and O. liner from Port Said to Bombay, on a British India Steam Navigation Company ship from Calcutta to Rangoon and Singapore,

then by way of another P. and O. boat from the
latter place via Saigon to Hong-Kong. From Hong-
Kong they are to take a Dollar liner bound for San
Francisco. For the present I would leave the party
in peace. Our quarry may think we have dropped
the matter and be off his guard. In a few days I
intend to dispatch a good man to Calcutta with
instructions to get in touch with the party from that
point on, in any manner that offers. I haven't
definitely decided, but I am thinking of sending
Sergeant Welby."

"One of the cleverest, Welby is, sir," Duff replied.

"Yes—and the type who could easily pass as a
ship's steward, or something of the sort. Cheer up,
my boy. If Welby hits on anything definite, you
shall join him and make the arrest. In the meantime, there is work to be done in the States. An
investigation of the Honywoods' past—the meaning
of those wash-leather bags—the search for a safety
deposit box with the number 3260. All that will be
left to you. But there is no need for you to be off
just yet. I want you to time your investigation in
America so that you can conclude it on the west
coast about the date when Lofton's travel party
lands at San Francisco.'

Duff was smiling again. "Very well planned, sir.
But may I make one suggestion?"

"Of course. What is it?"

"I should like to meet the party at Honolulu, sir."

"And why at Honolulu?"

"It would give me that last run from Honolulu to
the mainland, sir. Some of them may leave the
party at San Francisco. And furthermore——"

"Yes?"

"I have a very good friend at Honolulu. A chap
of whom I'm particularly fond. I believe I've spoken

to you about him—Inspector Chan, of the Honolulu police."

The superintendent nodded. "Ah, yes. Charlie Chan—the Bruce case. Do you think Inspector Chan would like to see you, Duff?"

Duff was puzzled. "I'm sure he would, sir. Why do you ask?"

His superior smiled. "Because I have long wanted to do a favour for Mr. Chan. Don't worry, my boy. Honolulu can undoubtedly be arranged."

CHAPTER XII

THE JEWELLER IN CHOWRINGHEE ROAD

THERE followed for Duff weeks of restless waiting.
He busied himself with minor tasks, but his heart was
elsewhere. Welby was off on a P. and O. boat, his
destination Calcutta. For several nights Duff had
coached him, read aloud from his notes, speculated
with him over the possibilities in the Lofton travel
party. Sergeant Welby, he realized with mixed
emotions, was a remarkably clever lad. Not like
most of the C.I.D. men, from some inland farm, but
a London product, a little cockney born within sound
of Bow bells. Within sound of those bells most of
his days had been passed, and the seven seas were
to him an uncharted emptiness. He had never even
read about them; he was having some difficulties with
his geography now; but he faced the future with
cool unconcern and unbounded confidence. He
examined again and again the little bags of pebbles;
they seemed to fascinate him. They formed, he said,
the essential clue. He trembled to be off.

Well, he was off now. Duff had gone with him to
the Royal Albert Docks, and had watched his fellow
detective until he faded from sight. Walking that
same night across Vauxhall Bridge, with the tide out
and a tang of sharpness in the air, the inspector
thought of Welby, some miles out at sea by this
time on his great adventure. Would Welby solve
the puzzle—the puzzle that was by all rights the

special task of Duff? He would try to be broad-
minded. He had wished Welby luck, and by gad,
he meant it.

In a little more than two weeks came the first
news of the Lofton party. It was contained in a
letter from Pamela Potter, postmarked at Aden.
The inspector opened it and read:

"DEAR INSPECTOR DUFF,—I'm so sorry. I meant to
send in my first report from Port Said. But the days
are so full and the nights are so wonderful—well, we
just drift along. I'm afraid you'd be feeling a bit impatient if you were with us. A murderer in our party—
and what of it? We've done all the bazaars, we've met
the Sphinx—I did remember to ask her that question
we so want answered, but she didn't reply.

"I've seen Port Said. It may be as wicked as it's
reputed to be, but Mrs. Luce wouldn't let me find out.
She said she'd tell me all about it—and she did. Yes,
she's as full of reminiscences as ever. You need an atlas
of the world when she talks to you. But she's an old
dear.

"We've put the Suez Canal behind us. Like a muddy
river, with lonely people sitting at the stations along
the way. I wanted to get off and tell them about
Maurice Chevalier in the talkies. On each side, oceans
of sand dotted with scrub acacias, and at night the nice
light air of the desert blowing across the ship. We're
nearly out of the Red Sea now, and the way I feel is,
thank heaven that's attended to. Hot—my word! The
flying fish flopped on to the deck with a sort of pleased-
to-meet-you air. The sun is a huge red ball when we
watch it go down every night, and we listen to hear it
sizzle when it hits the water. At least I do. Mark
Kennaway says it never touches the water at all, and
that the sound I hear is eggs frying in the crow's-nest.

"Faithful to my orders, I've been cultivating the men
in the party. The only result up to date is that I've
got myself heartily disliked by the women. Even Sadie
Minchin thinks I'm trying to steal her Maxy. Maybe
I have overplayed Maxy a bit—but he's quite amusing.
I've posed for Elmer Benbow so many times, I expect
to see his wife take his camera away from him at any

moment. As for the rest, well, I really believe I've got over big with Stuart Vivian.

"You remember that nice little row between Stuart and his lady friend at the San Remo station? About being superstitious? They didn't speak for days—that is, she didn't, and after a while he gave up trying. It was then I came into his life. I got to thinking we didn't know much about him, so I set to work. When the gentle Irene saw the speed I was making, she rose in her wrath and took him back. I'm not so sure he wanted to be taken. He squirmed considerably. A conceited man. As though I meant anything by my deep interest in his past. He's forty-five, if a day.

"All of which brings me—don't ask me how—to dear Captain Keane. I was going to my state-room the other night at twelve—I'd been sitting up on deck with somebody or other—a man, I believe it was. I'm trying to follow out your instructions to the letter, you see. Well, when I entered the alleyway—that's authentic and nautical—leading to my room, there was Captain Keane snooping just outside Mr. Vivian's door. He muttered something and hurried away. Still up to his old tricks, you will note. He's one of the slyest men I've ever met, but I'm afraid he's too obvious to mean anything, aren't you?

"As for the rest, I've listened to Doctor Lofton's erudite talks, to Mr. Ross on the subject of Tacoma and why does anybody live in the Middle West now that the Pacific coast has been discovered, until my ears ache. There's Mr. Tait, too—my one failure. Somehow, my charms seem to fall on barren ground when he is about. How would you explain it? Perhaps he's a bit miffed because I take up a little of Mark Kennaway's time. Did I say a little? Maybe that isn't quite accurate. You see, he is so young, and I am so beautiful—— But as I was saying, I've cultivated them all. And so far, I must admit I haven't turned up a single clue. I wouldn't call that about Keane a clue. Would you?

"We have nearly reached Aden. Mrs. Luce is taking me to luncheon there, at her favourite restaurant. Probably she will call the head waiter by his first name, and ask after all the little waiters. Aden, she tells me, is a melting-pot that somebody put on the stove and

forgot to remove. According to her, I shall get my first
smell of the East when we reach there. I believe I've
had a whiff or two already. I don't much like it. But
Mrs. Luce claims you grow to love it in time. That
when you're sitting in your patio at Pasadena you
suddenly remember it, and then it's just a case of engaging
a caretaker and locking the front door. Maybe. No
doubt I shall be able to tell you more about that when
I write again.

"Sadie Minchin has just stopped at my elbow, wondering about the jewellery shops in Aden. Maxy had better
arrange to have her met by an armoured truck at the
San Francisco dock. He owns a limousine with bullet-
proof glass—perhaps he'll have that there.

"Sorry I haven't proved more of a detective. Better
luck from here on. I'll have lots of time in the Indian
Ocean.

"Sincerely yours,
"PAMELA POTTER."

That night, in Vine Street station in London, Duff
discussed this letter with Hayley. There wasn't much
to discuss, as they both realized. Duff was inclined
to be impatient.

"First time in my life," he muttered, "that I ever
depended on a girl to keep me abreast of a case. And
the last, I hope."

"A charming girl, at any rate," Hayley smiled.

"What of that? She's not so charming that one of
those men will suddenly turn to her and say: 'Oh, by
the way, I murdered your grandfather.' And that's
all I want. Not charm, but the identity of Jim
Everhard."

"When does Welby join the party?" asked the
Vine Street man.

"Not for ages," sighed Duff. "There they are,
just drifting along, with no one watching them but a
girl. A big idea of the chief's."

"It will all come right in the end," Hayley answered.
"Something tells me."

"Please ask your something to come and talk to me," said Duff. "I need it."

He needed it even more before he heard again. Every night he studied the itinerary Lofton had given him. In his thoughts he followed the little party across the Indian Ocean to Bombay, then by the long route—they would take the long route—to Mt. Abu, Delhi, Agra, Lucknow, Benares, Calcutta. It was while they were at Calcutta that he heard once more —a mysterious cable from the girl.

"If one of your men is in this neighbourhood, have him get in touch with me at once. At the Great Eastern Hotel, Calcutta, until this evening, then aboard British-India liner *Malaya* bound for Rangoon, Penang, Singapore."

Feeling an unaccustomed thrill of anticipation, Duff cabled Welby in care of certain British agents in Calcutta. Then—silence again. One dreary day succeeding another, and not an atom of news. Confound the girl—didn't she realize that he, too, had a deep interest in this affair, wanted to know what was happening?

He heard at last. A letter came in, postmarked Rangoon. Eagerly the man in London tore it open:

"DEAR INSPECTOR DUFF,—I am rather a dud as a correspondent, aren't I? No doubt my cable left you in a little fever, and the explanation has been slow in coming. But the mails, Inspector—you really must blame it on the mails. I couldn't very well cable the contents of this letter. Spies, you know, in this mysterious East—spies back of every tamarind tree.

"Let me see—where was I? We were just steaming into Aden, I believe. We went on steaming after we got there, and all the way across the Indian Ocean to Bombay. Tempers began to get a little frayed about the edges. You know, a party of this sort starts out as one great, big, happy family. It was a bit delayed in our case by certain events at the beginning, but the peak of comradeship and mutual love and esteem was reached in Italy and Egypt. Everyone was very confidential. Then gradually, as the weather got hotter, our ardour for one another began to cool. It's got so now that nobody enters a room without a preliminary survey to make sure no other member of the party, thank God, is inside.

"Well, we did the Indian Ocean. We came into Bombay, said good-bye to the dear old ship, and staggered up to the Taj Mahal Hotel. And who do you think was in the lobby? Mr. Fenwick, and his silent sister, from Pittsfield, Massachusetts. It seems that after they left us at Nice they said to themselves, we've started out on a world tour, so why not go through with it? In Naples, it appears, they signed on for a cruise—you know, one of the big wonder ships that goes right on around without a change. At least, that's what they told us, and as we'd seen such a ship in the harbour, I presume it was the truth. Little Norman was insufferable. He asked us if we'd had any more murders, and gave us a long talk on the superiority of their method of travel over ours. We were so happy to see a comparatively new face—even one like Mr. Fenwick's—that we listened meekly.

"We stayed in Bombay a couple of days, and then set out over the hills and far away in the direction of Calcutta. I got a good look at the Taj Mahal, and a terrible cold. Eventually we reached our destination, feeling a little sad about India and rather wishing there wasn't any such place. In Calcutta something happened —and so I come at last to my long delayed story of the cable.

"On our final morning in Calcutta, Doctor Lofton herded us into a jewellery shop on Chowringhee Road. I presume he gets a commission on sales, he was so passionate about having us go there. Imri Ismail, I believe, was the proprietor's name. Once I got inside, I was glad I'd come. Really, the most gorgeous jewels you ever saw in your life—star sapphires, rubies, diamonds —but of course you're not interested. Sadie Minchin went haywire on the spot. Even Maxy turned a bit pale to see her buying.

"Most of the others in the party just looked casually around and then drifted out. But I happened to see a necklace of diamonds, and my will-power certainly failed me. A little weathered clerk with a drooping eyelid and a most villainous expression saw the condition I was in, and fastened himself on me. While I was hovering on the brink, Stuart Vivian came up and advised me to wait a minute. He said he knew a little about diamonds, and that these were good stones, but not worth what my pirate friend was asking. After a bitter argument, the price began to drop amazingly, until finally Mr. Vivian said it was a good buy. At that point Irene Spicer swept down on him, evidently after a long search, and carried him off.

"It was while the clerk was removing the fictional price tag from the necklace that a surprising thing happened. Another clerk came along behind him, and as my man pressed close to the counter to let the other pass, he said something in a foreign tongue. Right in the middle of that string of strange sounds, two English words stood out like a house afire. He said 'Jim Everhard' as clearly and distinctly as a radio announcer.

"My heart stood still. The other man paused, as though he were idly curious, and looked towards the door. No one was there. I had to get busy at once with travellers' checks, and when I handed them over, I said casually to the man with the drooping eyelid: 'You know Jim Everhard, too?' That was where I made my big mistake. I should have said it before he got his hands on the checks. Now it was all a closed incident as far as he was concerned. He calmly pretended he didn't understand English any longer, and bowed me out.

"I went for a walk in the Maidan and wondered what to do. I thought maybe I'd send you a postcard with the message: 'Wish you were here.' I certainly wished it. Then I evolved the brilliant idea of the cable.

"I didn't hear anything all day. Mr. Kennaway and I went for a stroll in the Eden Gardens that afternoon, and then rode down to Diamond Harbour to get the British-India boat. We were quite late, and everybody else was aboard. As we started up the gang-plank, which they were about to draw in, who should come rushing down it but my friend of the drooping eyelid?

He'd evidently been aboard to see somebody off. Who?
Jim Everhard? Or was this merely a last minute effort
to make a few more sales?

"Late that night I was walking along the deck of the
Malaya when a steward stopped me and told me someone in the second class wanted to see me. I was startled
at first, then I remembered my cable, and so I followed
the steward down a ladder to the lower deck. In the
shadow of a lifeboat I met the queerest little man. I
was a bit dubious about him at first, but he was all
right. He was your friend, Mr. Welby, of the C.I.D.
I liked him. He was cute. And such a quaint cockney
accent.

"I told him what had happened in the jewellery shop,
and he was naturally interested. When I added that I
had seen the clerk leaving the ship a few hours ago, he
nodded. He said that he had been up in the first class
about that time himself, talking with a friend among
the stewards, and that the man from Imri Ismail's
had attracted his attention. He had followed him and
noticed which cabin he visited. 'And,' added Mr. Welby,
'it was a cabin occupied by two members of the Lofton
travel party, Miss Potter.'

"Of course I wanted to know which two. Did I find
out? You know better. Mr. Welby just thanked me
heartily for my information. 'You may have lightened
my job considerably,' he said. Then he asked me how
much Stuart Vivian seemed to know about diamonds.
I said I couldn't tell, but that like all men he claimed
to know everything about everything. Mr. Welby
nodded again, and intimated that I could run along now.
He told me he was hoping to obtain a position as steward
on the Dollar boat out of Hong-Kong, and that in the
meantime he would be hovering about, but that I
mustn't speak to him unless he spoke first. I assured
him I was always the perfect lady in such matters, and
we parted. I haven't seen him since.

"Well, there you are, Inspector. That's the situation
on this hot April night in Rangoon, where our boat lies
over two days. Speaking of the smell of the East, I
know all about it now. The odour of fetid narrow
streets, vegetables rotting in the tropic sun, dead fish,
copra, mosquito lotions—and of too many people trying
to be in one place at one time. I'm used to it. I can

look forward to China and Japan with an unconquerable nose.

"I'll probably write again from Singapore—it will depend on what happens next. Please pardon this long letter, but I told you I was garrulous with a fountain pen. And I really had something to write about this time.

"Warmly yours—it's the climate—
"PAMELA POTTER."

An hour after reading this epistle, Inspector Duff was in conference with his chief. The superintendent read it too, and with an interest almost as great as Duff's.

"Welby appears to be playing a lone game," he remarked, and his tone suggested a certain lack of approval.

"He probably has nothing definite to report as yet, sir," Duff replied. "But if the girl has narrowed his search to one of two people, then there ought to be news very soon. Of course, it may all come to nothing. She may even be mistaken about what she heard in the jeweller's shop."

The superintendent considered. "Why did Welby ask her how much Vivian knew about diamonds?" he said at last.

"Couldn't say, sir," Duff answered. "He's deep, Welby is. No doubt he has a theory of some sort. We might cable to Calcutta and have that clerk questioned about Jim Everhard."

His superior shook his head. "No—I prefer to leave it to Welby. To do what you suggest might interfere with his game. A cable of warning from the clerk to Everhard, and Everhard might disappear from the party. Besides, I'm certain we should get nothing from Miss Potter's friend with the drooping eyelid. He doesn't sound like the sort who would be eager to assist Scotland Yard."

Duff had taken out a pocket calendar. "I figure that the Lofton party is in Hong-Kong to-day, sir. They're to stop at that port a week, I believe, making a side trip to Canton. If I'm to carry through the investigation you suggested, and then get on to Honolulu——" He waited.

"You want to be off, I suppose," the superintendent smiled. "How soon can you start?"

"To-night—if there's a boat, sir," Duff answered.

"To-morrow, at any rate," agreed his superior.

On the morrow Duff, radiantly happy that the moment for action had arrived at last, set out for Southampton. This time it was Hayley who sped the parting traveller, with many expressions of encouragement and hope. That night the inspector was aboard one of the swiftest of Atlantic liners. The steady turn of the screw was music in his ears; he stood at the starboard rail and watched the prow of the ship as it cut with amazing speed through the dark water. His heart was light. Every moment was carrying him nearer the puzzle that had so rudely left him to travel round the world.

His inquiries into the past of the Honywoods, which he pursued diligently once he had reached New York, got him nowhere. They had arrived in that confusing city some fifteen years ago, and none of the friends whose names Mrs. Honywood's maid had given him appeared to know whence they had come. It was not, it appeared, customary to inquire in New York. To-day was all that mattered, yesterday was nobody's business. Blank looks met any mention of the wash-leather bags. Duff found himself baffled, and somewhat resentful towards this teeming, heedless city.

In the matter of a safety-deposit box number 3260, he was equally helpless. With the aid of the New

York police, he was able to ascertain the number of Tait's box at his bank, and also that of the one kept by Lofton. Neither meant anything. A helpful commissioner pointed out to the Britisher that a man might have any number of secret boxes at banks where he did not regularly do business. This part of it, Duff began to realize, was nothing but a wild goose chase.

Nevertheless he plodded on, patient to the end. He went to Boston and looked up Mark Kennaway's position there. An excellent family, he discovered, and even he, an outsider, sensed what that meant— in Boston. Next he visited Pittsfield, where the continued absence of the Fenwicks was deplored by a circle of the best people. Painfully respectable, it seemed, the Fenwicks. At Akron the air was less rarefied, but the situation appeared much the same. Duff was taken out to lunch by Benbow's partner, who told him to tell old Elmer to hurry home. Business, it was rumoured, had definitely turned the corner, and was on the up grade.

In Chicago he found the friends of Maxy Minchin reticent in the extreme. Tight-lipped, they listened to the inspector and had nothing at all to say. Duff gathered that there was no great public demand for the gangster's return. He moved to Tacoma. John Ross, he found, was an important figure in the lumber trade. Dropping down to San Francisco, he made inquiries about Stuart Vivian. The man was known to many of the leading citizens; they all spoke highly of him. A call at the office of Irene Spicer's husband revealed that he was away in Hollywood, and was not expected back for some time.

Sitting down one mild May evening in his room at the Fairmont Hotel, Duff summed up the results of his long trek. They were nil. He had looked into the home standing of every man in the Lofton travel party, and with the exception of Maxy Minchin, all appeared to be above reproach. As for Maxy, it seemed unlikely that he could be involved in any such affair as this. Every man in the party? Well, it was true he had found no track of Keane in New York, where the captain claimed to reside. The name was in no directory. But Duff gave this little thought. From the first, for some reason he couldn't quite define, he had refused to suspect Keane.

With that one exception, then, he was familiar with the home environment of all of them, and he was no nearer than ever to knowing which one was capable of murder. Yet there was a murderer in that group —there must be, if Honywood's letter spoke true. "Jim Everhard is travelling with the party. Jim Everhard, who has sworn to kill me—and you, too."

Duff got up and walked to the window. From his lofty perch he saw the lights of Chinatown, of the ferries in the harbour, of the tall buildings across the bay. Memories of his previous visit to this fascinating city came back to him. Memories of Charlie Chan.

A bell-boy knocked at his door and handed him a cablegram. It was from his chief at the Yard.

"Cable from Kobe. Welby anticipates early success. Proceed to Honolulu. Luck."

A few words only, but Duff was mightily cheered. Welby, at least, was making progress. Would the little cockney solve the problem in the end? Not usually an imaginative man, Duff was able none the less to picture a gratifying scene. A meeting with Welby on the Honolulu dock, Welby with proofs such as would satisfy the most exacting jury, Welby pointing out some not quite—at this moment—clearly discerned figure. "Tyke him, Duff. He's guilty as hell." Not quite so gratifying, of course, as it would have been if Duff had gathered those proofs himself. But what of that? Scotland Yard always worked as a team. He would do something for Welby some day.

The next morning but one, Duff sailed for Honolulu on the *Maui*. It would bring him, he knew, into Honolulu harbour some twenty hours before that Dollar liner from Yokohama docked beneath the Aloha Tower. A brief time to renew old acquaintance with Charlie Chan, to tell him about this new case on which he had been working—and then, the Lofton travel party and action. Quick action, he hoped. He had decided not to cable Charlie of his coming. Why take the edge off the surprise?

For two days Duff loafed about the ship, at peace with the world. A glorious rest, this was. When the big moment arrived, he would be strong and ready. On the evening of the second day, a boy came up to him and handed him a radiogram. Tearing open the envelope, he glanced at the signature. The message was from his chief.

"Welby found murdered on dock at Yokohama shortly after sailing of liner carrying Lofton party. Get Everhard dead or alive."

Crushing the message savagely in his hand, Duff sat for a long time staring into the darkness beyond the rail of the ship. Before his eyes was a picture of Welby as he had seen him last in London, smiling, confident, serene. The little cockney who had never hitherto strayed beyond the sound of the bells of St. Mary le Bow, killed on a Yokohama dock.

"Dead or alive," said Duff through his teeth. "Dead, if I have my way."

CHAPTER XIII

A KNOCK AT CHARLIE'S DOOR

A FEW mornings later, in the police court on the second floor of Halekaua Hale at the foot of Bethel Street in Honolulu, three men were on trial—a Portuguese, a Korean and a Filipino. They were charged with gambling in the street, and on the witness-stand at the moment sat a placid and serene Chinese. The East, we are told, has a deep respect for obesity; in China as a mandarin increases in weight, he gains in prestige; in Japan the wrestlers, heroes of the crowd, are enormous. The Oriental in the witness-box was equipped, on this count, for high standing among his own.

"All right, Inspector Chan," said the Judge. "Let us have your story, please."

The witness sat, immobile as a stone Buddha. He opened his narrow black eyes a trifle wider, and spoke.

"I am walking down Pawaa Alley," he remarked. "With me is my fellow detective, Mr. Kashimo. Before us, at the door of Timo's fish shop, we perceive extensive crowd has gathered. We accelerate our speed. As we approach, crowd melts gradually away, and next moment we come upon these three men, now prisoners in the dock. They are bent on to knees, and they disport themselves with dice. Endearing remarks towards these same dice issue from their lips in three languages."

"Come, come, Charlie." said the prosecuting

attorney, a red-haired, aggressive man. "I beg your pardon—Inspector Chan. Your language is, as usual, a little flowery for an American court. These men were shooting craps. That's what you mean to say, isn't it?"

"I am very much afraid it is," Chan replied.

"You are familiar with the game? You know it when you see it?"

"As a child knows its mother's face."

"And you identify these men absolutely? They are the crap shooters?"

"No question whatever," Charlie nodded. "They are, unfortunately for them, the three."

The lawyer for the defence, a slick little Japanese, was instantly on his feet. "Now I object," he cried. "Your Honour, I question propriety of that word 'unfortunately.' The witness speaks as though my clients had already been tried and found guilty. Mr. Chan, kindly restrain such comment, if you will do so."

Chan bowed his head. "Overwhelmed with chagrin, I am sure," he replied. "Pardon me for assuming inevitable has already occurred." The lawyer gave a little cry of rebuke, but Charlie went blandly on. "To continue testimony, next moment the three look up and behold myself and the redoubtable Kashimo. At simultaneous moment, expressions of faces take on startling change. They leap up to feet to accomplish escape. Down the alley they race, myself after them. Before end of alley occurs, I have them."

The lawyer for the defence gave Charlie a hard look. He pointed to the three lean men, his clients. "Is it your purpose to tell the court that your avoirdupois conquered those thin legs?" he demanded.

Chan smiled. "He who runs with a light conscience makes the most speed," he answered gently.

"Meantime, how does Kashimo occupy himself?" inquired the lawyer.

"Kashimo knows his duty, and performs it. He remains behind to gather up abandoned dice. Such was the proper move." Chan nodded with grave approval.

"Yes, yes," broke in the judge, a bald-headed man with an air of infinite boredom. "And where are the dice?"

"Your Honour," Charlie answered, "unless I am much mistaken, the dice have only this moment entered the Court, in pocket of the active Mr. Kashimo."

Kashimo had indeed come in. He was a nervous little Japanese, and at sight of the bleak look on his face, Charlie's heart sank. Stepping hastily inside the enclosure, the Japanese whispered excitedly into Charlie's ear. Presently Chan looked up.

"I *was* much mistaken, your Honour," he said. "Mr. Kashimo has lost the dice."

A roar of laughter swept through the Court, while the judge idly hammered on his desk. Charlie sat motionless and seemingly undisturbed, but his heart was bitter. Like all Orientals, he did not relish laughter at his own expense, and much of this was no doubt directed at him. As a matter of fact, he was now in a ridiculous position. The lawyer for the defence, grinning broadly, addressed the Court.

"Your Honour, I move charge be dismissed. There is no material evidence. Even famous Inspector Chan will tell you there is no material evidence, when he regains composure and speaks again."

"Inspector Chan," said Charlie, with a grim look at the slant-eyed little attorney, "would much prefer to make oration on efficiency of Japanese race."

"That will do," cut in the judge. "Once more the

time of this Court has been wasted. Charge is dismissed. Call the next case."

With all the dignity he could muster, Chan left the
witness-box and moved slowly down the aisle. At
the rear of the room he encountered Kashimo, crouching on a bench. He took him gently by one brown ear,
and led him into the hall.

"Again," he remarked, "you let me down with
terrible tumble. Where do I obtain all this patience I
squander on you? I astound myself."

"So sorry," hissed Kashimo.

"So sorry, so sorry," repeated Charlie. "Those
words fall from your lips in never-ending stream. Can
good intentions atone for so many blunders? Can
the morning dew fill a well? Where were dice lost?"

The contrite Kashimo tried to explain. This
morning, on his way to Court, he had stopped at the
barber shop of Kryimota, on Hotel Street, for hair
cut. He had hung coat on rack.

"After first showing dice to entire shop, no doubt?"
Chan suggested.

No—he had shown them only to Kryimota, an
honourable man. While he submitted to the cut of
the hair, various customers had come in and gone out
of the shop. The operation finished, he had again
donned his coat, and hastened to the Court. On his
way up the stairs, he had made the unhappy discovery
that he was bereft.

Charlie regarded him sadly. "You began work as
supreme fumbler," he remarked, "but I think you
improve as you go forward. What laughter there
must have been among the gods when you were made
detective."

"So sorry," Kashimo said again.

"Be sorry out of my sight," sighed Chan. "While
you are in it, my vision blurs and I feel my self-control

under big strain." He shrugged his broad shoulders and turned away down the stairs.

The police station was on the ground floor, just beneath the Court, and at the rear was a small private office which was Chan's pride and joy. It had been turned over to him by his chief after he had brought to a successful conclusion the case of Shelah Fane, more than a year ago. He went inside now, closed the door, and stood looking through the open window into the alleyway that ran along behind the building.

He was still smarting from the incident upstairs, but that was merely a climax to a year of frustration. "Oriental knows," he had written to Duff in the letter the Inspector had read aloud in the Vine Street station, "that there is a time to fish, and a time to dry the nets." But, as he had confessed farther along in the same epistle, this eternal drying of the nets was beginning to distress him.

He had for some months past been troubled by a restlessness such as the Chinese are not supposed to know. He was troubled by it now as he stared out into the peaceful alley. Over a year since his last big case, and nothing of note had happened. Chasing slightly annoyed gamblers down obscure by-paths, invading odorous kitchens in search of stills, even sent to tag cars along King Street—was this the career for a Charlie Chan? Honolulu—he loved it—but what was Honolulu doing for him? A prophet is not without honour, save in his own country. Honolulu did not take him seriously—it had laughed at him only this morning. Like that alley out there, it was narrow—narrow as was his life.

With a ponderous sigh, he sat down at his roll-top desk. It was swept clean—clean as the desk of an old man who has retired from business. He swung slowly about in his chair, which creaked in alarm.

Getting older every day—well, his children would carry on. Rose, for instance. A brilliant girl, Rose. Making a grand record at that mainland univer-sity——

There was a knock on Charlie's door. He frowned. Kashimo, perhaps, with more of his apologies? Or the chief, to learn what had happened upstairs?

"Come!" Chan called.

The door opened, and there on the threshold stood his good friend, Inspector Duff, of Scotland Yard.

CHAPTER XIV

DINNER ON PUNCHBOWL HILL

A CHINESE does not, as a rule, register surprise, and a good detective learns early in his career the wisdom of keeping his emotions to himself. When you get the two in one package, as in the case of Charlie Chan, you are likely to have something pretty imperturbable. Yet now his eyes widened amazingly, and for a moment his mouth stood open. One would have said that he was, at the least, slightly taken aback.

In another moment he had leaped nimbly to his feet, and was moving swiftly towards the door. "My celebrated friend," he cried, "for an instant I question the reliability of my sight."

Smiling, Duff held out his hand. "Inspector Chan!"

Charlie took it. "Inspector Duff!"

The C.I.D. man tossed a brief-case down on the desk. "Here I am at last, Charlie. Did I surprise you? I meant to."

"For a brief space the breath left me," grinned Charlie. "Putting it more forcefully, I might say I gasped." He held ready a chair for his visitor, and inserted himself again into the one behind the desk. "I had so long desired this tremendous honour and happiness that I feared I endured hallucination. First question is now in order. What is your opinion of Honolulu, as far as you have got with it?"

Duff considered. "Well, it seems to be a nice clean town," he admitted.

Chan was shaking with silent mirth. "Almost I am drowned in the flood of your enthusiasm," he remarked. "But with you it is deeds, not words, I know. Busy man like yourself has no time for tourist nonsense. I make the wager you are here on case."

The other nodded. "I certainly am."

"I wish you no bad luck, but I am hoping you must remain for a lengthy visit."

"Only a few hours," Duff replied. "I'm here to meet the *President Arthur* at this port to-morrow morning, and I expect to go out on her when she sails for San Francisco to-morrow night."

Chan waved a hand. "Too brief, my friend. I am desolate to hear it. But I too know call of duty. You have, no doubt, a suspect on the ship?"

"Seven or eight of them," Duff answered. "Charlie, I've had suspects on boats and trains and at railway stations and hotels until I feel like Thomas Cook, or at least like one of the sons. I'm on the strangest case—as soon as your work permits, I want to tell you about it."

Charlie sighed. "Even if story requires one week to relate," he replied, "I possess plenty time to listen."

"Not much happening in your line, you wrote me?"

"The Indian philosopher who sat under one tree for twenty years was offensive busybody compared with me," Chan admitted.

Duff smiled. "I'm sorry. But perhaps in that event you can think about my troubles a bit, and it may be you can make a few suggestions."

The Chinese shrugged. "Does the mosquito advise the lion?" he inquired. "But I burn to hear what brings you to this somnolent paradise."

"A murder, of course," Duff answered. "A murder in Broome's Hotel, in the city of London, on the morning of February 7. Other murders too along the way, but only the first concerns me." And he launched into his story.

Chan listened, paying the rare tribute of silence as he did so. A casual observer might have supposed his interest slight, for he sat like a statue, seemingly as somnolent as the paradise he had mentioned. The little black eyes, however, never left Duff's face. Though the hands of the British detective busied themselves from time to time with his brief-case, though he took out letters and notes and read from them, still Charlie's gaze remained riveted where it had been when the long tale began.

"And now it's Welby," Duff finished at last. "Poor little Welby, shot down in a dark corner of the Yokohama docks. Why? Because he had located Jim Everhard, no doubt. Because he had learned the identity of as cruel and ruthless a killer as I have ever been called upon to hunt. By gad, I'll get him, Charlie! I must. Never before have I wanted a man so badly."

"A natural feeling," agreed Chan. "I am a mere outsider, but I can understand. Would you deign to partake of a terrible lunch at my expense?"

Duff was slightly shaken at this abrupt dismissal of an affair that was, to him, the most important in the world. "Why—er—you lunch with me," he suggested. "I'm stopping at the Young Hotel."

"No debate, please," Chan insisted. "You arrive over eight thousand miles of land and water, and you think to buy me a lunch. I am surprised. This is Hawaii, land of excessive hospitality. We will go to the Young, but I will demand check in strident terms."

"About my notes, Charlie. And these letters. I see you have a safe."

Chan nodded. "Yes, station-house safe is in this room. We will lock up your valuable papers there."

They walked up Bethel Street to the main thoroughfare, King, and along that in the direction of the Young. The penetrating midday sun shone down upon them, taxi-drivers slept fitfully at their wheels, a radio in a shop doorway was playing *My South Sea Rose*. Duff felt that some further comment was required of him.

"Hawaii's a sort of bright place, isn't it?" he said. "I mean the light's rather strong, you know."

Charlie shook his head. "My dear old friend," he replied, "please do not think that the matter must be attempted. Later I will hand you folders from Hawaii Tourist Bureau, and there you will find the words that now escape you. In the meantime, enjoy yourself. Here is the hotel, where inspeakably humble lunch awaits us."

When they were seated in the Young dining-room, Duff returned to the topic nearest his heart. "What did you think of my story, Charlie? Did you get a psychic wave about any of the members of that party? Chinese, I'm told, are very psychic people."

Chan grinned. "Yes—and psychic wave from unknown Chinese in Honolulu would rouse great sensation in London, I am sure. A locality where, if my reading is correct, more definite evidence of guilt is demanded than any other place in world."

Duff's face went grave. "You're right. That's the thought which haunts me constantly. I might discover to my own satisfaction which of those men is Jim Everhard, I might be positive I was right, yet I might still lack enough evidence for a warrant at home. They ask a lot of us at Scotland Yard, Charlie. Every man innocent until proved guilty, and we mean it on the other side. And that affair in Broome's Hotel on February 7 is a long way in the past now—slipping farther away each minute, too."

"I do not envy you your task," Chan told him. "All the greater triumph, however, when you win success at last. Was the soup possible? Yes? That is good. One meets so much impossible soup in Hawaii." His eyes narrowed. "You seek evidently two men," he added.

"What do you mean—two men?" Duff was startled.

"Great writer who once lived in these islands wrote book named 'Dr. Jekyll and Mr. Hyde.' The Jim Everhard who had some strange adventure with Honywood couple long ago is now, no doubt, stranger almost to himself. For years he has lived, under new name, respected life without violence. All time former self lies buried from sight, but it simmers there, nursing old grievance, promising to keep old vow. What wakes it—what brings it to life again—the bitter, half-forgotten self that throws off respectability with wild gesture and is able to strangle and to shoot —to shoot so straight without error? Ah, if we only understood queer twists and turns of human mind. But here is waiter with alleged chicken fricassee."

"It looks very good," remarked Duff.

"Looks," added Charlie, "are sometimes frightful liar. That is important thing for you to remember as you sail away to-morrow night with Lofton round world party. Jim Everhard looks good, I think. Looks respectable, without doubt, wearing disguise of new life so perfect from much use. But do not forget, my friend—many times honey in the mouth means poison in the heart."

"Of course," agreed Duff impatiently. He was bitterly disappointed to be met in this anxious hour

with general moralizing. It meant nothing, and
Charlie must know that himself. Almost the Chinese
acted as though he were not interested in the problem.
Was it that—or was it merely that Chan's talents were
rusty from lying unused so long? Duff yawned.
Wouldn't be surprising, here in this sunny land
where life was so easy, so effortless. A detective
needed constant activity, he needed too the tang of
sharp winds, flurries of snow. Southern people were
always languid, always slow.

"If respectability is, in this case, the mark of the
criminal," the Englishman continued, seeking to draw
the conversation on to more definite ground, "we have
several suspects to offer. Maxy Minchin, of course,
is out, and so, to my way of thinking, is Captain
Keane. But we have Doctor Lofton, cool, aloof,
the intellectual type. And we have Tait, a cultivated
man of brilliant ability—oddly enough, in the criminal
field himself; he has spent his life defending criminals.
We have Vivian, Ross and Benbow, all men of un-
impeachable standing in their own small worlds. And
we have Fenwick, whom we mustn't forget—a man
who holds a high position in a society that struck me
as most select."

"You have interest in Fenwick?" inquired Charlie.

"Have you?" asked Duff quickly.

"I could not fail to note how he hovers about like
brooding hawk above," Chan replied. "He leaves
party at Nice, and you think you are finished with
him. Yet there he is, at San Remo. In the hotel of
the Taj Mahal at Bombay he still persists."

Duff sat up. The easy manner with which Charlie
rattled off these names suggested that, after all, the
matter was interesting him more than his sleepy eyes
would indicate. Once again, Duff thought, he had
been wronging the Honolulu policeman. Once again,

as had frequently happened several years ago in San Francisco, he must hastily revise his opinion of this Chinese.

"But how about Yokohama?" he said. "How about the jeweller's shop in Calcutta? In neither of those places did anyone see Fenwick."

"You are certain of that?" Chan inquired.

"In point of fact, I'm not," Duff replied. "I must look further into the matter. Particularly if you fancy the man, Charlie——"

Chan grinned. "I have not said I fancied him. Maybe it was his name catches my attention. For a moment only. No—I have no fancies. Except, perhaps, chocolate ice cream. I make bold to suggest it as final course for this unworthy lunch."

"A bully good lunch," Duff assured him.

When they had finished, Charlie led his English friend back to the station and proudly introduced him to the force—to his chief, who was obviously impressed and even to Kashimo, who showed no sign of any emotion, whatever.

"Kashimo studies to be great detective like you are," Chan explained to Duff. "So far fortune does not favour him. Only this morning he proved himself useful as a mirror to a blind man. But"—he patted the Japanese on the shoulder—"he perseveres. And that means much."

Later in the afternoon Charlie got out, with marked pride, a shining new car, and took Duff for a tour of Honolulu and the surrounding section of the island. The Inspector looked, struggled gallantly to express his admiration, proved indeed a perfect guest, but his mind was uneasy. He could not 'forget that his big problém was still unsolved; in the midst of a conversation about something entirely different, that fact would slip back into his thoughts to torment him.

At dinner that night at the Royal Hawaiian, where Chan insisted on playing host, Duff was still in the same troubled frame of mind. He longed for the morrow and a return to action.

The next morning at ten he stood with Charlie on the dock and watched the *President Arthur* come in. For a time he had considered remaining in the background while the ship was in port, but he told himself there was nothing to be gained by that course; he must see them all again as soon as the liner sailed. He had insisted that Charlie come along and meet the members of the Lofton party. In the back of his head was a dim idea that the Chinese might have a sudden inspiration, a really helpful suggestion to offer. Overnight he had been thinking of Charlie on the trail of that other killer in San Francisco, and his confidence in his confrère had returned stronger than ever.

The big liner docked, and the gang-plank was put down. There was a moment's confusion at the top and then a motley crowd began slowly to descend. There is always a strange variety to the throng that lands from a through boat at Honolulu—a feeling in the onlooker—who are these people? Salesmen who have carried the creed of pep and hustle to far corners, raw Australians, bowing little Orientals, Englishmen walking secure in the feeling that under their feet is always a little bit of England, pale missionaries, washed-out Colonials, and the eternal tourist. Duff watched eagerly, and at his side stood Charlie, as one who hears an oft-told story.

Finally Lofton, in a pith helmet, appeared at the top of the plank and then started slowly to walk down it. After him came the twelve members of his party, until at one time on that plank Duff knew the man he sought must be walking. The man who had struck down Welby—a sudden anger flamed in the inspector's heart. As Doctor Lofton reached the pier-shed, Duff stepped forward with outstretched hand. Lofton glanced up. It was not precisely an expression of hearty welcome that crossed the conductor's face. Rather a look of keen annoyance—almost of dislike. Chan was watching him closely. Was it merely that Lofton hated to be reminded of certain events now put far behind?

"Ah, Doctor," Duff cried. "We meet again."

"Inspector Duff," said Lofton, and managed a wan smile. But now Duff was busily shaking hands with the Benbows, then with the Minchins, with Mrs. Spicer and Vivian, with Kennaway, Ross and the others— last of all with Tait, who looked more tired and ill than ever.

"Near the end of your journey, eh?" the Englishman said.

They all talked at once; it appeared that they were not sorry to step foot on U.S. soil again. Benbow did a little jig on the dock, his camera, hanging from the strap across his shoulder, flying wildly about him.

"Ladies and gentlemen, may I present my old friend, Inspector Chan, of the Honolulu Police?" Duff said. "I just dropped over for a little visit with the inspector, who happens to be the best detective in the Pacific Ocean. We once worked together on a case."

Vivian spoke. "Here for a long stay, Mr. Duff?"

"Unfortunately, no," Duff told him. "I'm booked out on your ship to-night. I hope none of you will mind."

"Delighted," Vivian murmured. The scar on his forehead shone suddenly crimson in the dazzling light of Honolulu.

"There are supposed to be cars waiting for us,"

Lofton announced. "We're going out for a swim at Waikiki, and lunch at the Royal Hawaiian." He bustled about.

Duff's eyes fell on Pamela Potter who was standing, a lovely vision in white, a little away from the others. There was a question in her own eyes; he shook his head ever so slightly as he approached her.

"How did I come to overlook you?" he inquired, taking her hand. "You're more charming than ever. The tour must have agreed with you." And in a lower voice: "Stick to the party, I shall see you later to-day."

"We're taking rooms at the Young," she answered. "Where in the world is——"

"Tell you later," Duff murmured. He shook hands with Mrs. Luce.

"Hello—we've missed you," the old lady said. "Well, here I am. Nearly around the world, and haven't been murdered so far."

"You're not home yet," he reminded her.

He refused Lofton's half-hearted invitation to join them for lunch. "You'll see plenty of me on the ship," he said jovially. The party entered waiting automobiles and was driven off in the direction of Waikiki. Duff and Charlie walked back to King Street.

"Well, there's my travel crowd," said the Englishman. "Did you notice a murderer among them?"

Chan shrugged. "Brand of Cain no longer legible," he returned. "Hasty glance such as I had then was not enough. Can you dispel fog with a fan? One matter I did note. Nobody boiled over with happiness to see you again. Except maybe beautiful young lady. That Doctor Lofton now——"

"He did seem annoyed, didn't he?" agreed Duff. "But, you see, I recall the unpleasant past, and I may also bring him some very un'ortunate publicity before I'm through. He's worried about his business."

"No more terrible worry than that in modern world," Chan nodded. "Ask Chamber of Commerce."

They lunched together again, this time with Duff as host. Afterwards Charlie was forced to return to the station to attend to some of the minor details of his work. At about two o'clock the Englishman was alone in the lobby of the Young, when Mrs. Luce and Pamela Potter came in. The rest of the party, it appeared, had driven to the Pali, but Mrs. Luce had seen it often, and the girl was eager for a chat with Duff. The two women went to the desk and engaged a sitting-room, bedroom and bath for the remainder of the day. Duff waited until he felt that they were comfortably settled in the suite, then went upstairs.

The girl was alone in the sitting-room. "At last," she greeted him. "I thought I was never going to be able to see you alone. Please sit down."

"Tell me your story first," Duff said. "When did you see Welby again?"

"What was the last letter you had from me?" she inquired.

"The one from Rangoon," he told her.

"I wrote another from Singapore, and still another from Shanghai."

"I'm sorry. They're probably following me about."

"Well, I hope they catch up with you. There wasn't any news in them, but they were masterpieces of descriptive writing. You'll do very wrong if you miss them."

"I shall read every word when they finally arrive. But no news, you say?"

"No—nothing much happened. I didn't see Mr. Welby again until I went aboard the *President Arthur* at Hong-Kong. He was steward for my cabin, and several others. He told me he'd learned how to do the work on the British-India boat, and he was efficiency itself. I imagine he began to search the cabins at once, but nothing happened until we got to Yokohama."

"Something happened there?" asked Duff.

"Yes, it did. We spent the day ashore, but I was rather fed up on sightseeing. So I came back to the ship for dinner, though we weren't scheduled to sail until late that night. Mrs. Luce came too. We——"

"Pardon me—just a moment. Did you note any other members of the party on the ship at dinner that evening?"

"Yes—Mr. Tait was there. He'd been feeling quite badly and hardly ever made any shore trips. And—oh, yes—Mr. Kennaway. If any of the others were aboard, I didn't see them."

"Very good. Go on, please."

"As I was leaving the dining-saloon, I saw Mr. Welby. He motioned to me and I followed him up to the top deck. We stood by the rail, looking out at the lights of Yokohama. I saw he was very excited. 'Well, Miss,' he whispered, 'the fun's over.' I stared at him. 'What do you mean?' I asked. 'I mean I've got my man,' he told me. 'I've located that duplicate key—number 3260, and no other.'

"'Where is it?' I cried. I meant, of course, who has it, but he took me literally. 'It's right where I found it,' he said. 'I'm leaving it there until I can get my man to the States and into the hands of Inspector Duff. It's rather late now to make an arrest in Japan, and I think the other plan would be better. I know Mr. Duff wants to get his hands on this lad himself, and I understand he's already in San Francisco. I'm going ashore now to send him a cable. care of the Yard, telling him to be on the

Honolulu dock without fail. I'm not taking any chance beyond that point.'"

The girl stopped, and Duff sat in silence. Welby had taken too much of a chance as it was; he had blundered, that was all too plain now. But he had meant well. And he had paid for his blunder.

"I wish to heaven," said the English detective savagely, "you had made him tell you the name of the holder of that key."

"Well, I certainly tried," the girl answered. "I begged and pleaded, but Mr. Welby simply wouldn't listen. He said it would be dangerous for me to know —and aside from that, I could see he had old-fashioned ideas about women. Never trust them with a secret —that sort of thing. He was a nice little man—I liked him—so I didn't nag. I told myself I would know all in good time. He went ashore to send that cable. And the next morning, when we were well out at sea, I discovered that he had never come back."

"No," said Duff quietly. "He never came back."

The girl looked at him quickly. "You know what happened to him?"

"Welby was found dead on the dock soon after your ship sailed."

"Murdered?"

"Of course."

Duff was startled to see that the girl, for all her sophistication, was weeping. "I—I can't help it," she apologized. "Such a nice little man. And— oh, it's abominable. That beast! Shall we ever find him! We must!"

"Indeed we must," returned Duff gravely. He got up and walked to the window. Honolulu was dozing in the blazing sun, under a palm tree in the little park across the way a brown-skinned, ragged boy was sprawled, his steel guitar forgotten at his side. That was the life, Duff thought, not a care in the world, nothing to do until to-morrow and perhaps not then. He heard a door open behind him, and turning, saw Mrs. Luce enter from the bedroom.

"Just taking a nap," she explained. She noted the girl's tears. "What's wrong now?"

Pamela Potter told her. The old lady's face paled, and she sat down suddenly.

"Not our little steward," she cried. "I've had millions of stewards all over the world, but I'd taken a particular fancy to him. Well, I shall never make a long trip like this again. Maybe a little run over to China, or down to Australia, but that's all. I begin to feel old, for the first time in seventy-two years."

"Nonsense," said Duff. "You don't look a day over fifty."

She brightened. "Do you mean that? Well, as a matter of fact, I'll probably get over this soon. After I've had a good rest in Pasadena—I've never been to South America, you know. I can't think how I came to miss it."

"I've got an invitation for the two of you," Duff announced. "It sounds quite interesting. That Chinese you met on the dock this morning—he's a good fellow and a gentleman. He's invited me to his home for dinner to-night, and he told me to bring you along. Both of you. The honour, it appears, is all his."

They agreed to go, and at six-thirty Duff was waiting for them in the lobby. They drove up to Punchbowl Hill in the cool of the evening. The mountains ahead of them were wrapped in black clouds, but the town at their backs was yellow and rose in the light of the setting sun.

Charlie was waiting on his lanai, in his best American clothes, his broad face shining with joy.

"What a moment in the family history," he cried. "Over my threshold steps my old friend from London, in itself an honour almost too great to endure. Additions to the party make me proud man indeed."

With many remarks about his mean house and its contemptible furniture, he ushered them into the parlour. His unflattering picture of the hospitality he was offering was, of course, merely his conception of what was due his guests. The room was a charming one, a rare old rug on the floor, crimson and gold Chinese lanterns hanging from the ceiling, many carved teakwood tables bearing Swatow bowls, porcelain wine jars, dwarfed trees. On the wall was a single picture, a bird on an apple bough, painted on silk. Pamela Potter looked at Charlie with a new interest. She wished certain interior decorators she knew could see this parlour.

Mrs. Chan appeared, stiff in her best black silk, and very careful about her English. A number of the older children entered and were ceremoniously presented.

"I will not burden you with entire roll-call," Chan explained. "The matter would, I fear, come to be an ordeal." He spoke of his eldest daughter, Rose, away at college on the mainland. His voice softened, and his eyes took on a look of sadness. If Rose were here—Rose, the flower of his flock—how well she would meet this situation, which had somewhat upset his wife's accustomed calm.

An aged woman servant appeared in the doorway and said something in a high shrill voice. They moved on into the dining-room, where Charlie explained that he was giving them a Hawaiian dinner, rather than a Chinese. The initial stiffness wore off, Mrs. Chan finally ventured a smile, and after Mrs. Luce had chatted breezily for a few moments, everybody felt at ease.

"My favourite race, the Chinese, Mr. Chan," the old lady remarked.

Charlie bowed. "After your own, of course."

She shook her head. "Not at all. I've just been cooped up in close quarters with my own for nearly four months, and I repeat—the Chinese are my favourite race."

"On trip round world you see many of my people," Chan suggested.

"One certainly does—doesn't one, Pamela?"

"Everywhere," nodded the girl.

"The Chinese are the aristocrats of the East," Mrs. Luce went on. "In every city out there—in the Malay States, in the Straits Settlements, in Siam—they are the merchants, the bankers, the men of substance and authority. So clever and competent and honest, carrying on among the lazy riff-raff of the Orient. A grand people, Mr. Chan. But you know all that."

Charlie smiled. "All I know, I do not speak. Appreciation such as yours makes music to my ears. We are not highly valued in the United States, where we are appraised as laundrymen, or maybe villains in the literature of the talkative films. You have great country, rich and proud, and sure of itself. About rest of world—pardon me—it knows little, and cares extremely less."

Mrs. Luke nodded. "Quite true. And sometimes the most provincial among us we reward with a seat in the Senate. Have you visited China recently, Mr. Chan?"

"Not for many years," Charlie told her. "I saw it last through sparkling eyes of youth. It was peaceful land in those days."

"But not any more," Pamela Potter said.

Chan nodded gravely. "Yes, China is sick now. But as someone has so well said, many of those who send sympathy to the sick man will die before him. That has happened in China's past—it will happen again." There was a rush of wind outside, followed by the terrific beating of rain upon the roof. "Now I think there is going to be a shower," Charlie added.

Through the remainder of the dinner, the rain continued. It was still pouring down with tropical fervour when they returned to the parlour. Duff consulted his watch.

"I don't mean to be rude, Charlie," he explained. "This evening will remain one of the happiest memories of my life. But the *President Arthur* goes at ten, you know, and it's past eight-thirty. I'm a bit nervous over the thought of missing that ship—as you can quite understand. Hadn't I better telephone for a car——"

"Not to be considered," Chan protested. "I possess automobile completely enclosed that will hold four with spacious ease—even four like myself, if there were such. I know the burden on your shoulders, and will convey you down Punchbowl Hill immediately."

With many expressions of their pleasure in the dinner, they prepared to leave. "It's the high spot of my trip around the world," Pamela Potter said, and Charlie and his wife both beamed with delight. In a few moments the new car was on its way down the hillside, the lights of the water front blurred and indistinct in the distance.

They stopped at the Young for Duff's luggage, and the two small bags the women had brought ashore. As they set out for the dock, Duff put his hand to his head.

"Good lord, Charlie," he remarked, "what's wrong

with me, anyhow? I'd completely forgotten—all my notes about the case are in your safe at the station."

"I had not forgotten," Charlie answered. "I am taking you there now. I will drop you off, then I will transport ladies to the dock. When I return, you can have papers gathered up—chief or one of men will open safe for you. We will have last chat, and you shall smoke a final pipe."

"Very good," Duff agreed. He alighted in a torrent of rain before Halekaua Hale, and the other three went on.

At the dock, Charlie bade the women a polite farewell, then hurried back to the station. As he climbed those worn, familiar steps, his heart was heavy. Duff's coming had meant a happy break in the monotony, but the Englishman's stay was all too brief. To-morrow, Chan reflected, would be like all the other days. The roar of tropic rain still in his ears, he crossed the hallway and pushed open the door of his office. For the second time within thirty-six hours, he encountered the unexpected.

Duff was lying on the floor beside the desk chair, his arms sprawled helplessly above his head. With a cry of mingled anger and alarm, Chan ran forward and bent over him. The English detective's face was pale as death, but placing a quick finger on his pulse, Charlie could feel a slight fluttering. He leaped to the telephone and got the Queen's Hospital.

"An ambulance," he shouted. "Send it to the police station at once. Be quick, in name of heaven!"

He stood for a moment, staring helplessly about. The single window was raised, as usual; out in the murky alley the rain was beating down. The window —ah, yes—and a sudden bullet from the misty darkness. Chan turned to the desk. On it lay Duff's open brief-case. Its contents appeared to be intact; some of the papers were still in the case; a few were strewn carelessly about, scattered, it was clear, by the wind.

Charlie called, and the chief came in from his office near by. At the same instant, Duff stirred slightly. Chan knelt by his side. The Englishman opened his eyes and saw his old friend.

"Carry on, Charlie," he whispered, and again lapsed into unconsciousness.

Chan stood erect, glanced at his watch, and began to gather up the papers on the desk.

CHAPTER XV

BOUND EAST FROM HONOLULU

THE chief was bending over Duff. His face very grave, he rose from his knees and looked wonderingly at Chan. "What does this mean, Charlie?" he wanted to know.

The Chinese pointed to the open window. "Shot," he explained tersely. "Shot in back by bullet entering from there. Poor Inspector Duff. He comes to our quiet city in search of murderer in travelling party landing at this port to-day, and to-night murderer attempts to ply his trade."

"Of all the damned impertinence," cried the chief, suddenly enraged. "A man shot down in the Honolulu police station——"

Chan nodded. "Even worse than that. Shot down in my very office, of which I have been so proud. Until this killer is captured, I am laughing-stock of world."

"Oh, I wouldn't put it that way," the chief said. Chan had restored all Duff's papers to the brief-case, and was strapping it up. "What are you going to do, Charlie?"

"What should I do? Can I lose face like this and offer no counter-attack? I am sailing to-night on *President Arthur.*"

"But you can't do that——"

"Who stops me? Will you kindly tell me which surgeon in this town is ablest man?"

"Well, I suppose Doctor Lang——"

In another second, Chan had the telephone book in his hand, and was dialling a number. As he talked, he heard the clang of an ambulance at the door of Halekaua Hale, and white-coated orderlies entered the hallway with a stretcher. The chief superintended the removal of the unfortunate Duff, while Charlie consulted with the surgeon. Doctor Lang lived at the Young Hotel, and he promised to be at the Queen's Hospital almost as soon as the ambulance. Charlie put the receiver back on the hook, then removed it and dialled once more.

"Hello," he said. "This is you, Henry? You are home early to-night. The gods are good. Listen carefully. Your father speaking. I sail in one hour for the mainland. What? Kindly omit surprised feelings—the matter is settled. I am off on important case. Pull self together and get this straight— to quote language you affect. Kindly pack bag with amazing speed, toothbrush, other suit, razor. Ask yourself what I shall require and bring same. Your honourable mother will assist. Come in your car to dock where *President Arthur*, Dollar boat, is waiting, bringing my bag and your mother. Boat departs at ten. You will gather that speed is essential. Thank you so much."

As he rose from the telephone, the chief faced him. "Better think this over, Charlie," he suggested.

Chan shrugged. "I have thought it over."

"What do you suggest—another leave of absence? I'd have to take that up with the commissioners—it would require several days——"

"Then call it my resignation," Chan answered briefly.

"No, no," protested the chief. "I'll fix it some-how. But listen, Charlie. This job is dangerous— this man is a killer——"

"Who knows that better than I? Is it important? My honour is assailed. In my office, you recall."

"I'm not suggesting that you shouldn't risk your life, provided it's in the legitimate line of duty. But I'd—I'd hate to lose you, Charlie. And this looks to me like Scotland Yard's affair——"

Stubbornly Chan shook his head. "Not any more. My affair, now. You would hate to lose me—from what? From pursuing fleet gamblers down an alley? From tagging cars on King Street——"

"I understand. Things have been rather slow——"

"Have been—yes. But not to-night. Things are plenty fast again. I am on that boat when she sails, and I will have my man before the mainland is reached. If not, I say good-bye for all time to title of detective inspector, I retire for ever in sackcloth with ashes." He went to the safe. "I find here two hundred cash dollars. I am taking same. You will cable me more at San Francisco. Either it is necessary expense of catching criminal who performed black act on premises of Honolulu police station, or it is my money and I will repay it. Which does not matter. Now I am off for hospital. I am saying good-bye——"

"No, you're not," replied his chief. "I'll be at the dock when you sail."

Clasping Duff's precious brief-case under his arm, Chan hurried to the street. With that sudden change of mood characteristic of Honolulu weather, the rain had ceased, and here and there amid the clouds the stars were shining. Charlie went to the lobby of the Young, and accosted the first man he met in the uniform of a ship's officer. Luck was with him, for the man proved to be one Harry Lynch, purser of the *President Arthur*.

Chan introduced himself, and persuaded Mr. Lynch

to get into the car with him. While he drove to
Queen's Hospital, he hastily explained what had
happened. The purser was deeply interested.

"The old man told me a Scotland Yard detective
was coming aboard here," he remarked. "We knew
all about Welby, of course. It was quite a shock
when we lost him so abruptly. The word from Yokohama was simply that the man had been killed.
And now Inspector Duff has been wounded, eh?
Well, we'll be glad to have a police officer aboard.
There seems to be plenty of work waiting for you,
Mr. Chan."

Charlie shrugged. "My talents are of the slightest,"
he protested.

"Yeah?" said Mr. Lynch. "I heard different."

He said no more, but Chan's heart had warmed
towards him. After his long period of inaction, it
was good to know that he was remembered.

"I'll fix up the matter of your ticket," Lynch went
on. "We're running light this crossing, and I can
give you a good cabin to yourself."

They were at the hospital now, and Charlie went
inside, a feeling of deep anxiety weighing him down.
Doctor Lang was pointed out to him—a ghostly
figure all in white, his face lost somewhere in the
shadow of an eye shade.

"I've located the bullet," the surgeon announced,
"and I'm operating at once. Fortunately it was
deflected from its course by a rib. It's a ticklish
business, but the man looks to be in remarkably good
condition, and he ought to pull through."

"He must," Charlie said firmly. He told the
doctor who Duff was, and why he had come to
Honolulu. "If I could see him for one final
moment——" he suggested, timid in this unfamiliar
place.

204 CHARLIE CHAN CARRIES ON

"Come up to the operating-room," the surgeon invited. "The patient has talked a little, but it's delirious talk. However, maybe you can make something of it."

In the rather terrifying, odoriferous room upstairs, Charlie bent over the sheeted form of his friend. Had Duff caught a glimpse of the man who fired that shot? If he had, and spoke the name now, the case was finished.

"Inspector," said the Chinese gently. "This is Charlie Chan. Haie, what an awful thing has happened! I am so sorry. Tell me—did you behold face of assailant?"

Duff stirred slightly and spoke in a thick voice. "Lofton," he muttered. "Lofton—the man with a beard——"

Charlie held his breath. Was it Lofton who had appeared at the window?

"There's Tait, too," Duff muttered. "And Fenwick. Where's Fenwick now? Vivian—Keane——"

Charlie turned sadly away. Poor Duff was only running over once again the list of his suspects.

"Better leave him now, Mr. Chan," the surgeon said.

"I will go," Charlie replied. "But I must say this last thing. To-morrow or whenever he awakes, you will have most restless patient on your hands. He will warmly desire to rise from bed and follow trail again. When that happens, soothe him with this word from me. Tell him Charlie Chan has sailed for San Francisco on *President Arthur*, and will have guilty man before boat reaches shore of mainland. Make it in form of promise, and say it comes from one who has never yet smashed promise to a friend."

The surgeon nodded gravely. "I'll tell him, Mr. Chan. Thanks for the suggestion. And now—we're going to do our best for him. That's my promise to you."

It was nine-forty-five when Charlie and the purser drove on to the dock beside the *President Arthur*. Not far away, as he alighted, Chan saw his son Henry and with him a dumpy little figure in black silk—Mrs. Chan, still in her party finery. He went over, and led them up the gang-plank in the purser's company. An officer who stood at a little desk at the bottom of the plank eyed them curiously as they passed.

On the deck, Mrs. Chan stood looking up at her inexplicable husband with timid eyes. "Wheh you go now, please?" she asked.

He gave her a kindly pat on the back. "Events break suddenly like fire-crackers in the face of innocent passer-by," he said. He told her what had happened in his office, and of the need for his immediate departure in order to save his face and regain his lost prestige.

The gentle little woman understood. "Plenty clean clo'es in bag," she told him. She considered for a moment. "I think mebbe dangah wheh you go," she added.

Charlie smiled reassuringly. "What the gods have decreed, man cannot alter," he reminded her. "Can he dodge down bypath and avoid his fate? Do not fret. All will no doubt be well. And before many days I expect to see our Rose."

In the dim light he saw sudden tears shining on her chubby cheeks. "Much love," she said. "I send much love. She goes so fah away." A quick pathetic little wringing of her hands. "I do not unnahstand why she go so fah away."

"You will understand in the proud days to come," Charlie promised

Little groups of passengers straggled up the gangplank, lingered a moment on the deck, and then drifted off to their cabins. There was to be no excitement attending this sailing evidently. Chan's chief appeared.

"Ah, here you are, Charlie," he said. "I was able to dig up another sixty dollars for you." He handed over a roll of bills.

"You overwhelm me with kindness," Charlie answered.

"I'll cable you more to bring you home—after you've got your man," the chief went on. "You'll get him, I'm sure."

"Now that I have time to think it over, I am not so certain myself," Chan responded. "Seems this is pretty hard task I have selected. I know from talk with Inspector Duff only one thing will make him happy. I must discover identity of man who committed murder more than three months ago in Broome's Hotel, London. All time I have remained eight thousand miles away from scene of crime, and I must solve same when clues are cold, trail is covered, and no doubt the one vital point that might have brought about arrest is forgotten by all involved. It appears to me now that to-night I hotly elected myself to superman's job without possessing necessary equipment. Maybe I come crawling home before long, defeated and expunged of all honour."

"Yes, and maybe not," returned the chief. "It does look like a difficult task, that's true, but——"

He was interrupted by a small panting figure that appeared out of the night and faced Charlie. It was Kashimo.

"Hello, Charlie," the Japanese cried.

"Ah—this is kind of you to say good-bye——" Chan began.

"Never mind good-bye," Kashimo broke in. "I got important information, Charlie."

"Have you indeed?" Chan answered politely. "Of what nature, Kashimo?"

"I am going by end of alley soon after shot is fired injuring your honourable friend," went on the Japanese breathlessly. "I behold man coming out of alley into lighted street. He is tall man wrapped in big coat, hat over eyes."

"Then you didn't see his face?" Chan suggested.

"What's the matter," Kashimo replied. "Face not necessary. Saw something better. The man is very lame, like this — ." With great histrionic vigour he gave an imitation of a lame man there on the deck. "He carries walking-stick, light-coloured, maybe Malacca kind."

"I am very grateful," nodded Charlie, speaking in a voice such as he might have used to his youngest child. "You are observant, Kashimo. You are learning fast."

"Maybe some day I am good detective too," suggested the Japanese hopefully.

"Who can say?" Chan replied. A deep voice suggested that all who were going ashore had better do so. Charlie turned to his wife, and at that instant Kashimo burst into a torrent of words directed at the chief. The burden of it appeared to be that he should be sent to San Francisco as Chan's assistant.

"I am very fine searcher," the Japanese insisted. "Charlie says so himself."

"How about it, Charlie?" grinned the chief. "Could you use him?"

Chan hesitated for a second, then he went over and patted the little man on the shoulder.

"Consider, Kashimo," he remarked. "You do not weigh situation properly. Should you and I both be absent from Honolulu at identical moment, what an opportunity for the evil-doers! Crime wave might sweep over island, almost obliterating it. Run along now, and be good boy while I am gone. Always remember, we learn by our mistakes. First you know, you will be ablest man among us."

Kashimo nodded, shook hands and disappeared down the deck. Charlie turned to his son. "Please arrange that my car is taken up to garage on Punchbowl Hill at once," he said. "In my absence you will show your mother every deference, and guard whole family well."

"Sure," Henry agreed. "And say, Dad—can I use your bus until you come back? There's something wrong with that old car I inherited from you."

Chan nodded. "I foresaw that request. Yes, you may use my car, but please treat it with unusual kindness. Do not continually demand more than it has to give, like speed-mad young people you imitate. Good-bye, Henry." He said a few low words to his wife, kissed her in Occidental fashion, and led her to the top of the gang-plank.

"Good luck, Charlie," remarked his chief, and shook hands.

A chain clanked in the quiet night, and the plank was lowered, cutting Chan irrevocably off from the group on the dock. He saw them standing there looking up at him, and the sight touched him. There was, in their very attitudes, an expression of confidence in him and in his ultimate success. It was a confidence he did not share with them. What was this wild task he had set himself? He clutched Duff's brief-case tightly in his arms.

Slowly the big liner backed away, out into midstream. No orchestra playing *Aloha* to-night, no gaily coloured streamers floating between ship and shore, none of the picturesque gestures that usually attended island sailings. Just the grim business of getting on with it, the old story of a ship putting out to sea.

The little group on the shadowy pier faded finally from his sight; still he did not move from his post by the rail. The throb of the engines became more pronounced; the ship was settling down to it. Presently Chan saw the circle of lights that marked Waikiki Beach. How many nights he had sat on his lanai staring across the town towards that beach, vaguely wishing for action, for something to happen. Well, it had happened at last—yes, something had certainly happened when he saw the lights of Waikiki from a ship at sea.

He turned and regarded the huge bulk of the liner, dark and mysterious behind him. He was in a new world now, a small world, and in it with him was a man who had killed in London through error, had killed again in Nice and San Remo through grim intention, and then again on the Yokohama dock, no doubt through necessity. A ruthless man who had only to-night sought to remove the relentless Duff from his trail. Not a squeamish person, this Jim Everhard. Now for six days Chan and he would be together in a limited space, prisoners on this brave contraption of steel and wood, each seeking to outwit the other. Which would win?

Charlie started. Someone had come up noiselessly behind him, and he had heard a sudden hissing in his ear. He turned.

"Kashimo," he gasped.

"Hello, Charlie," grinned the Japanese.

"Kashimo—what does this mean?"

"I am hide-away," Kashimo explained. "I go with you to assist on big case."

Chan cast a speculative eye at the breakers between the boat and Waikiki Beach. "Can you swim, Kashimo?" he inquired.

"Not a single stroke," replied the little man gleefully.

Chan sighed. "Ah, well. He who accepts with a smile whatever the gods may send, has mastered most important lesson in life's hard school. Pardon me one moment, Kashimo. I am seeking to achieve the smile."

CHAPTER XVI

THE MALACCA STICK

In another moment Chan's inherent good-nature triumphed, and the smile was accomplished.

"You will pardon, Kashimo, if for one instant I was slightly appalled. Can you blame me? I remember our last adventure together—the affair of the dice. But enterprise such as yours is not to be met with a sneeze. I welcome you into present case —which was a most difficult one, even before you arrived."

"Hearty thanks," replied the Japanese.

The purser emerged from a near-by doorway, and came rapidly along the deck.

"Oh, Mr. Chan," he said, "I've been looking for you. Just had a chat with the captain and he told me to give you the best I've got. There's a cabin with bath—at the minimum rate, of course. I'm having one of the beds made up. If you'll bring your bag and follow me——" He stared at Kashimo. "And who is this?"

Chan hesitated. "Er—Mr. Lynch, condescend to meet Officer Kashimo, of Honolulu force. One of"— he choked a little—"our most able men. At last moment it was decided to bring him along in rôle of assistant. If you can find a place to lay him away for the night——"

Lynch considered. "He's going as a passenger, too, I suppose?"

A brilliant idea struck Charlie. "Kashimo is specialist, like everybody nowadays. He is grand searcher. If you could find him place in crew which would not consume too much brain power, he might accomplish brilliant results. In that way he could maintain anonymous standing, which I, alas, cannot do."

"One of our boys was pinched in Honolulu to-night for bootlegging," Lynch replied. "What's getting into those Federal men, anyhow? It means a few changes in our assignments. We might make Mr. Kashimo a biscuit boy—one of the lads who sit in the alleyways and answer the cabin bells. Of course, it's not a very dignified job——"

"But a splendid opportunity," Chan assured him. "Kashimo will not mind. His duty is first with him, always. Kashimo, tell the gentleman how you feel about it."

"Biscuit boys get tips?" inquired the Japanese eagerly.

Charlie waved a hand. "Behold—he pants to begin."

"Well, you'd better take him in with you to-night," Lynch said. "Nobody will know about it but your steward, and I'll tell him not to say anything." He turned to Kashimo. "Report to the chief steward at eight to-morrow. I don't mind your searching, but you mustn't get caught, you understand. We can't have innocent people annoyed."

"Naturally not," agreed Chan heartily. But he wasn't so sure. Annoying innocent people, he reflected, was another of Kashimo's specialities.

"The captain would like to see you in the morning, Mr. Chan," the purser remarked at the doorway of the cabin to which he led them. He departed.

Charlie and Kashimo entered the state-room. The

steward was still there, and Chan directed him to make
up the other bed. While they waited, the detective
looked about him. A large airy cabin, a pleasant
place to think. And he would have to do much thinking during the next six days—and nights.

"I will return presently," he said to his assistant.

He went to the top deck and dispatched a radiogram. It was addressed to his chief, and in it he
wrote:

"If you notice Kashimo has mislaid himself, I am
one to do worrying. He is with me on ship."

Going back to his cabin, he found the Japanese
there alone. "I have just broken news to chief about
your departure," he explained. "This biscuit boy
business is brilliant stroke. Otherwise question might
have come up who pays your passage, and I have deep
fear everybody would have declined the honour."

"Better go to bed now," Kashimo suggested.

Charlie gave him a pair of his own pyjamas, and
was moved to silent mirth at the resulting spectacle.
"You have aspect of deflated balloon going nowhere,"
he said.

Kashimo grinned. "Can sleep in anything," he
announced, and climbed into his bunk prepared to
prove it.

Presently Charlie turned on the light above his
pillow, put out all the others, and got into his own
bed with Duff's brief-case in his hand. He undid the
straps, and took out a huge sheaf of papers. Duff's
notes were on numbered pages, and Chan was relieved
to discover that none was missing. Honywood's
letter to his wife, together with all other messages
and documents pertinent to the case, remained intact.
Either Jim Everhard had been afraid to enter the
office after his shooting of Duff, or he had felt that

there was nothing in these papers he need bother
about.

"I trust I shall not disturb you, Kashimo,"
Chan remarked. "But stowaways must not be too
particular. It is my duty now to read the story of
our case, until I know it perfectly by the heart."

"Won't disturb me none," yawned the Japanese.

"Ah, all the fun and no responsibility," sighed
Charlie. "You have happy life. While I read, I
shall pay especial attention to lame man in the party.
What was he doing at mouth of alley when poor Mr.
Duff lay shot in my office? You gave me point of
attack on case with that news, and I am grateful."

He began to read and, in imagination, he travelled
far. London, all his life a name and nothing more,
became a familiar city. He saw the little green car
set out from Scotland Yard, he stepped inside the
sacred portals of Broome's Hotel, he bent above the
lifeless form of Hugh Morris Drake as it lay on the
bed in room 28. Descending to the musty sitting-
room of the hotel, he witnessed Tait's heart attack on
the threshold, noted Honywood's haunted look.
Then on to Paris, and Nice: Honywood dead in the
garden. San Remo, and that terrible moment in
the lift. Carefully he read Honywood's epistle to his
wife, which explained so much but left the vital
question unanswered. Every detail in the long case
burned itself into his mind now.

True, he had been all over it with Duff, but then
the affair had seemed so remote, so little to concern
him. It concerned him to-night. He was in Duff's
shoes, the case was his; nothing must escape him;
nothing could be safely overlooked. Last of all he
perused the report of Duff's talk with Pamela Potter
in Honolulu that very afternoon, in which she had
told of Welby's discovery of the key. It was a matter

of pride with Duff that he kept his notes up to the minute.

Chan finished reading. "Kashimo," he remarked thoughtfully, "that man Ross has intriguing sound. What about Ross? Always in the background, limping along, never a hint against him—until now. Yes, Kashimo, the matter of Mr. Ross must be our first concern."

He paused. A loud snore from the bed across the way was his only answer. Charlie looked at his watch, it was past midnight. He turned back to the beginning and read it all again.

It was after two o'clock when he finally put out his light. Even then, he was not ready to sleep. He lay there, planning the future.

At seven-thirty he rudely dragged his small assistant out of slumberland. Kashimo was lost in the clouds, and had to be gradually brought back to earth and a realization of where he was. While he made his sketchy toilet Charlie told him a little of the case, with special emphasis on the part the Japanese was to play. He was to search among the possessions of the travel party for a key bearing the number 3260. He might find it, he might not—perhaps by this time it was at the bottom of the Pacific. But the effort must be made anyhow. The Japanese nodded in a dazed, uncomprehending sort of way, and at two minutes to eight was ready for his interview with the chief steward.

"Remember, Kashimo, too much haste may have fatal ending," was Chan's final admonition. "Take plenty of time and know what you are doing before you do it. You are biscuit boy from now on, and if we meet on ship, you have never seen me before. All talks between us are conducted with utmost secrecy in this cabin. Farewell, and best of luck."

"So long," Kashimo responded, and went out. Charlie stood for a moment at the port-hole, gazing at the sunlit sea and breathing in great draughts of the bracing air. There is something invigorating about the first morning on a ship, the cool peace, the feeling of security away from the land's alarms. A sense of well-being and confidence flooded Chan's heart. It was a glorious day, and the future looked promising.

He was shaving when a boy knocked at his door and handed him a radiogram from his chief. He read:

"Surgeon reports operation O.K. Duff doing fine. Sincere condolences on Kashimo."

Charlie smiled. Great news, that about Duff. In a cheerful frame of mind he stepped out on to the deck to face his problems. The first person he saw was Pamela Potter, who was taking a morning stroll, accompanied by Mark Kennaway. The girl stopped, and stared.

"Mr. Chan," she cried. "What are you doing here?"

Charlie managed a low and sweeping bow. "I am enjoying a very good morning, thank you. You appear to be doing the same."

"But I'd no idea you were coming with us."

"I had no idea myself, until late hour last night. In me you behold quite worthless replacement for Inspector Duff."

She started. "He—you don't mean that he, too——"

"Do not be alarmed. Wounded only." Quickly he reported what had happened.

The girl shook her head. "There seems to be no end to it," she said.

"What begins, must finish," Chan told her. "Miscreant in this case is clever enough to play a fiddle behind his back, but even the cleverest have been known to blunder. I believe I saw this young man on the dock yesterday. The name——"

"Oh, I'm sorry," the girl replied. "I was so startled to see you. Inspector Chan—this is Mr. Kennaway. I've just been telling him what a wonderful party he missed last night. He's all upset. You know, he belongs to *such* a family in Boston, and he isn't accustomed to being left out."

"Nonsense," Kennaway said.

"He would have been very welcome," Charlie remarked. He turned to the young man. "I myself have keen interest in Boston, and some day we must enjoy small talk about same. Just now I will not further interrupt your perambulations. Since I was introduced to your entire party yesterday, full name and title, it will be useless for me to attempt dissemble my identity. So I propose to meet all of you presently for little chat about last night."

"Same old story," Kennaway replied. "We've been gathered together to meet policemen at frequent intervals ever since the tour started. Well, you're bringing a new face into it, and that's something. I wish you luck, Inspector Chan."

"Thank you so much. I shall do my best. True, I am coming into the case through the back door. But I am encouraged when I remember old saying which remarks, the turtle that enters the house at the rear gate comes finally to the head of the table."

"Ah, yes—in the soup," Kennaway reminded him.

Chan laughed. "Ancient proverbs must not be taken too literally. Pardon me while I sample the cuisine of this vessel. At some later hour I shall sample your society more extensively."

He went to the dining saloon, where he was given a good table to himself. After a hearty breakfast, he rose to leave. In a seat near the door, he saw Doctor Lofton. He stopped.

"Ah, Doctor," he said. "Perhaps you do me the honour to recall my face?"

Lofton glanced up. Few people could look at Charlie without a friendly smile, but the doctor managed it. In fact, his expression was a rather sour one.

"Yes," he said. "I remember you. A policeman, I believe?"

"I am inspector of detectives, attached to Honolulu station," Charlie explained. "May I sit down, please?"

"I suppose so," Lofton growled. "But don't blame me if my feelings are none too cordial. I'm a bit fed up with detectives. Where is your friend Duff this morning?"

Charlie raised his eyebrows. "You have not heard what happened to Inspector Duff?"

"Of course not," snapped Lofton. "I've got twelve people to look after, and I can assure you that they keep me busy. I can't bother with every policeman who tags along. What's happened to Duff? Come on, man—speak! Don't tell me he's been killed, too?"

"Not entirely," Chan answered gently. He told his story, his little black eyes fixed on Lofton's face. He was amazed at the lack of shock or sympathy on that bearded countenance.

"Well, that's the end of Duff, as far as this tour is concerned," the doctor remarked, when Chan had finished. "And now what?"

"Now I replace poor Duff."

Lofton stared at him. "You!" he cried rudely.

"Why not?" asked Charlie blandly.

"Well, no reason, I suppose. You'll pardon me, but my nerves have been completely upset by the events of the last few months. Thank God, we break up at San Francisco, and it's a question in my mind if I ever go out again. I've been thinking of retiring, and this is as good a time as any."

"Whether you do or not is a private and personal matter," Chan told him. "What is not so private is, what is name of the killer who has honoured you with his presence on this journey? It is an affair I am here to look into, with full authority to do so. If you will get your party together in the lounge at ten o'clock, I shall launch the campaign."

Lofton glared at him. "How long, O Lord, how long?" he said.

"I shall be brief as possible."

"You know what I mean. How long must I continue to gather my party together for these inquisitions? Nothing ever comes of them. Ever has, or ever will, if you ask me."

Charlie gave him a searching look. "And you would be sorry if anything did," he ventured.

Lofton returned the look. "Why should I try to deceive you? I am not longing for any final flare of publicity about this matter. That would mean the end of my touring days, and no mistake. An unpleasant end, too. No, what I want is a petering out of the whole business. You see, I intend to be frank with you."

"Quite refreshing, thank you," bowed Charlie.

"I'll get the party together, of course. But further than that, if you look for any help from me, you'll be looking in the wrong place."

"Looking in wrong place is always terrible waste of time," Chan assured him.

"I'm glad you realize that," Lofton answered, and rising, moved towards the door. Chan followed meekly at his heels.

Going up to see the captain of the ship, Charlie encountered a more cordial greeting. That old seadog heard the story of the chase with mounting indignation.

"All that I can say is, I hope you get your man," he remarked at last. "I'll give you every help possible. But remember this, Mr. Chan. A mistake would be a serious thing. If you came to me and asked me to have someone put under restraint, and he proved to be the wrong person, I'd be in a hell of a hole. The line would probably never hear the end of it—law-suits and all that. We'll have to be very sure what we are doing."

"Man who runs big ship like this should always be sure what he is doing," Chan suggested mildly. "I promise to use every care."

"And I know you will," smiled the captain. "I haven't been on the Pacific run these past ten years without hearing about you. I have every confidence in you, but I couldn't, under the circumstances, fail to point out my position. If an arrest becomes necessary, let's try to have it made on the San Francisco dock. That would avoid many complications."

"You call up pretty picture," Chan remarked. "I hope it eventuates."

"So do I," nodded the captain, "with all my heart."

Charlie went back to the promenade deck. He saw Kashimo flit by resplendent in a new uniform which fitted him only in spots. Pamela Potter was sitting in a deck chair, and waved to him. He joined her.

"Your friend Mrs. Luce is not yet about?" he inquired.

"No—she sleeps late at sea, 'and has breakfast in her cabin. Did you want to speak with her right away?"

"I wished talk with the two of you. But you alone suffice in a very pleasant manner. Last night I set you down on dock at about nine o'clock. Tell me—what members of travel party did you encounter between that hour and moment of retiring?"

"We saw several of them. The state-room was quite warm, so we went up and sat in steamer chairs near the top of the gang-plank. The Minchins came aboard presently, and Sadie stopped to show us her day's loot. A ukulele for that boy of hers at military school, among other things. Then Mark Kennaway came on, but he didn't stop with us. He thought Mr. Tait might want him for the eternal bedtime story. Then the Benbows, Elmer all loaded down with exposed film. That was all, I guess. Mr. Kennaway came back to us in a few minutes. He said Mr. Tait didn't seem to be aboard, and he appeared to think that rather surprising."

"Those were all. No man with a Malacca stick?"

"Oh—Mr. Ross, you mean. Yes, he was one of the first, I think. He came limping aboard——"

"Pardon me—at about what time?"

"It must have been about nine-fifteen. He passed where we were sitting—I thought he was limping even more than usual. Mrs. Luce spoke to him, but oddly enough, he didn't answer. He just hurried on down the deck."

"Can you tell me—is his the only Malacca stick in the party?"

The girl laughed. "My dear Mr. Chan—we spent three days in Singapore, and if you don't buy a Malacca stick there, they won't let you leave. Every man in our party has one at least."

Charlie frowned. "Indeed? Then how can you be absolutely certain it was Mr. Ross who passed you?"

"Well—this man was limping——"

"Simplest thing in the world to imitate. Think hard. Was there no other way in which you could identify him?"

The girl sat for a moment in silence. "How's this?" she remarked at last. "Getting to be some little detective myself. The sticks that were bought in Singapore all had metal tips—I noticed that. But Mr. Ross's stick has a heavy rubber tip on it. It makes no noise when he walks along the deck."

"And the stick of the man who passed you last night——"

"It made no sound. So the man must have been Mr. Ross. Am I good? Just to show you how good I am, I'll give you a demonstration. Here comes Mr. Ross now. Listen!"

Ross had appeared in the distance, and was swinging along towards them. He passed with a nod and a smile, and disappeared around the corner. Chan and the girl looked at each other. For accompanying the lame man like a chant they had heard the steady "tap-tap-tap" of metal on the hard deck.

"Well, of all things," cried the girl.

"Mr. Ross's stick has lost its rubber tip," Charlie said.

She nodded. "What can that mean?"

"A puzzle," Chan answered. "And unless I am much mistaken, the first of many aboard this ship. Why should I worry? Puzzles are my business."

CHAPTER XVII

THE GREAT EASTERN LABEL

At a little before ten, Lofton appeared in front of the chair where Chan was sitting. He still had the air of a much-abused man.

"Well, Inspector," he announced, "I've got my people together in the smoking-room. I chose that spot because it's always deserted at this hour. A bit odoriferous, perhaps—I trust you won't hold them there long. I suggest you come at once. Keeping a touring party intact in one place for any length of time is, I have discovered, a difficult feat."

Chan rose. "Will you also come, Miss Pamela?" he suggested. As they walked along, he added to the doctor: "Am I to understand that all members of band are present?"

"All except Mrs. Luce," Lofton told him. "She prefers to sleep late. But I'll have her roused, if you say so."

"Not at all," Chan replied. "I know where Mrs. Luce was last evening. Matter of fact, she dined at my house."

"Not really?" cried the doctor, with unflattering surprise.

"You would have been welcome yourself," Charlie smiled.

They entered the thick atmosphere of the smoking-room, redolent of old, unhappy, far-off things, and

bottles, long ago. The group inside regarded Chan
with frank curiosity. He stood for a moment, facing
them. A little speech seemed indicated.

"May I extend courteous good morning?" he
began. "Would say I am surprised to see you all
again as you must be to behold me. I am reluctant
to enforce my inspeakable presence upon you, but fate
will not have it otherwise. Inspector Duff, as you
know, was awaiting you at Honolulu, Paradise of
Pacific, intending to travel eastward in your company.
Last night in paradise history repeats and snake
appears, striking down the worthy Duff. He is much
better this morning, thank you. Maybe plenty soon
he sees you all again. In meantime, a stupid substitute for Duff has been pushed into position for which
he has not the brains, the wit, the reputation. Notably
—myself."

He smiled pleasantly and sat down. "All mischief
comes from opening the mouth," he continued.
"Knowing this, I am still forced to operate mine to
considerable extent from now on. Let us make the
best of it. My initial effort will be to find out from
each of you exact presence between hour of—may I
say—eight last evening, and sailing of boat at ten.
Pardon such outrageous hint, but any of you who
fails to speak true may have cause to regret same later
on. I have said I am dull and stupid, and that is the
fact, but often the gods go out of way to take care of
such. To recompense, they shower on me sometimes
amazing luck. Look out I don't get shower at any
moment."

Patrick Tait was on his feet. "My dear sir," he
remarked irritably, "I question your authority to
interrogate any of us. We are no longer in Honolulu——"

"Pardon interruption, but what you say is true,"

Charlie put in. "Legal side of matter is no doubt such as to give eminent lawyer bad attack of choleric. I judge from records of case same has happened before. Can only say captain of ship stands behind me firm as Gibraltar rock. We proceed on assumption every one of you is shocked and grieved by attack on Duff, and eager to see the attacker captured. If this is wrong—if there is man among you has something to hide——"

"Just a minute!" Tait cried. "I won't let you manœuvre me into that position. I've nothing to hide. I only wanted to remind you that there is such a thing as legal procedure."

"Which is usually the criminal's best friend," nodded Chan blandly. "You and I—we know. Do we not, Mr. Tait?" The lawyer sank back into his chair. "But we are some miles off the point," continued Charlie. "You are all friends of justice, I feel certain. You have no interest in that poor relation of same, legal procedure. Let us go forward on such basis. Doctor Lofton, since you are conductor of party, I begin with you. How did you spend two hours mentioned by me?"

"From eight to about nine-thirty," said Lofton sourly, "I was at the Honolulu office of the Nomad Travel Company, which manages my tours for me. I had a lot of accounts to go over, and some type-writing to do."

"Ah, yes. Of course, others were with you at that office?"

"Not a soul. The manager was due to attend a country club dance, and he left me there alone. Since the door had a spring lock, I had only to close it after me when I went out. I returned to the ship at about nine-thirty."

"Nomad Travel Company office is, I believe, on

Fort Street? Only few steps from mouth of alley wandering along rear of police station."

"It's on Fort Street, yes. I don't know anything about your police station."

"Naturally you don't. Did you encounter any members of travel party in neighbourhood of alley?"

"I have no idea what alley you're talking about. I saw none of my people from the time I went to the office until I returned to the ship. I suggest you get on with this. Time is pressing."

"Whom is it pressing?" asked Chan suavely. "Speaking for myself, I have six days to squander. Mr. Tait, do you cling to legal rights, or will you condescend to tell humble policeman how you spent last evening?"

"Oh, I've no objection," returned Tait, amiable with an effort. "Why should I have? Last night, about eight o'clock, we started a contract bridge game in the lounge. Aside from myself, Mrs. Spicer, Mr. Vivian and Mr. Kennaway took part in it. It's a foursome that has had many similar contests as we went round the world."

"Ah, yes—travel is fine education," nodded Chan. "You played until the boat sailed."

"We did not. We were having a splendid game when, at about eight-thirty, Mr. Vivian raised the most unholy row——"

"I beg your pardon," Vivian cut in. "If I broke up the game, I had an excellent reason. You have heard me tell my partner a thousand times that if I make an original two bid, I expect her to keep it open, even if——"

"So—you told me that a thousand times, did you?" flared Mrs. Spicer. "A million would be more like it. And I've explained patiently to you that if I had a flat hand, I wouldn't bid—no, not even if Mr. White-

head was sitting beside me with a gun.   The trouble
with you is, a little knowledge is a dangerous——"

"Pardon me that I burst in," Charlie said, "but
the matter becomes too technical for my stupidity to
cope with.   Let us seize on fact that game broke
up."

"Broke up in a row, at eight-thirty," Tait continued.   "Mr. Kennaway and I went out on to the
deck.   It was raining hard.   Mark said he thought
he'd get his rain-coat and take a stroll up to the town.
I saw him leave about ten minutes later.   I told him I
preferred to stay aboard."

"And did you?" Charlie asked.

"No, I didn't.   After Mr. Kennaway had gone, I
remembered that I'd seen a copy of the *New York
Sunday Times* hanging outside a news-stand on King
Street yesterday morning.   I'd meant to go back and
get it.   I hadn't seen one for ages, and I was keen to
have it.   The rain seemed to be letting up a bit.   So
I got a coat, my hat and stick——"

"Your Malacca stick?"

"Yes—I believe I carried the Malacca.   At about
ten minutes to nine I walked up-town, bought the
paper, and returned to the ship.   I'm a slow walker,
and I suppose it was about twenty minutes past the
hour when I came aboard again."

Chan took his watch from his left-hand vest pocket.
"What time have you now, Mr. Tait?" he asked
quickly.

Tait's right hand went to his own waistcoat pocket.
Then it dropped back to his lap, and he looked rather
foolish.   He extended his left wrist, and examined
the watch on it.   "I make it ten-twenty-five," he
announced.

"Correct," smiled Charlie.   "I make it the same,
and I am always right."

Tait's bushy eyebrows rose. "Always?" he repeated, with a touch of sarcasm.

"In such matters—yes," nodded the Chinese. For a moment he and the lawyer stared at each other. Then Chan looked away. "So many changes of time as you peruse way around world," he said softly. "I merely wished to be certain your watch is up to date. Mr. Vivian, what was your course of action after bridge table eruption?"

"I, too, went ashore," Vivian responded. "I wanted to cool off."

"With hat, coat and Malacca stick, no doubt?" suggested Charlie.

"We've all got Malacca sticks," snapped the polo player. "They're almost obligatory when you visit Singapore. I walked about the city, and got back to the ship a few minutes before it sailed."

"Mrs. Spicer?" Charlie's eyes turned in her direction.

She looked weary and fed-up.

"I went to bed when I left the bridge table," she told him. "It had been a somewhat trying experience. Bridge is only fun when you happen to have a gentleman for a partner."

"Mr. Kennaway, your actions have already been detailed by Mr. Tait."

Kennaway nodded. "Yes—I took my little stick and went ashore. I didn't stay long, however. I thought Mr. Tait might want me to read to him, so I came back to the ship soon after nine. But Mr. Tait, to my surprise, wasn't aboard. He appeared about nine-twenty, as he told you, and he had the *Times* under his arm. We went to our cabin, and I read to him from the paper until he fell asleep."

Charlie looked around the circle. "And this gentleman?"

"Max Minchin, Chicago. And nothing to hide, get me?"

Charlie bowed. "Then you will be glad to detail your actions?"

"Yes—and it'll take just one minute—see?" Mr. Minchin fondled an expensive, half-smoked cigar, from which he had failed to remove a shining gold band. "Me and Sadie—that's the wife—was doing the town, in the rain. Well, the evening wasn't so much on the up and up with me, so I dragged the frau into a pitcher show. But we seen that filum a year ago in Chi., and Sadie was itching to get back to the stores, so we made our get-away quick. After that, just buying right and left. We didn't have no truck with us, and when we couldn't handle no more, Sadie agreed to quit. We staggered back to the ship. I didn't have no gat on me, and I wasn't carrying no Malacca stick. When I carry a cane, it'll mean my dogs ain't no good no more—I told Sadie that in Singapore."

Charlie smiled. "Mr. Benbow?" he suggested.

"Same story as the Minchins," that gentleman replied. "We did the stores, though they're not much after those Oriental bazaars. Sat a while in the Young lobby and watched it rain. I said I wished I was back in Akron, and Nettie practically agreed with me. First time we've been in accord on that point since the tour started. But we were on good old U.S. soil, even if it was pretty sloppy, and we came back to the ship walking high, wide and handsome. I think we stepped aboard about nine-fifteen. I was dead tired—I'd bought a motion picture projector in Honolulu, and the weight of one of those things is nobody's business."

"Miss Pamela," said Chan. "I already know how your evening was spent. Leaving, I think, only two yet to be inquisitioned. This gentleman—Captain Keane, I believe."

Keane leaned back, stifled a yawn, and clasped his hands behind his head. "I watched the bridge for a while," he replied. "Not as a kibitzer, you understand." He glanced at Vivian. "I never interfere in affairs that don't concern me."

Recalling the captain's record outside various doors, Charlie felt the remark was somewhat lacking in sincerity. "And after the bridge——" he prompted.

"When the battle broke," Keane went on, "I took to the open air. Thought some of getting my own little Malacca stick and going ashore, but the rain gave me pause. Never did care for rain, especially the tropical kind. So I went to my cabin, got a book, and returned here to the smoking-room."

"Ah," remarked Chan. "You now possess a book."

"What are you trying to do, razz me?" said the captain. "I sat here reading for a while, and about the time the boat sailed, I went to bed."

"Was anyone else in this room while you were?"

"Nobody at all. Everybody ashore, including the stewards."

Charlie turned to the man whom he had purposely saved until the last. Ross was sitting not far away, staring down at his injured foot. His stick, innocent of its rubber tip, lay beside him on the floor.

"Mr. Ross, I believe you will complete the roster," Chan remarked. "You went ashore last evening, I have heard."

Ross looked up in surprise. "Why, no, Inspector," he replied. "I didn't."

"Indeed? Yet you were seen to come aboard ship at nine-fifteen."

"Really?" Ross lifted his eyebrows.

"On authority not to be impeached."

"But—I am sorry to say—in this case quite mistaken."

"You are sure you did not leave the ship?"

"Naturally I'm sure. It's the sort of thing I ought to know about, you must admit." He remained entirely amiable. "I dined aboard, and sat in the lounge for a while after dinner. I'd had a rather hard day—a lot of walking, and that tires me. My leg was aching, so I retired at eight o'clock. I was sound asleep when Mr. Vivian, who shares my cabin, came in. That was in the neighbourhood of ten, he told me this morning. He was careful not to wake me. He is always most considerate."

Chan regarded him thoughtfully. "Yet at nine-fifteen, as I have said, Mr. Ross, two people of unreproachable honesty saw you come up the plank, and you passed them on deck."

"May I ask how they recognized me, Inspector?"

"You carried stick, of course."

"A Malacca stick," nodded Ross. "You have seen what that amounts to."

"But more, Mr. Ross. You were walking with customary difficulty, owing to unhappy accident which is so deeply deplored by all."

For a moment Ross regarded the detective. "Inspector," he remarked at last, "I've watched you here. You're a clever man."

"You exaggerate shamelessly," Charlie told him.

"No, I don't," smiled Ross. "I say you're clever, and I believe that all I need do now is to tell you about a queer little incident that happened on this ship late yesterday afternoon." He picked up his stick. "This was not bought in Singapore, but in Tacoma some months ago just after I had my accident. After

I bought it, I looked around until I found a rubber tip—a shoe, I believe it is sometimes called—to 'fit over the end of it. This made walking easier for me, and it did not scratch hardwood floors. About five yesterday afternoon, I returned to the ship and took a brief nap in my cabin. When I rose and went down to dinner, I was conscious of something—something wrong—at first I didn't know just what. But presently I realized. As I walked, my stick was tapping on the deck. I looked down in amazement. The rubber tip was gone. Someone had taken it." He stopped. "I remember Mr. Kennaway came along at that moment, and I told him what had happened."

"That's right," Kennaway agreed. "We puzzled over the matter. I suggested somebody was playing a joke."

"It was no joke," remarked Ross gravely. "Someone, I now believe, was planning to impersonate me for the evening. Someone who was clever enough to recall that my stick made no sound when it touched a hard surface."

No one spoke. Mrs. Luce appeared in the distant doorway, and came swiftly to Chan's side. The detective leaped to his feet.

"What's this I hear?" she cried. "Poor Inspector Duff!"

"Not badly injured," Charlie assured her. "Recovering."

"Thank heaven," she replied. "The aim is wavering. The arm is getting weak. Well, too much shooting is bad for anybody. I take it you are with us in Inspector Duff's place, Mr. Chan?"

"I am unworthy substitute," he bowed.

"Unworthy fiddlesticks! You can't put that over on me. Known Chinese most of my life—lived among 'em. At last we're going to get somewhere. I'm sure of it." She glanced belligerently around the circle. "And about time, if you ask me."

"You arrive at good moment," Charlie said. "I will request your testimony, please. Last night, after I brought you to dock, you and Miss Pamela sat on deck near top of gang-plank. You beheld several members of party return to ship. Among them, Mr. Ross here?"

The old lady stood for a moment staring at Ross. Then she shook her head. "I don't know," she answered.

Chan was surprised. "You don't know whether you saw Mr. Ross or not?"

"No, I don't."

"But, my dear," said Pamela Potter, "surely you remember. We were sitting near the rail, and Mr. Ross came up the plank, and passed us——"

Again Mrs. Luce shook her head. "A man who walked with a stick, and limped, passed us—yes. I spoke to him, but he didn't answer. Mr. Ross is a polite man. Besides——"

"Yes?" Charlie said eagerly.

"Besides, Mr. Ross carries his stick in his left hand, whereas that man last night was carrying his in the right. I noticed it at the time. That's why I say I don't know whether it was Mr. Ross or not. My own feeling at the moment was that it was not."

Silence followed. Finally Ross looked up at Charlie. "What did I tell you, Inspector?" he remarked. "I did not leave the ship last evening. I had rather a hunch the matter would be proved in time, though I didn't expect the proof so soon."

"Your right leg is injured one," Charlie said.

"Yes—and anyone who has never suffered such an injury might suppose that I would naturally carry my stick in the right hand. But as my doctor pointed out to me, the left is better. I am more securely balanced, and I can move faster."

"That's O.K., Officer," put in Maxy Minchin. "A few years back an old pal of mine winged me in the left calf. I found out then the dope was to carry the cane on the opposite side. It gives you better support —get me?"

Ross smiled. "Thank you, Mr. Minchin," he said. He glanced at Chan. "These clever lads always slip up somewhere, don't they?" he added. "Here is one who had brains enough to want my rubber shoe so his stick couldn't be distinguished on that score— and then, in his haste, forgot to notice in which hand I carried mine. Well, all I can say is, I'm very glad he did." His eyes travelled questioningly about the little circle.

Charlie stood up. "Meeting now adjourns for time being," he announced. "I am very grateful to you all for kind co-operating."

They filed out, until Tait alone remained with the detective. He strolled over to Chan with a grim smile on his face.

"You didn't get much out of that session," he remarked.

"You believe not?" Chan inquired.

"No, but you did your best. And on one point, at least, you showed unusual acumen. That about the watch, I mean."

"Ah, yes—the watch," Charlie nodded.

"A man who has been accustomed all his life to carrying a watch in his vest pocket, and then switches to a wrist-watch, is inclined to put his hand to the old location when suddenly asked the time."

"So I noticed," the detective replied.

"I thought you did. What a pity you wasted that experiment on an innocent man."

"There will be more experiments," Chan assured him.

"I hope so. I may tell you that I purchased a wrist-watch just before I came on this tour."

"Before you came on the tour." The first word was accented ever so slightly.

"Exactly. I can prove that by Mr. Kennaway. Any time at all."

"For the present, I accept your word," Charlie replied.

"Thank you. I trust I shall be present when you attempt those other experiments."

"Do not worry. You are plenty sure to be there."

"Good. I like to watch you work." And Tait strode debonairly from the room, while Chan stood looking after him.

The investigation was young yet, Charlie thought, as he walked towards his cabin to prepare for lunch. No great progress this morning, but a good beginning. At least he had now a pretty shrewd idea as to the character and capabilities of the people with whom he had to deal. Know them better to-morrow. No place like a ship for getting acquainted.

A boy appeared with a radiogram. Chan opened it and read.

"Charlie, as a friend, I implore you to drop the whole matter. I am getting on beautifully and can take up the trail soon myself. Situation is far too dangerous for me to ask such a service of you. Believe me, I was quite delirious when I suggested you carry on. DUFF."

Charlie smiled to himself, and sat down at a desk in the library. After due deliberation, he composed an answering message:

"You were not delirious last night, but I have deep pain to note you are in such state now. How else could you think I would not pursue to very frontier of my ability this interesting affair? Remain calm, get back health promptly, and meantime I am willing replacement. Hoping you soon regain reason I remain your solid friend, C. CHAN."

After lunch, Charlie spent several hours meditating in his cabin. This was a case after his own heart, six long days to ponder it, while the person he sought must stay within easy reach of his hand.

That evening after dinner the detective came upon Pamela Potter and Mark Kennaway having coffee in a corner of the lounge. At the girl's invitation, he joined them.

"Well, Mr. Chan," she remarked, "one of your precious six days is gone."

"Yes, and where are you?" Kennaway inquired.

"Two hundred and fifty miles from Honolulu, and moving comfortably along," Chan smiled.

"You didn't learn much this morning?" the young man suggested.

"I learned that my friend the murderer still seeks to entangle the innocent, as he did when he stole Doctor Lofton's luggage strap in London."

"You mean that about Ross?" the girl asked.

Charlie nodded. "Tell me—you agree now with Mrs. Luce?"

"I do," she answered. "I thought at the time that person was limping very weirdly—much more than Mr. Ross ever had. Whom could it have been?"

"It might have been any of us," said Kennaway, looking at Chan over his cup.

"How right you are," returned the detective. "Any of you who wandered about rainy town, assisted on way by Malacca stick."

"Or it might even have been the lad who couldn't

tear himself away from his book," the young man
suggested. "Or claims he couldn't. I refer to jolly
old Captain Keane, the irrepressible reader."

"Ah, yes—Keane," Chan said. "Has anyone ever
determined cause of Keane's fondness for loitering
outside wrong doors?"

"Not so far as I know," Pamela Potter replied.
"As a matter of fact, he hasn't been doing it much
lately. Mr. Vivian caught him at it just after we
left Yokohama, and the row could be heard for blocks.
If there'd been any blocks, I mean."

"Mr. Vivian has special talent for rows," Charlie
noted.

"I'll say he has," Kennaway agreed. "That last
night made bridge look like one of the more hazardous
occupations. I thought Vivian started it with very
little reason. It almost looked as though he wanted
to break up the game."

Chan's eyes narrowed. "Mr. Kennaway, I understand your employer, Mr. Tait, bought a wrist-watch
just before he left New York?"

The young man laughed. "Yes—he warned me
you were going to ask that. He did. Thought it
would be more convenient on a long tour. He has his
old watch and chain in his trunk, I believe. Get him
to show them to you."

"Chain is intact, of course?"

"Oh, naturally. Or was when I saw it last—in
Cairo."

Tait came up to them. "Mrs. Luce and I are
getting up a bridge game," he announced. "You
young people are elected."

"But I'm a terrible player," the girl protested.

"I know you are," the lawyer replied. "That's
why I'm going to assign you to Mark as a partner. I
feel I'm going to win. I love to win."

Kennaway and the girl got up. "Sorry to leave you, Mr. Chan," the latter said.

"I would not interfere with your pleasure." he returned.

"Pleasure?" she repeated. "You've heard about the slaughter of the innocents. Haven't you an old Chinese proverb to comfort me?"

"I have one which might have warned you," Charlie told her. "The deer should not play with the tiger."

"That's the best bridge rule I ever heard," the girl answered.

After a time, Charlie rose and walked out on to the deck. He was standing in a dark corner by the rail when he heard a stealthy hiss out of the night. He had completely forgotten Kashimo.

His slim little assistant came close. Even in the dark it was evident that he bubbled over with mystery and excitement.

"Search all over," he whispered breathlessly.

"What!" breathed Charlie.

"I have discovered key," the Japanese replied.

Chan's heart leaped at the words. Welby, he recalled, had also discovered the key.

"You are quick worker, Kashimo," the Chinese said. "Where is it?"

"Follow me," directed Kashimo. He led the way into the corridor, and to a de luxe cabin on the same deck. At the door, he paused.

"Who occupies this room?" Charlie asked anxiously.

"Mr. Tait and Mr. Kennaway," the Japanese told him, and pushing open the door, flooded the cabin with light. Remembering the bridge game with relief, Charlie followed, closing the door behind him. He noticed that the port-holes, which opened on the promenade deck, were safely shuttered.

Kashimo knelt, and dragged from beneath one of the beds a battered old bag. It was plastered with the labels of foreign hotels. The Japanese made no effort to open it, but lovingly ran his fingers over a particularly gorgeous label—that of the Great Eastern Hotel, Calcutta.   "You do same," he suggested to Charlie.

Charlie touched the label. Underneath he felt the faint outline of a key, about the size of the one Duff had shown him.

"Good work, Kashimo," he murmured.

In gold letters near the bag's lock, he saw the initials "M.K."

CHAPTER XVIII

AFTER a few whispered instructions to Kashimo,
Charlie returned to the deck and stood by the rail,
staring thoughtfully out at the silver path of the
moon on the dark waters. His chief feeling at the
moment was one of admiration for his assistant. An
ingenious place to hide an object like a key—it had
made but the slightest protuberance on the rough
leather of the case. The eye would never have
detected it—only the fingers. Yes, Kashimo was
undoubtedly a blunderer, but in this matter of
searching, of meddling with the property of others,
the boy was touched with genius.

Gradually Chan began to consider the larger aspects
of the matter. How came this key, duplicate of the
one found in the dead hand of Hugh Morris Drake that
morning in a London hotel, to be on Kennaway's
bag? Of course he had not seen it, but Charlie felt
it safe to assume that it was the duplicate. The one
Welby had located the night he told Pamela Potter:
"The fun's all over." The fun had indeed been over
for poor Welby. A dangerous object to discover.

Where had Welby found it? In the same place
where it was now? He must have. For it was under
the label of the Great Eastern Hotel, Calcutta, and the
natural inference must be that it had been put there in
the Indian city. A man couldn't pick up a Calcutta

label anywhere save in Calcutta. Yes, it must have been in its present position in Yokohama, where Welby found it——

Wait a minute. Welby had spoken of this key to the girl as though he had actually seen it. Number and all. But had he? Perhaps he was merely assuming, as Chan was doing, that this was the duplicate key. It would have been a natural assumption. It might be that he had only run his fingers over the outline, as Chan had done. And someone had learned of his discovery, had followed him ashore and murdered him.

Who? Kennaway? Nonsense. It had without doubt been the same man who killed Honywood and his wife. Kennaway was a mere boy; what concern could he have with Jim Everhard and the Honywoods. With events that had happened long ago in some far place, and then remained in the shadows for many years?

Charlie put his hand to his head. Puzzles, puzzles. It couldn't have been Kennaway. The murderer's settled policy, evidently, was to implicate innocent men if he could. Witness the matter of the strap in London, the theft of the rubber tip from the stick belonging to Ross. Furthermore, he would hardly care to have this key discovered in his possession. What more natural than for him to attach it to the property of another man?

Who would have had the best opportunity to put that key on Kennaway's bag? Chan's eyes, fixed unseeing on the glittering water, narrowed suddenly. Who but Tait? Tait, who had been so prompt that morning to proclaim himself an innocent man, who had asserted that his change to a wrist-watch had been effected before the tour started. Tait, who had slept in the room next to that in which Drake died; Tait who had fallen in a terrific heart attack when he discovered next morning that Honywood, the man Everhard meant to kill, was still alive. Certainly Tait was old enough to have been Everhard in his day, to have acquired those little bags of pebbles, to have carried them for years, determined to return them when opportunity offered. What more likely than that Tait had made use of his companion's suitcase?

Chan began a slow stroll about the deck. No, the key was never Kennaway's. Suddenly he stood still. If Welby had found it where it was now, and it did not belong to Kennaway, then the little detective from Scotland Yard had not discovered the murderer. Why, then, had he been killed on the Yokohama dock?

Again Chan put his hand to his head. "Haie, I wander amid confusing fog," he murmured. "Much better I go to my pillow, seeking to gain clarity for the morrow."

He took his own advice at once, and the second night aboard the *President Arthur* passed without incident.

In the morning Charlie cultivated the society of Mark Kennaway. It meant considerable moving about, for the young man seemed restless and distraught. He roamed the ship, and Charlie roamed with him.

"You are youthful person," the Chinese remarked. "You should study calm. I should say to look at you you have few more than twenty years."

"Twenty-five," Kennaway informed him. "But I seem to have added about ten by this tour."

"It has been difficult time?" inquired Chan sympathetically.

"Ever been a nursemaid?" asked the young man. "Lord—if I'd known what I was letting myself in for!

I've read aloud at night until my eyes ached and my throat felt like the desert's dusty face. Then there's been the constant anxiety about poor Mr. Tait's condition."

"There have been other attacks since the one in Broome's Hotel?" Charlie suggested.

Kennaway nodded. "Yes, several. One on the boat in the Red Sea, and a quite terrible one at Calcutta. I've cabled his son to meet us at San Francisco, and believe me I'll be glad to see that Golden Gate. If I can get him ashore there still alive, I'll consider that I'm a fool for luck. I'll heave a sigh of relief that will be reported in all the Eastern papers as another California earthquake."

"Ah, yes," agreed Chan. "You must have been under much strain."

"Oh, I had it coming to me," Kennaway returned gloomily. "I should have started on law and let the map of the world alone. None of my people in Boston were in favour of this trip. They warned me. But I knew it all."

"Boston," repeated Charlie. "As I told you yesterday, a city in which I have great interest. The diction of its people is most superior. Some years ago I did small favour for Boston family, and never in my life was I thanked in better language."

Kennaway laughed. "Well, that must have been something," he replied.

"A great deal," Chan assured him. "I am old-fashioned person who feels that choice of words proclaims the gentleman. Or, in the case of which I speak, the lady. My children regard me old fogy on this point."

"Children don't show their parents enough respect these days," the young man nodded. "I say that as an ex-child. Well, I hope my parents don't find out

the hell I've been through on this trip. I'd hate to
hear the familiar: 'I told you so.' Of course, it
hasn't been only poor Mr. Tait. I've had other
troubles."

"I do not wish to penetrate any Boston reserve,"
Charlie remarked. "But could you name one,
please?"

"I certainly could. That Potter girl—well, perhaps
I shouldn't have said it."

Chan's eyes opened in surprise. "What is wrong
with Potter girl?" he inquired.

"Everything," returned the young man. "She
annoys me beyond words."

"Annoys you?"

"Yes. I've said it, and I'll stick to it. Doesn't
she get on your nerves too? So damned Middle
Western and competent? So sure of herself? She's
got more poise than a great-aunt of mine who's lived
on Beacon Hill for eighty-one years and met everybody
worth while." He leaned closer. "You know, I
actually believe the girl thinks I'll propose to her
before this tour's over. Would I take that chance?
Not I. And get her bank-book thrown in my face."

"You think that would happen?"

"I'm sure of it. I know these Middle Westerners
—nothing matters but money. How much have you
got? We don't feel that way in Boston. Money
doesn't count there. Ours certainly doesn't. Uncle
Eldred lost it all betting on the New York, New
Haven and Hartford. I—I don't know why I've
said all this to you. But you can see how I feel.
Worn out acting as a nursemaid—and this girl on
my mind all the time."

"Ah—then she is on your mind?"

"She certainly is. She can be mighty nice when
she tries. Sweet, and—er—you know, sweet—and

then all at once I'm run over by an automobile. One
of the Drake brand. Millions at the wheel."

Chan consulted his watch. "I see her now at far
end of deck. I presume you wish to flee?"

Kennaway shook his head. "What's the use?
You can't get away from people on a boat. I've
given up trying, long ago."

Pamela Potter came up to them. "Good morning,
Mr. Chan. Hello, Mark. How about some deck
tennis? I think I can trim you this morning."

"You always do," Kennaway said.

"The East is so effete," she smiled, and led the
captive Kennaway off.

Chan made a hasty tour of the deck. He found
Captain Ronald Keane seated alone near the bow of
the boat, and dropped into a chair beside him.

"Ah, Captain," he said, "a somewhat gorgeous
morning."

"I guess it is," Keane replied. "Hadn't noticed,
really."

"You have other matters that require pondering?"
Charlie suggested.

"Not a thing in the world," yawned Keane. "But
I never pay any attention to the weather. People
who do are nothing but human vegetables."

The chief engineer came strolling along the deck.
He paused at Charlie's chair. "About time for our
tour of the engine room, Mr. Chan," he remarked.

"Ah, yes," returned the Chinese. "You were
kind enough to promise me that pleasure when we
talked together last night. Captain Keane, I am
sure, would enjoy to come along." He looked
inquiringly at Keane.

The captain stared back, amazed. "Me? Oh, no,
thanks. I've no interest in engines. Wouldn't know
a gadget from a gasket. And care less."

Charlie glanced up at the engineer. "Thank you so much," he said. "If you do not object, I will postpone my own tour. I desire short talk with Captain Keane."

"All right," nodded the engineer, and moved away. Chan was regarding Keane grimly.

"You know nothing about engines?" he suggested.

"Certainly not. What are you getting at, anyhow?"

"Some months ago, in parlour of Broome's Hotel, London, you informed Inspector Duff you were one time engineer."

Keane stared at him. "Say, you're quite a lad, aren't you?" he remarked. "Did I tell Duff that? I'd forgot all about it."

"It was not the truth?"

"No, of course not. I just said the first thing that came into my head."

"A habit of yours, it seems."

"What do you mean by that?"

"I have been reading about you, Captain Keane. In Inspector Duff's note-book. Investigation of murder is serious business, and you will pardon me if I get plenty crude in my remarks. You are self-confessed liar, seemingly with no regrets. All through tour you have behaved strangely, listening outside doors. Not very lovable activity."

"No, I fancy it isn't," Keane snapped. "You must have found that out in your own work."

"I am not sneaky kind of detective," replied Chan, with dignity.

"Is that so?" replied Keane. "Then you can't be much good. I've been in the business six years, and I'm not proud of what I've done."

Charlie sat up. "You are detective?" he asked.

Keane nodded. "Yes—keep it under your hat. I represent a private agency in San Francisco——"

"Ah—private detective," nodded Chan, relieved.

"Yes, and don't be nasty. We're just as good as you are. I'm telling you this because I don't want you to waste your time on me. Mrs. Spicer has a husband and he's eager to get rid of her. Wants to marry a movie actress, or something like that. So he sent me on this trip to see what I could see."

Chan studied Keane's mean face carefully. Was this the truth? The man certainly looked well-suited to the rôle of private detective. So he didn't want Chan to waste any time on him? Unexpected consideration, this was.

"You have had no success?" the Chinese remarked.

"No—the thing was a flop from the first. I believe Vivian suspected me the moment he saw me. I dread meeting Spicer when we land at San Francisco—all this has cost him a pretty penny. But it wasn't my fault if love's young dream blew up right in my face. If they only hadn't been partners at bridge—that finished it. They're not even speaking now, and Vivian has threatened to break my neck if I come near him again. I'm fond of my neck. So I'm at a loose end from here on home. By the way, all this is on the quiet."

Charlie nodded.

"Your secret is safe with me."

"I was wondering," continued Keane. "Couldn't I help you out on this murder thing? Is there any reward, or anything like that?"

"The reward of work well done," Charlie replied.

"Tripe! You don't mean to say you've come into this without having an understanding with the Potter girl? Say—you need a manager. I'll go and have a talk with her. The family's got wads of money, and they naturally want to find out who killed the old man. We'll go fifty-fifty——"

"Stop!" cried Chan. "You have already said too much. Kindly remember that I am not private detective. You have no authority from me for your low plan——"

"Wait a minute. Let's argue this out——"

"No. The ignorant are never defeated in argument. What is more, there is nothing to debate. You will kindly keep out of this affair, which does not concern you in the least. I am bidding you good day."

"You're a hell of a business man," growled Keane.

Charlie walked rapidly down the deck, his accustomed calm rudely disturbed. What a worm this fellow Keane was! All that about being a private detective—was it true? Possibly. On the other hand, it might be merely a blind, a tall story designed to put Charlie off his guard. Charlie sighed. Mustn't forget Keane. Mustn't forget any of them.

The creaking ship ploughed on its way, making good time over the glassy sea. Kashimo reported the key still on Kennaway's bag. Long, leisurely talks with one member of the party after another yielded no result. The second day passed, and the third night. Not until the fourth night did Charlie begin to take hope again. It was on that evening that Maxy Minchin entertained—a grand party to celebrate the approaching end of the tour.

Maxy had passed about with his invitations and had been, much to his own surprise, cordially received. Familiarity had bred charity where he was concerned. The long weeks together had led the party to overlook his crudities. As Mrs. Luce put it: "We mustn't forget there's someone in this crowd who's even worse than Mr. Minchin."

Everyone accepted, and Maxy was delighted. When he brought the news to his wife she reminded him that, with Lofton, there would be thirteen at table.

"Don't let's take any chances, Maxy," she said. "You been gettin' all the breaks so far—don't trifle with your luck. You got to find a fourteenth."

Mr. Minchin found the fourteenth in Charlie. "I ain't got nothing against the dicks," he explained to the Chinese. "I give a party once in Chicago for a table full of 'em. One of the nicest feeds I ever pulled off. You come along. Informal. I'm leaving my Tux in the trunk."

"Thank you so much," Chan answered. "And may I hope that you will not be offended if at this dinner I make bold to refer to the subject of murder?"

"I don't get you," said Maxy, startled.

"I mean I have unlimited yearning to mention there the unfortunate fate of Hugh Morris Drake in Broome's Hotel. It would make me happy to hear conversation regarding this affair from one and all."

Maxy frowned. "Well, I don't know about that. I was hopin' we wasn't going to talk business. Just a good time for all and no questions asked—get me? Some guy in this gang's got a lot on his mind, and I wouldn't like him to have no anxious minutes while he's my guest. After that, you can put the cuffs on him any minute—see what I mean? He ain't no pal of mine. But for the one evening——"

"I will be discreet," Chan promised. "No questions of course."

Maxy waved his hand. "Well, have it your own way. Start the murder thing if you want to. They's no tags to my bids. It's Liberty Hall when Maxy Minchin is paying."

Liberty Hall turned out to be the deck café, where fourteen people sat down that evening around a lavishly decorated table. Knowing full well his duties as a sea-going host, Mr. Minchin had provided a comic hat for everyone. He himself put on a

Napoleonic tricorn with a scarlet cockade, and thus equipped, felt that the evening had begun auspiciously.

"Eat hearty, folks," he ordered. "And drink the same. It's all on the house. I told 'em to put out the best they got."

After the coffee, Maxy rose. "Well, here we are," he began, "near the end of the big hop. We seen the world together, and we had good times, and some not so good. Take it all and all, I'll say it's been a swell lay-out from the start. And if you're asking me, we had one dandy guide. Lift your glasses, people. To old Doc Lofton, the grandest guy afloat."

There were cries for a speech and Lofton arose, somewhat embarrassed.

"Thank you, friends," he said. "I have been conducting parties like this for many years, and I want to say that this has been in many ways one of my more—er—memorable experiences. You have given me very little trouble—that is, of course—most of you have. There have been differences, but they have been amicably settled. You have all been most reasonable, sometimes under great strain, and I am grateful. Of course, I would be foolish to overlook the fact that our tour began under very unusual and trying circumstances. If Miss Pamela will forgive me, I am referring to the unfortunate passing of—er —her grandfather that midnight at Broome's Hotel in London. That is to say, between midnight and morning—er—an occurrence that I regret more deeply than any of you—with, of course, the exception of the young lady I have mentioned. But that is now long in the past, and it seems best to forget it. If it remains among the unsolved mysteries, we must accept that as the will of fate. I shall land you all in San Francisco very soon, and we shall part"—his manner brightened noticeably—"but I assure you that I

shall always treasure memories of our companionship."

"Hear, hear," cried Mr. Minchin, as the doctor sat
down amid polite applause. "Well, folks, since the
Doc's brought it up, I may say that we're all sorry
about that kick-off at Broome's. And that brings me
at this time to mention our special guest here to-night
—the Chinese dick from Hawaii. Believe me, people,
I seen all kinds, but this is a new one on me. Mr.
Chan, spill a few words."

Charlie rose with dignity, despite his introduction.
He glanced calmly about the little room.

"The drum which makes the most noise is filled
with wind," he said. "I remember this in time so
I will not obtrude myself. But I welcome opportunity
to bow to my gracious host, and to his delightful lady,
obscured with plenty jewels. Fate is capricious stage
manager. She has introduced you to policemen round
the world. To my distinguished friend from Scotland
Yard, to the officers of France and Italy. Now you
get sample from melting-pot of Hawaii, you let your
gaze for fleeting moment rest on humble Chinese
who follows meagre clues left behind by the few
criminals who infest our paradise.

"I stand here before you in not entirely happy
position. Wise man has said, do not follow on the
heels of a sorrow, or it may turn back. Such would
be my own advice to Miss Pamela. But while I
remain thus in upright posture, old sorrow will not
fade from your minds.

"You must recall that had it not occurred, I would
not be here. You see pictures of Broome's Hotel,
old incidents, now long forgotten, come back to you.
It can happen they take on new meaning after extensive absence. I am desolate to know I recall
these things, and I make haste to erase myself. First

I would add—Doctor Lofton has told you that if matter is never solved, it is will of fate. I am Chinese, I accept will of fate, but I have lived so long among American people I feel inclination to give fate small tussle before I offer my meek acceptance. By this time my broad bulk has cast plenty shade on this gay feast. I am sitting down."

Mr. Minchin's roving eye fell on Mr. Tait. That gentleman rose with the manner of the experienced speaker.

"I am, perhaps, happier than any of you to be here," he began. "There have been times when it seemed I must leave you long before this. But the determination to live is strong, and I promise that I shall finish with you, as I began.

"In many ways, I feel that I am lucky. I have much to be grateful for. For example, referring again to my friend Mr. Hugh Morris Drake, and the night of February 6—the morning of the seventh—I might have been the occupant of the bed in room 28—the innocent victim of a murder that was purely——"

He stopped, and looked helplessly about him. "Pardon me. I am off on the wrong tack there. We are, I fear, making this a rather unhappy evening for the charming Miss Pamela. I only meant to say that I am happy to have survived thus far on our tour around the world, and that it has been a great pleasure to meet you all. Thank you very much."

He sat down abruptly amid subdued applause. Mrs. Luce obliged with a travelogue, and Pamela Potter said a few graceful words. Captain Keane arose.

"Well, it's been a great trip," he said. "However, I guess it's about over now, and those of us who have work to do can go and do it. We've had a lot of fun, and for my part I'd almost forgotten the incident at Broome's Hotel. That was a bit of a strain, and no mistake. Inspector Duff acted for a while as though he intended to spoil the tour—for some of us at least. His questions were pretty personal. I don't go in for murder myself, but I happened to be wandering about that night, as you may recall. I had my bad moments. And I guess some of the rest of us were on the anxious seat, too. I guess Mr. Elmer Benbow was a little bit worried—eh, Mr. Benbow? I haven't said a word to anybody about this before, but now we're all back in God's country and I guess we can take care of ourselves. I saw Mr. Benbow at three o'clock the morning of the murder, just as he was slipping back into his room from the hall. I imagine you're glad you didn't have to explain that to Scotland Yard—eh, Benbow?"

Keane's air was one of light-hearted banter, but it deceived no one. Underneath was a cheap malice that was unpleasant to contemplate. Even Maxy Minchin, though he couldn't have defined the feeling, knew that here was an exhibition of bad taste that took the palm. The little gangster leaped to his feet.

"The way things is going you don't need no toast-master here," he announced. "Mr. Benbow, you been elected the next speaker."

The man from Akron got slowly to his feet. "I've been doing a lot of speaking the past few years," he began, "but I don't know that I ever had to make a speech like this before. It's quite true—I was out of my room that night in Broome's Hotel. After we got home and got to bed, I suddenly remembered that February 6 was my daughter's birthday. We'd been intending all day to send her a cable, but we'd been so busy we both forgot. Well, I was upset, and no mistake. Then I remembered the change of time— that it was six hours earlier in Akron. It came to me

that maybe I could still get my cable to her that day
—late at night, perhaps, but still on her birthday. I
jumped out of bed, dressed, and hustled out. There
were some scrubwomen in the hotel lobby, but I didn't
meet any of the other servants, coming or going. Of
course, I should have told the police about this, but I
certainly didn't feel like getting mixed up in the affair.
It was a foreign country—different—you know how
it is. If I'd been at home—well, I'd have told the
chief of police all about it. But England. Scotland
Yard. I got cold feet.

"I'm glad Captain Keane brought the matter up
here to-night. I'm glad to explain the thing, and I
hope you believe me. Now—er—I had a speech
ready, but it's clean gone. Oh, yes—one thing I do
remember. I've been taking pictures all the way
around, as I guess you know. You're all in 'em. I
bought a projector in Honolulu and Friday night—
our last night aboard—well, Mrs. Benbow and I are
entertaining then. We want you all to be our guests,
and I'll run off the whole trip for you. That's—that's
about all, now."

He sat down amid loud and friendly applause.
Several rebuking looks were cast at Keane, who
received them nonchalantly. Mr. Minchin rose again.

"I guess it's up to me to make the next selection,"
he remarked. "Mr. Ross, we ain't heard from you
yet."

Ross stood up and leaned heavily on his stick. "I
have no belated accusations to offer," he remarked,
and a little round of applause circled the table. "All
I can say is, this has been an interesting tour. I've
been looking forward to it for many years—how many
I wouldn't like to tell you. It has been somewhat
more exciting than I bargained for, but I have no
regrets. I'm glad I came on this party with Doctor

Lofton—and with all of you. I only wish I had been as wise as Mr. Benbow and made a record of my experiences, to solace the long hours when I get back to Tacoma. As for the unfortunate night in London, when poor Hugh Morris Drake lay dead in that stuffy room in Broome's Hotel, with Doctor Lofton's luggage strap about his throat——"

Suddenly from far down the table, Vivian spoke. "Who says it was Doctor Lofton's luggage strap?" he demanded brusquely.

Ross hesitated. "Why—why—I understood at the inquest," he replied, "that it was taken from the doctor's room——"

"We're all telling our real names to-night," went on Vivian in a clear, cool voice. "That wasn't Lofton's luggage strap. In point of fact, it wasn't a luggage strap at all. It was a camera strap—the kind you use to carry the motion picture camera over your shoulder. And I happen to know that it was the property of Mr. Elmer Benbow."

With one accord they all turned and stared at Benbow, sitting with a stricken look on his face near the foot of the table.

CHAPTER XIX

THE FRUITFUL TREE

In the tense silence Maxy Minchin got slowly to his feet. He removed the Napoleonic hat from his head, and with a gesture of abdication, cast it aside.

"Well, you bimbos are certainly making some dinner out of this," he remarked. "Sadie, I guess we never give one like it before, did we? Way I figure it, guys that put on the feed-bag together ought to act nice and friendly at the table, even if they do pull a gat on the stairs going out. Still, I ain't one to tell my guests how to behave. Mr. Benbow, you spoke once, but it looks to me like you gotta speak again."

Benbow leaped to his feet. The stricken look had faded, and he appeared grim and determined.

"Well," he said, "I guess I made a mistake. When I was telling you that about the cablegram to my daughter, it flashed through my mind I ought to say something about the strap——"

"I suppose you sent her that as a birthday present," Keane sneered.

Benbow turned on him. "Captain Keane, I don't know what I have done to win this hostility from you. I've regarded you from the first as a cheap and contemptible light-weight, but I thought I had kept my opinion of you hidden. I did not send that strap to my girl as a birthday present. I wish I had. Then it would not have been put to the use it ultimately was."

He took a sip of water, and continued. "I heard about Mr. Drake's murder early that next morning, and I went to his room to see if there was anything I could do. That's what I would have done in Akron —it seemed the neighbourly and kindly thing. There was no one in the room at the moment but an hotel servant—the police hadn't come. I went over and looked at Drake. I saw the strap about his throat, and I thought it was almighty like my camera strap. It gave me a shock, I can tell you. I went to my room, hunted up my camera—and found that the strap was missing from the case.

"Well, we talked it over, Nettie and I. Our door was always unlocked—I didn't like to go out and leave it that way, but the maid had requested us to do it. The camera had been there all the previous afternoon, as well as in the evening, when we went to the theatre. It had been easy enough for somebody to slip in and get that strap. My wife suggested that I go and talk things over with Doctor Lofton." He looked at the doctor. "I'm going to tell the whole business," he added.

Lofton nodded. "By all means," he remarked.

"Well, the doctor pooh-poohed my fears at first, but when I told him I had been out the previous night to send that cablegram, he began to look serious. I asked him if he thought I'd better tell Scotland Yard it was my strap, and also that I had been away from my room between two and three o'clock on the morning of the murder. Men have been hung on less than that. And there I was, in a strange country, first time I'd ever been out of the good old United States, and—well, I was scared stiff. 'It looks like I leave your party here and now,' I said to the doctor. He patted me on the shoulder. 'Say nothing,' he told me. 'Leave everything to me. I'm sure you didn't kill Drake, and I'll do all I can to keep you out of the investigation.' Believe me—it was a good offer. I took it. The next thing I heard about the strap, Doctor Lofton had claimed it as his own. That's all I've got to say. Oh, yes—Vivian asked me on the channel boat where my strap was. He asked in sort of a nasty way. When I bought another in Paris, he made some crack about it. I saw that he was on to the situation, but he didn't seem inclined to do anything about it."

For the first time in many moments, Chan spoke. He turned to Vivian with interest.

"Is this true, sir?" he inquired.

"Yes, it is," replied Vivian. "I knew from the first it was Benbow's strap. But there we were, in a foreign country—and I didn't really think Benbow was guilty. I didn't know what to do. So I consulted the one man in our party who ought to know about such things. A celebrated criminal lawyer. Mr. Tait, I mean. I outlined the matter to him, and he advised me to say nothing."

"And now you disregard his advice?" Charlie said.

"Not precisely. He and I were speaking about it to-day, and he told me he thought it was about time to get to the bottom of the strap business. He suggested I tell you. He said he thought yours the best mind that had yet come into the case."

Chan bowed. "Mr. Tait does me too much honour," he protested.

"Well, there's nothing more I can say," Benbow went on, mopping his perspiring brow. "Doctor Lofton claimed the strap, and that let me out." He sat down.

They all looked at Lofton. His manner showed that he was decidedly annoyed; his eyes were flashing.

"Everything that Mr. Benbow has told you is true,"

he remarked. "But consider my position, if you will. There I was, with a murder in my party, and up against the most celebrated man-hunting organization in the world. My only object was to cut off their investigation at the earliest possible moment, and get out of England with my party intact. I felt that if Mr. Benbow admitted those two damaging facts, he would certainly be held in London. One of them alone might not have sufficed, but both together—well, that would have been too much. I saw myself losing at the very start of the tour a couple of my best clients. And I was morally certain Mr. Benbow was entirely innocent.

"When the matter of the strap was brought up by Inspector Duff, I saw my way out immediately. I had not left my room the night before, and no one could say I had. True, there had been a little matter of warm words between Mr. Drake and myself, but that meant nothing, as the inspector was quick to see. I was not connected with the crime in any way. The strap was not unlike one I had about an old bag— not quite so wide, but the same colour, black. I told Duff I possessed a strap similar to the one he was showing me. I went to my room, removed it from my bag, and hid it beneath a wardrobe that reached nearly to the floor. If my plan failed, I could pretend to discover it there and simply tell Duff I had been mistaken. Then I went back to Drake's room and told the inspector that I believed the strap used to strangle the old gentleman was mine.

"It worked like a charm. From that point on the matter of the strap was of no further interest to Scotland Yard. Mr. Benbow was safe and——"

"And so were you," suggested Captain Keane, blowing a ring of smoke towards the ceiling.

"I beg your pardon, sir," glowered Lofton.

"I say, Benbow was safe, and so were you," Keane went on calmly. "If there had been any disposition on the part of Duff to suspect you of the crime, you rather took him aback by claiming that strap on the spot. He figured that if you'd been guilty, you'd hardly have committed the murder with your own strap, and then admitted the ownership immediately. Yes, my dear Doctor, it worked like a charm——"

Lofton's face was scarlet. "What the devil are you driving at——"

"Oh, nothing, nothing. Don't get excited. But nobody's been paying much attention to you in this affair. There you were—broken-hearted because such a thing had happened on a tour of yours. But were you? Mightn't there have been something more important to you than your tour——"

Lofton tossed aside his chair, and strode over to where Keane sat.

"Stand up," he cried. "Stand up, you dirty cur. I'm an old man, but by heaven——"

"Gentlemen, gentlemen," shouted Maxy Minchin. "Remember they's ladies present."

Charlie inserted his great bulk between Doctor Lofton and the captain. "Let the refreshing breeze of reason blow over this affair," he suggested gently. "Doctor Lofton, you are foolish man to listen to unresponsible talk of this plenty flippant person. He has no basis whatever for evil insinuations." He took the doctor by the arm and led him a few feet away.

"Well, folks," announced Maxy Minchin, "I guess the dinner's over. I was going to suggest we all join hands and sing *Auld Lang Syne* at the finish, but mebbe we better chop that. Open the doors. An' for the sake of my boy at school, I hope they won't be no rods drawn in the hallway."

Chan quickly escorted Lofton outside. Behind him, as he left, he heard the scraping of chairs, the breaking up of Maxy's interesting dinner party.

"Hot words will cool here on windy deck," he suggested. "Accepting my advice, you will abstain from presence of Keane until you feel less fiery."

"Yes, I fancy I'd better," the doctor admitted. "I've hated that sneering whelp from the moment I saw him. But of course, I mustn't forget my position." He gave Charlie a searching look. "I was happy to hear you say that he had no basis for his accusations."

"None whatever that I discover," answered Chan blandly.

"I don't know—now that I come to think of it, it was a rather silly move, my claiming that strap. I can't explain it except for the fact that after you've travelled with groups like this for a few years, you begin to look upon them as children. Somewhat stupid children, too, helpless and needing protection. My first instinct is always to furnish the protection. One of my people was in trouble so, as had happened many times before, I simply shifted his burden to my own shoulders, and carried on."

Charlie nodded. "I understand plenty well," he reassured the older man.

"Thank you, Mr. Chan," Lofton replied. "You seem an understanding person. I'm inclined to think I underrated you when we met."

Charlie smiled. "That is customary. I do not let it distress me. My object is to arrange so people are not still underrating me when we part."

"I imagine your object is usually attained," the doctor bowed. "I think I'll go to my cabin now. I have a lot of work to do."

They parted, and Chan set out on a walk about the deck. His step was brisk, his manner serene and composed. Much had happened at Maxy Minchin's dinner. Charlie smiled to himself as he recalled how much had happened. Someone called to him from a steamer chair.

"Ah, Mr. Tait," he remarked. "I will sit down at your side, if you have no inclination for objecting."

"I am delighted," replied Tait.

"Ah, yes. You were kind enough to speak to Mr. Vivian in flattering terms of my poor brain-power."

"I meant every word of it," the lawyer assured him.

"Then you judge on the smallest grounds."

"No, I never do that." Tait struggled with his rug, and Chan assisted him. "Thanks," he said. "Well, that was quite a little dinner, as it turned out. Was it, by any chance, another of your experiments?"

Chan shook his head. "No—it was idea of hospitable Mr. Minchin. But who knows—I may be able to turn it to my purpose."

"I'm sure you can."

"Detective is in happy luck," Charlie continued, "when he can stand aside and hear murderer talk about incidents attending crime. To-night many men spoke—possibly murderer among them. Was there some indiscreet admission?"

"Did you note any?" inquired Tait.

"I am much afraid I did. It came—you will pardon my rudeness—it came from you."

The lawyer nodded. "You justify my belief in you. I hardly expected you would overlook my indiscretion."

"We are talking, no doubt, about same thing?"

"Oh, no doubt at all."

"Will you tell me, then, of what we speak?"

"Gladly. It was rather a slip for me to admit that

any one of us might have been in Hugh Morris Drake's position that night in Broome's Hotel."

"It was, indeed. You knew, of course, that Honywood and Drake changed rooms that night. Inspector Duff told you same on train between Nice and San Remo."

"Yes—that was where he told me about the change. You know Duff's notes pretty thoroughly I perceive?"

"I must. They are my only hope. I find no record that you ever read a letter written by late Mr. Honywood to his wife."

"I didn't even know there was such a letter."

"Yet you knew that Drake was killed by someone seeking to kill Honywood. You understand that poor man's taking off was, as you started to say, purely accidental. That it might have happened to any man in the party."

"Yes—I'll have to admit that I knew that. I'm sorry I let it out, but it's too late now for regrets."

"How did you know it? Duff never told you."

"No, of course—Duff never told me."

"Then who did?"

Tait hesitated. "I suppose I shall have to confess. I got the information from Mark Kennaway."

"Ah, yes. And Mr. Kennaway got it from——"

"According to his story, he got it from Pamela Potter."

A brief silence, then Charlie stood up. "Mr. Tait, I congratulate you. You are out of that in neat fashion."

Tait laughed. "And in simple fashion," he added. "Just by telling the truth, Mr. Chan."

"A pleasant evening," Charlie said. "I leave you to enjoy your no doubt interesting thoughts." He strolled away.

Seeking the dancers on the promenade deck, he noted Pamela Potter circling that restricted floor in Mark Kennaway's arms. He waited patiently until the music stopped, and then approached the couple.

"Pardon," he announced. "But this lady has next fox trotting with me."

"Just as you say," smiled Kennaway.

Gravely Chan offered his arm, and led the girl off. The music was beginning again.

"I spoke with metaphor," Charlie remarked. "My avoirdupois and dancing do not make good mixture."

"Nonsense," she answered. "I'll bet you've never tried."

"The wise elephant does not seek to ape the butterfly," he told her, and escorted her to a shadowy corner by the rail. "I have brought you here not only for the fragrance of your society, which is delectable, but also to ask a question."

"Oh—and I thought I'd made a conquest," she laughed.

"Surely same would be ancient story for you," he replied, "and hardly worthy of recording. Tell me this, if you will be so kind. You have related to others the matter you read in Mr. Honywood's letter to his wife? You have told fellow members of tour that murder of grandfather was accident?"

"Oh, dear," she murmured. "Shouldn't I have done it?"

Chan shrugged. "Old saying has it, two ears, one mouth. Hear twice as much as you tell."

"I'm properly rebuked," she said.

"Do not fret. No harm may have been done. I merely wish to know whom you told."

"Well, I told Mrs. Luce."

"That was natural. And how many more?"

"Just one more. Mark—Mr. Kennaway."

"Ah, yes. You noted to-night, perhaps, that Mr. Kennaway has passed information along to Mr. Tait?"

"Yes, I did note it—and it made me rather angry. I didn't tell Mark it was a secret, but he should have known. He irritates me very much, that lad."

"Irritates you? I should have said——"

"Yes, I know—I'm with him a lot. But heavens— what have I to choose from? Vivian? Keane? It's hopeless. When there's anything doing that calls for a man—a dance, for instance—naturally I select Mark. But all the same, he irritates me."

"So you said."

"I meant it. You must have seen yourself how he acts. So frightfully superior—Boston and Harvard and all that. I can tell you—it gets on my nerves ——"

"Suppose," smiled Chan, "that this irritating young man should ask you to marry him?"

"Do you think he will?" asked the girl quickly.

"In what way should I know?" Charlie said.

"Well—it's almost uncanny, Mr. Chan, how you invite confidences. I may tell you that I hope he will ask me to marry him. As a matter of fact, I've been leading him on—a little. I want him to propose to me."

"And then?"

"Then I shall turn him down. What a triumph! The flower of Boston turned down by something crude and vulgar from the terrible Middle West."

Chan shook his head. "A woman's heart," he remarked, "is like a needle at the bottom of the sea."

"Oh, we're not so darned hard to fathom. My motives are perfectly clear. Of course, in a way, it will be a pity—he can be so nice when he wants to be——"

"Yes?"

"Yes, but he seldom wants to be. Usually he's just cold and lofty and Bostonian, and I know that he's sneering at my money." She laid a slender hand on Charlie's arm. "Can I help it," she added wistfully, "if my grandfather had brains enough to get rich?"

"No honourable man would hold you accountable," Charlie answered soothingly. "But if you are leading this young man on—a little—we should get back to the work."

They walked along the deck towards the music.

"He should never have told that to Mr. Tait," the girl said. "I ought to call him down for it—but I don't think I will. The mood to-night is one of tenderness."

"Let it remain so," urged Chan. "I like it better that way myself."

Kennaway, he noted, showed no signs of annoyance when he saw the girl again. Nor did Pamela Potter seem especially irritated. As Charlie turned away, the purser faced him.

"Come with me, Mr. Chan," Lynch said. He led the way to his office.

In a chair drooped Kashimo, evidently much depressed.

"What has happened?" Charlie inquired.

Kashimo looked up. "So sorry," he hissed, and Chan's heart sank.

"Your helper here has got himself into trouble," the purser explained.

"How do I know she will come back?" the Japanese said.

"You speak in riddles," Chan told him. "Who came back?"

"Mrs. Minchin," the purser put in, "returned to her cabin a few moments ago and found this boy searching there. She's got a billion dollars' worth of knick-knacks in her luggage, and her screams could be heard as far away as the Astor House bar, in Shanghai. I promised her I'd throw the lad overboard myself. We'll have to take him off those cabins and put him somewhere else. I'm afraid his usefulness to you is ended."

"So sorry," Kashimo repeated.

"One minute," Charlie said. "You will have plenty time to be sorry later. Tell me first—did you find anything of interest in Maxy Minchin's cabin?"

Kashimo leaped to his feet. "I think so, Charlie. I find—I search hard and I am good searcher—you said so——"

"Yes, yes. What did you find?"

"I find nice collection of hotel labels not pasted on to anything. Pretty labels from all hotels visited by these travellers—labels that say Grand Hotel, Splendid Hotel, Palace Hotel——"

"And there was one from the Great Eastern Hotel, Calcutta?" Chan inquired.

"No. I look twice. Label from that hotel is not among those present."

Chan smiled, and patted the little Japanese on the back. "Do not belittle own attainments any longer, Kashimo," he advised. "Stones are cast alone at fruitful trees, and one of these days you may find yourself in veritable shower of missiles."

CHAPTER XX

MISS PAMELA MAKES A LIST

CHARLIE turned to the purser, and within a few minutes the question of Kashimo's future status on the ship was settled. It was arranged that he was to be transferred to a series of cabins on a lower deck, and that he must keep out of the way of the loudly vocal Sadie Minchin as much as possible from that moment on to the end of the journey. The little Japanese, crestfallen, slipped away, and Chan returned to the deck. Standing once more by the rail, he considered this latest development.

If there were loose hotel labels available aboard the *President Arthur*, then it became more unlikely than ever that the key had been attached to Kennaway's bag at Calcutta, and had consequently been in its present position when Welby located it in Yokohama. No, it had unquestionably been elsewhere, in the possession of its owner. That person, not wanting to throw it away, but somewhat shaken by the Welby episode, had evolved the happy idea of planting it on Kennaway's suitcase, under the label of an hotel long since visited and left behind. He had known where such a label could be had. He might even have owned such a label himself. He might have been Maxy Minchin.

Chan smiled to himself, and after spending a few moments in the library, went to his cabin. His first act there was to take out Duff's notes, and study them once again. What he read seemed to please him, and he went cheerfully to bed, where he enjoyed the most complete rest he had yet encountered aboard the boat.

Early the next morning Charlie met Maxy Minchin pacing the deck, grimly determined on exercise. He fell into step beside the gangster.

"Hello, Officer," Maxy said. "Swell morning after the storm."

"Storm?" Chan inquired.

"I mean that snappy little party I give last night. Say, maybe them birds didn't mix it, hey? Hope you had a good time?"

"An excellent one," smiled the Chinese.

"Well, I was a little anxious myself," Maxy returned. "A guy that's host, he can't get much of a kick out of a rough-house like that. I thought for a minute it was going to end in a pair of bracelets for some bimbo. But after all was said and done, I guess you was just as far from a pinch as ever."

Chan sighed ponderously.

"I fear I was."

"It's sure some mystery," Maxy went on. "Me, I can't figure why any guy'd want to rub out that nice old gentleman. Something Tait said made me think mebbe it was all a mistake—mebbe Drake got took for a ride because they thought he was somebody else. Such things do happen. I remember once in Chicago —but why should I let a bull in on that? What I was going to say, we had a little excitement in our cabin last night."

"Yes? Of what nature?" Charlie was mildly curious.

"Us rich millionaires," Maxy continued, "we gotta keep our eyes peeled every minute. The word goes round we're rolling in jack, and after that, good night! I don't know what the world's coming to. No respect for property rights no more—it's disgusting. Sadie went back to the cabin, and there was a biscuit boy going through things like a Kansas cyclone."

"What a pity," Chan answered. "I trust nothing valuable was taken."

"That's the funny angle on it. There was all that jewellery Sadie's been copping on to—valuable stuff. I ought to know, I come across for it. And when Sadie went into the cabin, there was this Chink——"

"Ah—er—no matter——" cried Chan, catching himself in time.

"There was this Chink, with bunch of old hotel labels in his hand."

"You have collection of such labels?" Charlie inquired.

"Yeah—I been picking 'em up from each hotel we been to. Going to take 'em home to little Maxy— that's my son—so he can paste 'em on his suitcase. He wanted to come along with us, but I tells him an education comes first. You stay here and learn to talk right, I says. Even a bootlegger's got to speak good language nowadays, associating with the best people the way he does. Not that I want Maxy in the racket—he'll have all he can do to manage the estate. I'll bring you the labels, I says to him. It'll be as good as taking the trip. And as I just been telling you, with all Sadie's valuables laying around, it was them labels that caught the Chink's eye. But he only had time to pinch one of 'em."

"Ah—one is missing?"

"Yeah. The wife noticed it right off the bat. The swellest one in the bunch—we both remembered speaking of it when we got it—how pleased little Maxy would be. A Calcutta hotel. But it was gone. We couldn't dig it up nowhere."

Charlie turned and stared at the gangster. The

simple innocence of that dark face amazed him.
Nothing there save the anxiety of an indulgent
father.

"I tossed in a kick to the purser," Mr. Minchin
went on, "but he tells me he searched the Chink and
he was clean. I guess he'd made away with the label.
In Chi. in the old days he'd'a' got a pineapple in his
soup for this. But—oh, well—let it ride. Little
Maxy won't know what he missed—and that's something."

"I congratulate you," said Chan. "Life has made
you philosopher, which means peaceful days ahead."

"That's the kind I got a yen for now," Minchin
replied. They finished the walk in silence.

Early that afternoon Charlie met the unpleasant
Captain Keane. The Chinese was inclined to ignore
the encounter, but the captain stopped him.

"Well?" Keane began.

"Yes?" returned Chan.

"That dinner last night. Quite a few develop-
ments."

"Plenty," nodded Charlie.

"Plenty for me," Keane replied. "As far as I can
see, the matter begins to look pretty plain."

"You mean Mr. Benbow?"

"Benbow, my hat! Don't try to kid me. Lofton's
my choice, and has been from the start. Do you know,
he told me at San Remo that the tour was off? Why?
Elementary, my dear Mr. Chan. Duff forced him to
go on, but he didn't want to do it. He'd finished his
job."

"You think that is proof enough to convict in
English courts?"

"No—I know it isn't. I'm working on the case,
though. Miss Potter has authorized me to go ahead,
and she's promised to pay up if I make good."

Chan glared at him. "You did not mention my name?"

"Why should I? You're going to be on the outside looking in before this case is ended. Go ahead— look wise. I suppose you think I'm on the wrong track."

"Not at all," Chan answered.

"What?"

"Why should I think that? The stupidest man in the town may point out the road to the school."

"And just what do you mean by that?"

"Nothing. Old Chinese saying."

"I don't think much of it," answered Keane, and went on his way.

The afternoon passed swiftly, while the ship sailed on across a calm and sunlit sea. Evening came—the last of his evenings but one—and Chan was as calm as the sea. He prepared for dinner and, stepping out on to the deck, saw Tait about to enter the smoking-room.

"Won't you join me, Mr. Chan?" the lawyer invited.

Charlie shook his head. "I am seeking Mr. Kennaway," he replied.

"Still in the cabin when I left," Tait said.

"And the number is——" the Chinese inquired.

Tait gave him this quite unnecessary information, and Chan walked away. He found Mark Kennaway busy with a black tie.

"Oh, come in, Mr. Chan," the young man greeted him. "Just trying to beautify the old façade."

"Yes—the time in Miss Pamela's society is growing brief," Charlie smiled.

"Why bring that up?" asked Kennaway. "Always look your best—that's my motto. There may be somebody about who wants to hire a lawyer."

Chan closed the door. "I have called for a private talk with you," he announced. "I must have your word of honour you will keep what is said in dark."

"Naturally." Kennaway seemed surprised.

Charlie dropped to his knees and dragged from beneath one of the beds the suitcase with the interesting label. He pointed to the latter.

"You will regard that, please."

"You mean the label from the Great Eastern Hotel in Calcutta? What about it?"

"Do you recall—was it there when you left Calcutta?"

"Why, of course. I noticed it after I got on the boat at Diamond Harbour. It's so striking one could hardly overlook it."

"You are certain this is the label you saw on that occasion?"

"Well—how could I be certain of that? I saw one just like it."

"Precisely," answered Chan. "You saw one just like it. But you did not see this one."

Kennaway came closer. "What do you mean?" he inquired.

"I mean that at some later date, second label was pasted neatly over the first. And between the two—— Will you kindly run fingers over surface?"

The young man did so. "What's this?" he frowned. "Feels like a key."

"It is a key," Charlie nodded. "Duplicate of the one found in hand of Hugh Morris Drake one February morning in Broome's Hotel."

Kennaway whistled softly. "Who put it on my bag?" he asked.

"I wonder," said Chan slowly.

The young man sat down on the edge of his bed,

thinking deeply. His eyes strayed across the room to another bed, on which lay a pair of pyjamas. "I wonder, too," he said. He and Charlie exchanged a long look.

"I will put suitcase back in place," remarked the detective with sudden briskness. He did so. "You will say nothing of this to living soul. Keep eye on key. It will, I think, be removed before ship reaches port. Kindly inform me the moment it is gone."

The door opened abruptly, and Tait came in. "Ah, Mr. Chan," he said. "Pardon me. Is this a private conference?"

"Not at all," Charlie assured him.

"I found I had no handkerchief," Tait explained. He opened a drawer and took one out. "Won't you join me for an appetizer—both of you?"

"So sorry not to do so," the Chinese answered. "What I require mostly is non-appetizer." He went out, smiling and serene.

After dinner, he found Mrs. Luce and Pamela Potter seated together in deck chairs.

"May I intrude my obnoxious presence?" he inquired.

"Sit down, Mr. Chan," the old lady said. "I'm not seeing much of you on this trip. But then, I suppose you're a busy man?"

"Not so much busy as I expected to be," he answered quietly.

"Really?" She gave him a questioning look. "Lovely evening, isn't it? This weather reminds me of the South African veldt. I spent a year there once."

"You have pretty well investigated the map."

"Yes—I've been about. Think now I'll settle down in Pasadena—but that feeling is usual with me just as I finish a long tour. Some day I'll pass a window

filled with steamship folders—and then I'll be off
again."

Charlie turned to the girl. "May I, with rude
boldness, inquire about last evening? Maybe you led
young man on—a little farther?"

"When I was a small girl," she smiled, "I used to
build snow men. It's been interesting to meet one
who can walk about."

"You have two more nights—with plenty good
moon shining."

"It wouldn't help if they were Arctic nights, and
six months long," she told him. "I'm afraid the last
returns are in."

"Do not despair," Chan replied. "Perseverance
wins. A matter I have proved in my own endeavours.
By the way, did you promise Captain Keane reward
if he finds slayer of your grandfather?"

"Why, no."

"But he has talked with you about it?"

"He hasn't talked with me about anything."

Chan's eyes narrowed: "The truth is not in him.
We will say no more of that." He glanced at a sheet
of paper and pencil in the girl's hand. "Pardon me
—I think I interrupt. You are writing letter?"

She shook her head. "No, I—I—well, as a matter
of fact, I was merely puzzling over our mystery. The
time is getting rather short, you know."

"No one could know it better," he nodded gravely.

"And it doesn't seem to me that we're getting anywhere. Oh—I'm sorry—but you came into the case
rather late. You really haven't had a chance. I was
just making a list of the men in our party, and opposite
the name of each, I've been putting down the things
against him. So far as I can see, every single one of
them except Mr. Minchin and Mark Kennaway has
been under a cloud at one time or another——"

"Your list is not correct. Those two, also, have no claim to clean record."

She gasped. "You mean every man in the party has been involved?"

Chan rose, and gently removed the paper from her hand. He tore it into tiny fragments and, walking to the rail, tossed them overboard.

"Do not worry pretty head over matter," he advised, coming back. "It is already settled."

"What do you mean?" she cried.

"Of course, there remains stern quest for proofs acceptable to English courts, but these will yet be found."

"You mean you know who killed my grandfather?"

"You yourself do not know?" inquired Charlie.

"Of course I don't. How should I?"

Charlie smiled. "You had same opportunities as I. But then, your mind was filled with young man who irritates you. As for me, I laboured under no such handicap."

With a beautiful bow which included both of them, he strolled casually off down the deck.

CHAPTER XXI

THE PROMENADE DES ANGLAIS

HER eyes wide with amazement, Pamela Potter looked at Mrs. Luce. "What in the world," she cried, "did Mr. Chan mean by that?"

Mrs. Luce smiled. "He meant that he knows who killed your grandfather, my dear. I rather thought he'd find it out."

"But how did he find it out? He said I ought to know, too. And I can't imagine——"

The old lady shrugged. "Even for your generation," she said, "you're a clever girl. I've noticed that. Bright as a dollar, as we used to say. But you're not so clever as Charlie Chan. Not many people are. I've noticed that, too." She stood up. "Here comes young Kennaway—I think I'll go into the lounge."

"Oh, please don't run away."

"I may be a chaperon, Pamela, but I was young once myself." And she moved towards a distant door.

Kennaway sat down tentatively on the foot of the deck chair the old lady had deserted.

"Well," he remarked. "Another day gone."

The girl nodded.

"You don't seem very talkative," the young man suggested.

"That should be a relief," she answered. "I—I was very busy thinking. Mr. Chan has just told me the most surprising thing."

"What, for instance?"

She shook her head. "No, I mustn't repeat it to

you. I told you something once—and you failed to keep it secret."

"I don't know what you mean."

"No matter. We needn't go into it now."

"Whatever I've done, I'm sorry," he said. "Really, I am." He looked quite contrite, and very handsome in the light of the newly risen moon. For a moment neither spoke. Then a sudden expression of concern crossed the young man's face. "I say—Mr. Chan didn't tell you that—that he had his man?"

"Why should he?"

"I don't know—but something that happened to-night——" Again he was silent, staring into space. "I wonder," he added at last, and his voice was strained, even frightened.

Pamela Potter glanced at him. A boy in Detroit had once been the recipient of a similar glance, and had never been the same since. "Our next to the last night aboard the ship," she reminded him.

"I know," he replied gloomily.

"We shall miss this old war when it's over."

"I shall," he nodded. "But you—you'll be back in Detroit, having a grand time. The little princess of the automobiles. All the peasants bowing low."

"Nonsense. You'll be back in Boston—that's where the royal blood is. One of the Beacon Street Kennaways. I presume the Browning Society will call a special meeting when you arrive."

He shook his head. "Don't kid me, please. Somehow, I don't seem to enjoy it any more."

"What's the matter? I supposed you'd be in high spirits. The end of the tour so near, and all. Rid of poor Mr. Tait at last—and of me."

"I know," he agreed. "I ought to be the happiest man in the world. But I'm not. Oh, well—that's life, no doubt."

"And that nice girl waiting for you in Back Bay."

"What girl?"

"The one you're engaged to."

"Me—engaged? Do I look as feeble as that? They're lots of nice girls in Boston, but I'm not engaged to any of them, thank heaven."

"You ought to try it sometime. It's fun, rather."

"I suppose you've tried it?"

"Oh, yes—frequently."

"One of those fellows who's been writing to you?"

"One of them? I'm no piker. All of them, at various times."

"Well, make a selection," he suggested. "Get it over with. We're none of us as young as we used to be."

"I am—and I mean to stay so. Shall you write to me, after we part?"

"What for?"

"I love to get letters."

"I hate to write them. Besides, I'll be terribly busy. It will take me a lifetime of hard work to put by even a modest competence. We can't all manufacture automobiles."

"Heaven forbid! The roads are crowded enough now. Then—when we say good-bye, it will be for ever?"

"And a day," he added, with forced cheerfulness.

"That will make it so much more romantic, don't you think? You'd better go in and play bridge. I imagine Mr. Tait is waiting."

"No doubt he is," the young man agreed.

"Would you like me to play?"

"Suit yourself. You're pretty bad, you know."

"I guess I am," she sighed.

"But of course, you make poor old Tait happy. As long as you aren't his partner."

"It's tough on you—having me for a partner, I mean."

He shrugged, and stood up. "Oh, I don't mind. I realize that it isn't permanent."

She started to rise, and he gave her his hand. "Since you insist," she said, "I *will* join you."

"Thanks so much," he smiled grimly. They went inside.

Mrs. Luce and Tait were seated at a bridge table, the latter looking wistfully about the room. His face lighted when he saw Kennaway.

"Ah, my boy," he cried. "Will you join us?"

"Surely," Kennaway answered.

"That's good of you. I didn't like to ask. I've taken so much of your time—and this is one of your last nights aboard."

"Quite all right," the young man assured him. "I have nothing else to do."

"God bless the man who invented bridge," remarked Pamela Potter. "Come on, old son—say it."

"Say what?" Kennaway inquired.

"Your proper come-back to that should have been: 'You ought to learn it some time.'"

He laughed. "I couldn't be so rude as that," he protested.

"Oh, couldn't you!" she answered.

Meanwhile Charlie, having gone to the library and selected a book, was sitting there reading with the air of a man who has joined a book club and hopes none of his friends will call him up for a year. He read until ten o'clock, and after a leisurely stroll around the deck, sought his cabin. Sleep came to him without delay, the dreamless sleep of one who hasn't a care in the world.

At eight o'clock the next morning, he was abroad on the sunlit deck. The final twenty-four hours of a most momentous journey were impending. If the realization of this was hanging over him, it evidently left him calm and undisturbed. From his manner it was clear he was one of those who feel that what is to be, will be.

Later that morning he had a long radiogram from Duff. He retired with it to his cabin. There, with the sun streaming over his shoulder, he read:

"Splendid news. How can I ever thank you? Get the proofs, Charlie. But I know you will. Cable from chief says investigation clerk jewellery shop Calcutta reveals him once I.D.B. in South Africa. Meaning illicit diamond buyer. Inquiries among diamond merchants Amsterdam brought out further fact another I.D.B. around Kimberley some fifteen years back by name Jim Everhard. May be help. Remember bags of stones. Scotland Yard man Sergeant Wales in New York time my accident now in San Francisco by chief's order. Will meet you at dock prepared to make arrest. With him our friend Flannery. Like old times. Sorry can't be there. Mending rapidly, be on coast soon, wait there for my thanks. Cheerio. Best of luck.
"DUFF."

Chan read the message a second time, and when he came to the mention of Captain Flannery, an amused smile spread over his broad face. Fate was a wonderful stage manager, he reflected. He would be happy to see Flannery again. He tore Duff's message to bits, and tossed them through the port-hole.

The day wore on without incident. Benbow came to him late in the afternoon.

"I don't know whether or not you understand, Mr. Chan," he remarked, "but you're invited to that party of ours to-night. Couldn't get along without you. Policemen round the world—you said it."

Chan bowed. "I accept with unbounded pleasure. You will show your films?"

"Yes. I've arranged to have the sitting-room of

one of the empty de luxe suites. We'll meet there about eight-thirty. I'll put up a screen I've borrowed from the purser. I must say nobody seems to be much interested."

"I am deeply interested," Charlie assured him.

"Yes—but the rest of them—you'd think they'd be keen to see those pictures. Their own trip." He sighed. "But that's the way it goes. A man with a camera never gets any encouragement. I suppose I'll have to lock the doors when I try to show those films in Akron. At eight thirty, then, in Cabin A."

"You are so very kind," Chan returned. "I am honoured beyond words."

By eight o'clock the clear skies that had for so long looked down on the *President Arthur* were lost behind an impenetrable curtain. The ship moved cautiously along through a thick fog that recalled London on the morning Hugh Morris Drake lay dead in Broome's Hotel. At intervals the voice of the fog-horn, deep and sonorous, claimed for a moment the sole attention of everyone aboard.

When, at eight-thirty, Charlie pushed open the door of Cabin A, all the members of the party appeared to be already gathered inside. They were moving about, chatting aimlessly, but Mrs. Benbow, an efficient woman, soon had them seated in a little semi-circle facing a white screen. Before this Benbow laboured, busy with the many details that oppress a man about to show his own motion pictures.

While they waited, Charlie spoke. "All life long," he remarked, "I have unbearable yearning to travel —to take same extended tour you people in this room are now completing. One thing I have unquenchable desire to learn. What sight envisioned on your long journey stands out in outline of fire amid great crowd of memories? Mrs. Luce, you are agile traveller. On

recent circle of world, what that you witnessed
interests you most?"

"I can tell you in a minute," the old lady replied.
"A troupe of trained cats I saw at a vaudeville theatre
in Nice. I'll never forget them. Greatest sight I
ever saw in my life."

Doctor Lofton smiled. "You needn't look so
surprised, Mr. Chan," he said. "I always ask that
same question at the close of a tour, and often the
answers leave me breathless. Mrs. Spicer—if I were
to ask it of you——"

"Let me think." The San Francisco woman's eyes
grew dreamy. "There was a gown I saw at the Opera
in Paris. It wasn't just a gown—it was a little bit
of heaven. Any woman could have looked young in
that," she added wistfully.

"As far as I'm concerned," said Vivian, "the
bright spot of this tour is still to come. When we
pass the Farallones to-morrow morning, and Russian
Hill rises out of the mist—well, ask me your question
then, Mr. Chan. I know it's impolite to point, but
that's what I'll have to do."

Maxy Minchin took out a large cigar, looked about
the crowded room, and then put it back in his pocket.
"They was a kid drivin' an ox cart in Italy," he
remarked. "Gee, I wish little Maxy coulda seen him.
It woulda give him a new slant on that Straight Eight
I bought him just before we left."

"Do any of you remember the trees in the Forest
of Fontainebleau?" Ross inquired. "I'm very fond
of trees. Something so solid and serene and comfortable about them. Great timber, that was."

"Miss Pamela, you have not spoken," Chan
reminded her.

"I have so many memories," she answered. She
was wearing a delphinium blue gown she had saved

for this final evening. All the women had noticed it
—and even a few of the men. It could have been the
one that haunted Mrs. Spicer's dreams. "I find it
difficult to say what interested me most," the girl went
on. "But there was one flying fish that hopped
aboard our ship in the Red Sea. He had such sad,
romantic eyes—I just can't forget him." She turned
to the young man at her side. "You remember—I
named him John Barrymore."

"He looked more like Eddie Cantor to me," smiled
Kennaway.

"It's all been wonderful," Mrs. Benbow said. "So
different from Akron, and I wanted a change. I'll
never forget the afternoon I was walking in Delhi,
and a maharajah drove by in a Rolls-Royce. He had
on the most wonderful clothes—gold brocade, they
were——" She looked severely at her husband, busy
with the projector. "You've got to go to your tailor
the minute you get home, Elmer," she announced.

"A lot of things have interested me on this trip,"
Keane put in. "There's one night that sticks in my
mind—the last in Yokohama. I was walking round
the town, and I dropped into a cable office. Doctor
Lofton was there—and that little steward named
Welby. I asked the doctor if he was going back to
the ship, but he put me off—I could see he wanted to
be alone. So I went along by myself—down to the
water front—dark and mysterious—the godowns—the
funny little people running around in the dark—the
lights of the sampans—picturesque, I'd call it. It sort
of gave me the feel of the East." He stopped and
looked meaningly at Lofton, a malicious light in his
eyes. "That was the place where Welby was found
dead, you know——"

"All ready, folks," cried Mr. Benbow. "Mr.
Kennaway, will you snap off the lights? Thanks.

The first pictures, as you can see, are the ones I took on the deck of the ship just as we were leaving New York harbour. We didn't know one another very well then. I think I got the Statue of Liberty—yes, here she is. Take off your hats, boys. Now we're coming to some I got on the way across the Atlantic. Not many of you people in these—I guess most of you had a date with the little old berth down below. Here's poor Mr. Drake—lucky he didn't know what was coming."

He continued his prattle as the film unwound. They saw London again, and Broome's Hotel. They had a few minutes with the Fenwicks, whom Benbow had met on a street corner and insisted on recording for posterity. The little man from Pittsfield was obviously somewhat resentful of the honour being done him. Then came the pictures of Inspector Duff, driving away from the doorway of Broome's, and evidently as unwilling an actor as Fenwick. Dover and the channel boat. Paris, and after that, Nice.

Mr. Benbow's audience sat in attitudes that betokened an increasing interest. As the pictures of Nice were unrolled, Charlie suddenly uncrossed his plump legs and leaned forward. He was recalled to his surroundings by the voice of Tait, who sat by his side. The lawyer spoke in a low voice.

"I'm leaving, Mr. Chan," he said. "I—I feel rather ill." Charlie saw, even in that dim light, that his face was like chalk. "I'll not say anything to Kennaway—it's his last night and I don't want to trouble him. I shall be all right when I've rested for a moment on my bed." He slipped out noiselessly.

Benbow was starting on a new reel. His pictorial record seemed endless, but now his audience was with him. Egypt, India, Singapore, China—the man had really shown remarkable intelligence in the scenes he had selected.

He came at last to the end, and after thanking him, the party drifted from the room, until only Chan and the Benbows were left. The detective was examining the little spools on which the film was wound. "A very interesting evening," he remarked.

"Thanks," Benbow replied. "I believe they did enjoy it, don't you?"

"I am certain they did," Charlie told him. "Mrs. Benbow, it is not just that you should oppress frail self with that burden. Your husband and I will together transport this material to your cabin." He took up the many reels of film, and moved towards the door. Benbow carrying the projector, followed. They went below.

Once inside the Benbow state-room, Charlie laid the film on the bed, and turned to the man from Akron.

"May I inquire who has cabins on either side of you?" he said.

Benbow seemed startled. "Why—Mrs. Luce and Miss Pamela are on one side. The cabin forward is empty."

"One moment," Chan answered. He disappeared, but returned almost at once. "At this instant," he announced, "both cabins quite empty. Corridor also is entirely deserted by one and all."

Benbow was fumbling nervously with the projector. He got it into its case, and began to buckle up a long black strap. "What—what's it all about Mr. Chan?" he stammered.

"That is very valuable film of yours?" Charlie suggested blandly.

"I'll say it is."

"You have trunk with good strong lock?"

"Why, yes." Benbow nodded towards a wardrobe trunk in the corner.

"Making humble suggestion, would you be good enough to bestow all reels of film in that, and fasten lock securely?"

"Of course. But why? Surely nobody——"

Chan's little eyes narrowed. "Person never knows," he remarked. "It would grieve me greatly if you arrived in beloved home town lacking important reel. The reel, for example, that includes pictures taken at Nice."

"What is all this, Mr. Chan?" Benbow asked.

"You noticed nothing about those particular pictures?"

"No, I can't say I did."

"Others were perhaps more observant. Please do not distress yourself. Merely lock pictures all away. They have told their story to me, and may never be required by Scotland Yard——"

"Scotland Yard!" cried Benbow. "I'd like to see them try to——"

"Pardon that I interrupt. I must ask just one question. Do you now recall exact date when the photographs of street in Nice were taken?"

"You mean of the Promenade des Anglais?" Removing a worn bit of paper from his pocket, Benbow studied it. "That film was exposed on the morning of February 21," he announced.

"An excellent system," Chan approved. "I am grateful. Now, you will stow away all reels, and I will assist. This is snap lock, I perceive. There—it has nice strong appearance." He turned to go. "Mr. Benbow, I am much in your debt, first, for taking so many pictures, second, for showing them to me."

"Why—why, that's all right," returned the dazed Benbow.

Chan departed. He went at once to the topmost

deck and entered the radio room.   For a moment he
thought deeply, then he wrote a message:

"Sergeant Wales, care Captain Flannery, Hall of
Justice, San Francisco: Without delay request Scotland
Yard authorities obtain from Jimmy Breen, English
Tailor, Promenade des Anglais, Nice, France, full de-
scription man who had work performed on or about
February 21, calling for same on morning of that date,
also nature of work done.   Expecting you without fail
on dock to-morrow morning.

"CHARLIE CHAN, Inspector."

With light heart, Charlie descended to a lower deck
and began a thoughtful turn about it.   Damp,
dripping, clammy fog surrounded the ship on all
sides.   In marked contrast to previous nights he
walked a deserted path, the passengers had with one
accord sought the brightly lighted public rooms.
Twice he made the circle, well pleased with himself
and the world.

For the third time he was crossing the after deck,
which was shrouded in darkness.   Suddenly, amid the
shadows at his right, he saw a black figure moving,
caught the faint glint of steel.   It must be set down
for ever to his credit that he was rushing in that
direction when the shot was fired.   Charlie dropped
to the deck and lay there, motionless.

There followed the stealthy sound of quickly
retreating footsteps, then a moment of grim silence.
It was broken by the voice of the purser, leaning over
Chan.

"In heaven's name, Inspector," he cried.   "What
has happened?"

Charlie sat up.   "For a moment I found the
recumbent position more comfortable," he remarked.
"I am, you will observe, conservative by nature."

"Somebody shot at you?" the purser said.

"Briefly," replied the Chinese. "And missed—by one inch."

"I say—we can't have this sort of thing here," the officer objected plaintively.

Chan got slowly to his feet. "Do not fret," he advised. "The man who fired that shot will repose in arms of police to-morrow morning, moment ship docks."

"But to-night——"

"There is no occasion for alarm. Something tells me there was no real effort to hit target. Kindly note size of same. And that aim has never failed before."

"Just a warning, eh?" remarked the purser, relieved.

"Something of that nature," Charlie returned, and strolled away. As he reached the door leading to the main companionway, Mark Kennaway ran up to him. The young man's face was pale, his hair sadly rumpled.

"Mr. Chan," he cried. "You must come with me at once."

Silently Charlie followed. Kennaway led the way to the state-room he shared with Tait, and pushed open the door. Tait was lying, apparently lifeless, on his bed.

"Ah—the poor gentleman has had one of his attacks," Chan said.

"Evidently," Kennaway replied. "I came in here a moment ago and found him like this. But see—what does this mean? I heard that somebody had taken a shot at you—and look!"

He pointed to the floor beside the bed. A pistol was lying there.

"It's still warm," the young man added hoarsely. "I touched it, and it's still warm."

Charlie stooped and carelessly picked up the weapon. "Ah, yes," he remarked, "it remains over-heated. And for good reason. It was only a moment ago discharged at my plentiful person."

Kennaway sat on the edge of his own bed, and put his face in his hands. "Tait," he muttered. "Good lord—Tait!"

"Yes," Charlie nodded. "Mr. Tait's finger-prints will indubitably be found on bright surface of pistol." He stooped again, and drew Kennaway's bag from beneath the bed. For a moment he stared at that innocent-seeming Calcutta label. Then he felt it with his fingers. There was a slit little more than the length of a key just above the centre, but the heavy paper was pasted back into place. One spot was still rather damp. "Plenty neat job," the detective commented. "It is just as I thought. The key is gone."

Kennaway looked wildly about. "Where is it?" he asked.

"It is where I want it to be," Charlie answered. "On the person of the man who fired this revolver a moment ago."

The young man stared at the other bed. "You mean he's got it?"

"No," replied Charlie, shaking his head. "It is not on Mr. Tait. It is on the person of a ruthless killer—a man who was not above putting to his own uses the misfortune of our poor friend there on the bed. A man who came here to-night for his key, found Mr. Tait unconscious, saw his chance. A man who rushed out, fired at me, then returned here and after pressing Tait's hand about revolver to attend to finger-prints, dropped weapon suggestively on floor. A clever criminal if ever I met one. I shall experience great joy in handing him over to my old friend Flannery in the morning."

CHAPTER XXII

TIME TO FISH

KENNAWAY stood up, a look of immense relief on his face. Charlie was putting the revolver away in his pocket.

"Thank heaven," the young man said. "That's a load off my shoulders." He glanced down at Tait, who was stirring slightly. "I think he's coming out of it now. Poor chap. All evening I've been wondering—asking myself—but I just couldn't believe it. He's a kind man, underneath his bluster. I couldn't believe him capable of—all those terrible things."

Chan was moving towards the door. "Your lips, I trust, are sealed," he remarked. "You will repeat no word of what I have told you, of course. We have yet to make our capture, but I am certain our quarry is unsuspecting. Should he feel that his little stratagem here has succeeded, I think maybe our future path becomes even smoother."

"I understand," Kennaway answered. "You may rely on me." He put his hand over the lawyer's heart. "It begins to look as though I'm going to get poor Mr. Tait safely home, after all. And from then on—no more jobs like this for me."

Charlie nodded. "To supervise his own destiny is task enough for any man," he suggested.

"I'll say it is," Kennaway agreed warmly. Chan opened the door. "Er—just a moment, Inspector. If you should happen to run across Miss Potter, will you kindly ask her to wait up for me? I may be here for a half-hour or so, but as soon as Mr. Tait falls asleep——"

"Ah, yes," smiled Chan. "I shall be happy to take this message."

"Oh—please don't go out of your way to find her. I merely thought—it's our last night, you know. I really ought to say good-bye to her."

"Good-bye?" Charlie repeated.

"Yes—and nothing more. What was that you just told me? To supervise his own destiny is task enough——"

"For the timid man," finished Chan quickly. "Mind is so filled with other matters, regret to say I stupidly misquoted the passage when I spoke before."

"Oh," said Kennaway blankly. Chan stepped into the corridor and closed the door behind him.

The ship's captain was waiting for him in the main companion way. "I've just heard what has happened," he remarked. "I have an extra berth in my cabin and I want you to sleep there to-night."

"I am immensely honoured," Charlie bowed. "But there is no need for such sacrifice——"

"What do you mean, sacrifice? I'm doing this for myself, not for you. I don't want any accidents on my ship. I'll be expecting you. Captain's orders."

"Which must, of course, be obeyed," Chan agreed.

He found Pamela Potter reading in a corner of the lounge. She put down her book and looked at him with deep concern.

"What's all this about your being shot at?" she wanted to know.

Charlie shrugged. "The matter is of no consequence," he assured her. "I am recipient of slight attention from a shipmate. Do not give it thought. I arrive with message for you. Mr. Kennaway requests you loiter up for him."

"Well, that's an offer," the girl replied.

"Mr. Tait has suffered bad attack——"

"Oh, I'm so sorry."

"He is improving. When chance offers, Mr. Kennaway will seek you out." The girl said nothing. "He is plenty fine young man," Charlie added.

"He still irritates me," she replied firmly.

Charlie smiled. "I can understand feeling. But as favour to me, please wait up and let him irritate you for final time."

"I might," she answered "But only as a favour to you."

When Chan had gone, she picked up her book again. Presently she laid it aside, put on a wrap, and stepped out on to the deck. To-night the Pacific belied its name, it was dark, angry and tempestuous. The girl went over to the rail and stared into the mist. The fog-horn somewhere above her head spoke at frequent intervals in a voice that seemed hoarse with anxiety.

Kennaway appeared suddenly at her side. "Hello," he remarked. "Mr. Chan gave you my message, I see."

"Oh, it didn't matter," she replied. "I had no intention of going to my cabin. Never be able to sleep with that thing blowing."

They waited until the end of a particularly insistent blast.

"Jolly old horn, isn't it?" Kennaway went on. "Once when I was a kid I got a horn for Christmas. It's a pretty good world."

"Why the sudden cheerfulness?" asked the girl.

"Oh, lots of reasons. I've been worried about something all evening, and I've just found out there was nothing to worry about. Everything's fine. Going ashore in the morning—Mr. Tait's son will be waiting—after that, freedom for me. I tell you, I——"

The horn broke in again.

"What were you saying?" asked the girl, when it stopped.

"What was I? Oh, yes. Only myself to take care of, beginning to-morrow."

"It will be a glorious feeling, won't it?"

"I'll say it will. If I shouldn't see you in the morning——"

"Oh, you'll see me."

"Just wanted to tell you that it's been fun knowing you—you're awfully nice, you know. Charming. Don't know what I'd have done without you on this tour. I'll think of you a lot—but no letters, remember——"

The horn shrieked above them. Kennaway continued to shout indistinguishable words. The girl was looking up at him, she seemed suddenly very lovely and appealing. He took her in his arms and kissed her.

"All right," she said. "If you insist."

"All right what?" he inquired.

"I'll marry you, if you want me to. That's what you were saying, wasn't it?"

"Not exactly."

"My mistake. I couldn't hear very well. But I did think I caught the word 'marry'——"

"I was saying I hoped you'd marry some nice boy, and be very happy."

"Oh! Excuse it, please."

"But look here. Do you mean you'd actually marry me?"

"Why bring that up? You haven't asked me."

"But I will. I do. I am."

The horn again. Kennaway wasted no time in words. He released her when the blast was over.

"You really do care for me, after all?" she asked.

"I'm crazy about you. But I was sure you'd turn me down. That's why I didn't like to ask you. You're not going to turn me down, I take it?"

"What a ridiculous idea," she answered.

"Wonderful night," the young man said, and so it seemed, to him. "I know where there are a couple of chairs—in a dark corner on the after deck."

"They've been there ever since Hong-Kong," the girl replied. They went to find them.

As they walked along through the dripping fog, the horn blared forth again. "The lad who's working that," Kennaway remarked, "is going to get a big surprise in the morning. I intend to tip him within an inch of his life."

Meanwhile, amid the unfamiliar surroundings of the captain's cabin, Charlie Chan lay wide awake. He wondered if all old sea-dogs snored as loudly as this one.

He was aroused next morning by a knock at the door, and leaping up, he discovered that his cabin-mate was already about and dressed for the day. The captain took a radiogram from a rather flustered boy, and handed it to Chan.

"From Captain Flannery, of the San Francisco police," Charlie announced when he had read it. "He and Sergeant Wales of Scotland Yard will be aboard immigration launch."

"Good," said the other. "The sooner the better, as far as I am concerned. I've been wondering, Inspector. Hadn't I better put our friend under restraint until they come?"

Chan shook his head. "Not necessary, thank you. I prefer to remain unsuspecting to the end. Mr. Tait will no doubt spend morning in cabin, and I shall spread underground word among Lofton party we have our man in him. Believe real quarry will assume extra carelessness when he hears that."

"Just as you say," the captain nodded. "I'm not keen about taking action myself, as you know, though after what you told me last night, I'd gamble a year's pay that you're right. I will instruct the second officer not to lose sight of your man until he's in the hands of the police. People have been known to disappear from boats, you know."

"A wise suggestion," Charlie agreed. "I am grateful for your help." He had been rapidly dressing while they talked, and now moved towards the door with his bag. "I will continue toilet in my own room, please. Many hearty thanks for lodging of the night."

"Not at all. By gad, Inspector, you've been on the job this time. Ought to get a lot of kudos for your work on this case."

Chan shrugged. "When the dinner is ended, who values the spoon?" he replied, and went out on to the bridge. The fog was rapidly dispersing, and a hint of sun was in the eastern sky.

Back in his own cabin, he went about his preparations for the day with characteristic deliberation. On his way to breakfast, he stopped at the state-room occupied by Tait and Kennaway. Both were awake, and the lawyer looked to be much improved.

"Oh, I'm fine," he said, in answer to Chan's query. "I promised you I'd make San Francisco, didn't I? And I'll make a lot of other towns, too, before I'm through. Mark thinks I'd better stay in bed until we're ready to land. It's all nonsense, but I've agreed to do it."

"A splendid idea," nodded Chan. "Has Mr. Kennaway told you of last night's happenings?"

Tait frowned. "He has. There's one criminal I wouldn't defend—not for a million dollars."

Charlie outlined his plan for the morning, and the lawyer readily agreed.

"All right with me," he said. "Anything to get him. But of course, you'll let the members of the party know the truth before we land?"

"Naturally," Chan answered.

"Then go to it. You say you've got your man? I don't suppose——"

"Later, please," smiled Chan as he left.

After breakfast, he met the purser on the deck. "I've got a landing card for you," that gentleman said. "But as for Kashimo—well, I don't know. He's never been over here before, and of course he has no record of his birth in the islands. He came as a stowaway—he's admitted as much to me—and he'd better go back at once. One of our boats will be at the same pier, due to sail at two o'clock to-day, and I'll simply turn him over to her purser with instructions to return him to Honolulu."

Chan nodded. "I approve of plan, and so, no doubt, will Kashimo. His work is done—it was good work, too—and already he shows signs of yearning for home. I know he will be glad to hurry back and face the plaudits of his chief. Kindly arrange he goes as passenger. I will supply the money." The busy purser nodded, and hurried away.

Farther down the deck, the detective came upon Stuart Vivian. The San Franciscan stood at the rail, a pair of glasses in his hand, the empty case from which they had been taken hanging from his shoulder.

"Good morning," he said. "Just had a glimpse of Russian Hill. By heaven, I was never so glad to see it before."

"There is no vision so restful to weary eyes as that of home," Charlie remarked.

"You've said it. And I've been fed up with this tour for weeks. I'd have dropped out long ago, but I was afraid you policemen might think—— By the way, I hear a rumour that you've found out who the killer is?"

Charlie nodded. "A very distressing affair."

"It is, indeed. Ah—er—I presume the man's name is a secret?"

"Not at all. Mr. Tait has granted full permission to make the matter public."

"Tait!" cried Vivian. He was silent for a moment. "That's interesting, isn't it?" He looked at his watch. "We're having a farewell meeting in the library in ten minutes. Lofton's giving out the tickets to those who travel beyond San Francisco—and his final blessing, I suppose. What a riot this news will stir up!"

"I think maybe it will," smiled Chan, and went on down the deck.

Twenty minutes later the ship's engines were stilled at last, and they waited on the grey, rolling sea for the launch bearing the customs men and the immigration officials.

When the small motor-boat arrived, Charlie was at the top of the ladder. Presently the crimson face and broad shoulders of Flannery hove in sight.

"Hello, there," the officer cried. "It's my old pal! Sergeant Chan, as I live."

They shook hands. "So happy to see you again," Charlie said. "But since the day, long time ago, when I stood by and noted your admirable work on Bruce case, there have been changes. For one thing, I am now promoted to inspector."

"Is that so?" Flannery answered. "Well, you can't keep a squirrel on the ground. An old Chinese saying."

Charlie laughed. "I perceive you have not forgotten me." Behind Flannery stood a solid mountain of a man. "This, I presume, is——"

"Excuse me," said Flannery. "Shake hand with Sergeant Wales, of Scotland Yard."

"Highly honoured," Chan remarked.

"What's your latest word from Duff?" inquired the sergeant.

"Steady improvement has set in," Charlie told him. "And speaking of Duff, you have come for his assailant, of course. The murderer of Hugh Morris Drake in your London hotel?"

"I certainly have," Wales said.

"I am happy to hand him over to you," Chan replied. "So that the matter may not encounter too much publicity, I fix up little plan. Will you come with me, please?"

He led them to a state-room, on the door of which was the number 119. Escorting them inside, he indicated a couple of wicker chairs. There were two beds, one on either side of the cabin, and beside each was a pile of luggage.

"If you will wait here, your quarry will come to you," he announced. He turned to Wales. "One thing I would inquire about. You had message from me last night?"

"Yes, I did," the sergeant replied. "And I got in touch with the Yard at once. It was morning over there, you know, and within a few hours they had an answer. The news arrived in San Francisco just before we left Captain Flannery's office. It's great stuff. Jimmy Breen told our representative your man brought him a coat to be repaired on February 20, and called for it the next morning. It was the coat of a grey suit, and the right-hand pocket was torn."

"Ah, yes," nodded Charlie. "Torn by hand of aged porter in hallway of Broome's Hotel on early morning of February 7. Murderer should have discarded that coat. But it is not his nature to discard, and from the first, he has felt himself so safe. I would wager he shipped it from London to Nice, addressed to himself, and then engaged the able Mr. Breen. It was excellent choice. I behold on many tailors' signs nowadays the words 'Invisible Repairing.' Screen was too small for me to note them on Breen establishment, but they should have been there. Many times I have examined that coat, but Mr. Breen was evidently master of invisibility." He stepped to the door. "However, talk will not cook rice. You will await guilty man here," he added, and disappeared.

He found the Lofton party, with the single exception of Tait, gathered in the library, and evidently in a state of great excitement. At the only door leading into the room, Charlie met the second officer. With him the detective held a brief conversation.

"All right, people," shouted the officer. "The baggage is examined on the ship here, you know. The customs men are now ready. Go to your rooms, please."

Mark Kennaway and Pamela Potter were the first to emerge. They were both in high spirits.

"Just like Yale tap day," laughed the young man. "Go to your room. We'll see you later, Mr. Chan. We've news for you."

"That has happy sound," Charlie replied, but his face was grave.

Minchin and his wife came out. "Should I fail to see you again," Charlie remarked, shaking hands, "my kindest regards to little Maxy. Tell him to be good boy and study hard. An idle brain is the devil's workshop."

"I'll tell him, Officer," the gangster said. "You're one bull I been glad to meet. So long."

Mrs. Spicer passed, with a nod and a smile of farewell. Mrs. Luce followed.

"You let me know when you reach southern California," she said. "The greatest country on God's footstool——"

"Hold back your judgment on that, Mr Chan," broke in Benbow, coming up. "Wait until we've shown you Akron——"

"Then forget them both and come and look at the North-west," added Ross.

"You're all wrong," protested Vivian. "He'll be in God's country in half an hour."

Keane and Lofton were approaching, but Charlie did not wait. Leaving the second officer at the door, he hurried away.

Meanwhile, in cabin 119, Captain Flannery and the man from Scotland Yard were growing a bit restless. The latter got up and moved anxiously about.

"I hope nothing goes wrong," he muttered.

"Don't you worry," said Flannery generously. "Charlie Chan is the best detective west of the Golden Gate——"

The door opened suddenly, and Flannery leaped to his feet. Vivian was standing in the doorway.

"What's all this?" he demanded.

"Come in," the policeman said. "Shut that door —quick—and step inside. Who are you?"

"My name is Vivian, and this is my cabin——"

"Sit down there on the bed."

"What do you mean—giving me orders——"

"I mean business. Sit down and keep still."

Vivian reluctantly obeyed. Wales looked at Flannery. "He would be the last, of course," the sergeant remarked.

"Listen," Flannery whispered.

Outside, on the hard surface of the alleyway, they heard the "tap-tap-tap" of a cane.

The door opened, and Ross stepped inside. For a

moment he looked inquiringly about him. Then he glanced back at the door. Charlie Chan was standing there, and to say he filled the aperture is putting it mildly.

"Mr. Ross," said Charlie, "you will shake hands with Captain Flannery, of San Francisco police." The captain seized Ross's unresisting hand. Stepping forward, Chan made a hasty search. "I perceive," he added, "that weapon supply, which you have replenished so many times along the way, is exhausted at last."

"What—what do you mean?" Ross demanded.

"I am sorry to say Captain Flannery has warrant for your arrest."

"Arrest?"

"He has been asked by Scotland Yard to hold you for the murder of Hugh Morris Drake in Broome's Hotel, London, on the morning of February 7, present year." Ross stared about him defiantly. "There remain other matters," Chan continued, "but you will never be called upon to answer for those. The murder of Honywood in Nice, the murder of Sybil Conway in San Remo, the murder of Sergeant Welby in Yokohama. The brutal attack on Inspector Duff in Honolulu. Murder round the world, Mr. Ross."

"It's not true," Ross said hoarsely.

"We will see. Kashimo!" Charlie's voice rose. "You may now emerge from your hiding-place."

A bedraggled little figure rolled swiftly from beneath one of the beds. The Japanese was covered with lint, stray threads and dust. Chan helped him to his feet.

"Ah, you are somewhat stiff, Kashimo," he remarked. "I am sorry I could not dig you out sooner. Captain Flannery, the Oriental invasion becomes serious. Meet Officer Kashimo, of the

Honolulu force." He turned to the boy. "Is it too much to hope you know present whereabouts of precious key?"

"I know," the Japanese answered proudly. He dropped to his knees, and from the turn-up of Ross's right trouser leg extracted the key, which he held aloft in triumph.

Charlie took it. "What is this? Looks like plenty good evidence to me, Sergeant Wales. Key to safety-deposit box in some bank, with number 3260. Ah, Mr. Ross, you should have thrown it away. But I understand. You feared that without it you would not dare approach valuables again." He handed the key to Wales.

"That's the stuff to give a jury," remarked the Englishman, with satisfaction.

"The key was planted there," cried Ross. "I deny everything."

"Everything?" Charlie's eyes narrowed. "Last night we sat together, watching Mr. Benbow's pictures. Flickering film revealed you emerging from doorway of a shop in Nice. Did you think that I failed to notice? I might have—but for days I have known you guilty——"

"What!" Ross was unable to conceal his surprise.

"I will explain in moment. Just now, I speak of Nice. Jimmy Breen, the tailor, remembers. He recalls grey coat with torn right pocket——"

Ross started to speak, but the detective raised his hand.

"Cards lie against you," Charlie went on. "You are clever man, you have high opinion of yourself, and it is difficult for you to believe that you have failed. Such, however, is the situation. Clever—ah, yes. Clever when you hid that key on Mr. Kennaway's bag—a bag that would naturally be thrust under bed and forgotten until hour of landing was imminent once more. Clever when you discarded rubber tip from stick, then carried same in wrong hand, hoping some keen eye would notice. So many were under suspicion, you thought to gain by being suspected too, and then extricating yourself in convincing manner—which I must admit you did. You were clever again last night when you fired wild shot at me and dropped smoking revolver beside poor Mr. Tait. It was cruel act—but you are cruel man. And what a useless gesture! For, as I remarked before, I have known for several days that you were guilty person."

"You don't tell me," Ross sneered. "And how did you know it?"

"I knew it because there was one moment when you were not quite so clever, Mr. Ross. That moment arrived at Mr. Minchin's dinner. You made a speech there. It was brief speech, but it contained one word—one careless little word. That word convicted you."

"Really? What word was that?"

Charlie took out a card and wrote something on it. he handed it to Ross. "Keep same as souvenir," he suggested.

The man glanced at it. His face was white, and suddenly very old. He tore the card into shreds and tossed them to the floor.

"Thanks," he said bitterly, "but I'm not collecting souvenirs. Well—what happens next?"

CHAPTER XXIII

TIME TO DRY THE NETS

WHAT happened next was that a customs inspector knocked on the door, and in that strained atmosphere made his examination of the hand luggage belonging to both Vivian and Ross. He was followed by a steward who carried the bags below. Vivian slipped out, and Kashimo, after a brief word with Charlie, also departed.

Captain Flannery took out a handkerchief and mopped his brow. "Getting pretty hot down here," he remarked to Wales. "Let's take this bird up to the library and hear what he's got to say for himself."

"I have nothing to say," Ross put in grimly.

"Is that so? Well, I've seen men in your position change their minds." Flannery went first, then Ross, and Wales was close behind. Charlie brought up the rear.

They passed Mark Kennaway on the stairs. Chan stopped for a word.

"We have our man," he announced.

"Ross!" Kennaway cried. "Good lord!"

"I suggest you pass among members of travel party, clearing name of poor Mr. Tait."

"Watch me," the young man replied. "I'll beat the time of Paul Revere—and he had a horse."

Coming out on to the open deck, Charlie realized for the first time that they were moving again. On the right were the low buildings of the Presidio, and up ahead the fortress of Alcatraz Island. All about him the ship's passengers were milling, in a last frenzy of farewell.

Flannery and Wales were sitting with their quarry in the otherwise deserted library. Charlie closed the door behind him, and the racket outside subsided to a low murmur.

As the Chinese went over to join the group, Ross gave him a look of bitter hatred. In the man's eyes there was now a light that recalled to Chan's mind a luncheon over which he had sat with Duff a week ago. "You seek evidently two men," he had said to the English detective on that occasion. This was no longer the gentle, mild-mannered Ross the travel party had known; it was the other man, hard, merciless and cruel.

"You'd better come across," Flannery was saying. Ross's only reply was a glance of contempt.

"The captain is giving you good advice," remarked Wales pleasantly. His methods were more suave than those of Flannery. "In all my professional career I never encountered a case in which the evidence was quite so strong as it is here—thanks, of course, to Inspector Chan. It is my duty to warn you that anything you say may be used against you. But my suggestion would be that you plan to plead guilty——"

"To something I didn't do?" flared Ross.

"Oh, come, come. We have not only the key, but the information from the tailor who——"

"Yes, and how about a motive?" The voice of the accused man rose. "I don't give a damn for all your keys and your coats—you can't prove any motive. That's important, and you know it. I never saw any of these people I'm supposed to have murdered before—I've lived on the west coast of the States for years—I——"

"You had a very obvious motive, Mr. Ross,".
Wales answered politely. "Or perhaps I should say
—Mr. Everhard. Jim Everhard, I believe."

The man's face turned a ghastly grey, and for a
moment he seemed about to collapse. He was fight‑
ing for the strength that had sustained him thus far,
but he fought in vain.

"Ah, yes, Mr. Everhard—or Ross, if you prefer,".
Wales went on evenly. "Judging by information that
came in to the Yard only a few days ago, your motive
is only too clear. We haven't worried recently about
motive—we've worried only as to your identity.
Inspector Chan has cleverly discovered that. When
the jury asks for a motive, we have only to tell them
of your days in South Africa—of how Honywood stole
your girl——"

"And my diamonds," cried Ross. "My diamonds
and my girl. But she was as bad as he was——"
He had half risen from his chair, now he fell back,
suddenly silent.

Wales glanced at Charlie. Their eyes met, but
they were careful to conceal the elation with which
they heard those words from Ross.

"You went out to South Africa some fifteen years
ago, I believe," the sergeant continued, "as a violinist
in a musical comedy company orchestra. Sybil
Conway was leading woman in the troupe, and you
fell in love with her. But she was ambitious, she
wanted money, stardom, success. You came into a
small inheritance, but it wasn't enough. It was
enough, however, to launch you into a business—a
shady business—the trade of the I.D.B. Buying
diamonds from natives, from thieves. Inside a year
you had two bags filled with these stolen stones.
Sybil Conway promised to marry you. You went on
one last tour to the vicinity of the diamond fields.

leaving those two bags with your girl in Capetown.
And when you came back to her——"

"I saw him," Ross finished. "Oh, what's the use
—you're too much for me—you and this Chinese. I
saw him the first night after I got back—Walter
Honywood Swan, that was his name. It was in the
little parlour of the house where Sybil Conway was
living."

"A younger son," Wales suggested. "A ne'er-
do-well at home—out there a member of the South
African police."

"Yes, I knew he was with the police. After he'd
gone, I asked Sybil what it meant. She said the
fellow was suspicious, that he was after me, and that
I'd better get away at once. She would follow when
the show closed. There was a boat leaving at midnight—a boat for Australia. She hurried me aboard
—in the dark on the deck just before I sailed, she
slipped me the two little bags. I could feel the stones
inside. I didn't dare look at them then. She kissed
me good-bye—and we parted.

"When the boat was well out, I went to my cabin
and examined the bags. The little bags of stones.
That's what they were—wash-leather bags, each filled
with about a hundred pebbles of various sizes. I'd
been done. She preferred that policeman to me.
She'd sold me out."

"So you went to Australia," Wales gently urged
him on. "You heard there that Sybil Conway and
Swan were married, and that he now called himself
Walter Honywood. You wrote, promising to kill
them both. But you were broke—it wasn't so easy
to reach them. The years went by. Eventually you
drifted to the States. You prospered, became a
respectable citizen. The old urge for revenge was
gone. And then—suddenly—it returned."

Ross looked up. His eyes were bloodshot. "Yes," he said slowly, "it returned."

"How was that?" Wales continued. "Did it happen after you hurt your foot? When you lay there, idle, alone, plenty of time to think——"

"Yes—and something to think about," Ross cried. "The whole affair came back to me as vividly as yesterday. What they'd done to me—do you wonder I thought? And I'd let them get away with it." He looked wildly about him. "I tell you, if ever a man was justified——"

"No, no," Wales protested. "You should have forgotten the past. You'd be a happy man to-day if you had. Don't expect any mercy on that score. Were you justified in killing Drake——"

"A mistake. I was sorry. It was dark in that room."

"And Sergeant Welby—as fine a chap as I ever knew?"

"I had to do it."

"And your attempt to kill Duff——"

"I didn't attempt to kill him. I'd have done it if I had meant to. No, I only wanted to put him out for the moment——"

"You have been ruthless and cruel, Ross," Wales said sternly. "And you will have to pay for it."

"I expect to pay."

"How much better for you," Wales went on, "if you had never attempted your belated vengeance. But you did attempt it. When your foot was better, I see you gathering up all your valuables, your savings, and leaving Tacoma for ever. You put all your property in the safety-deposit box of a bank in some strange town. Where? We shall know presently. You set out for New York to find the Honywood pair. Walter Honywood was about to make a tour around the world. You booked for the same party.

"In Broome's Hotel you attempted your first murder. It was a ghastly mistake. But you hung on. You sent that coat to Nice, where you had it repaired. You had lost part of your watch-chain, one of the keys to your safety-deposit box. You debated with yourself—should you throw the duplicate key away? You knew Scotland Yard would make every effort to find the owner of a safety-deposit box numbered 3260. Could you go into a bank where you were practically unknown and call undue attention to yourself by admitting you had lost both keys? No, your only hope of ever seeing your valuables again was to hang on to that other key.

"The party went on. Walter Honywood knew you now, but he was as eager to avoid publicity as you were. He warned you of a letter that would incriminate you if anything happened to him. You searched until you had it, and that same night, in the hotel gardens at Nice, you got him. You heard that Sybil Conway was in the next town. You didn't dare leave the party. You went along, hoping for the best—and that lift—it was made for your purpose.

"After that, it seemed smooth sailing. You began to think luck was with you. Duff was baffled, and you knew it. You moved on in peace, until Yokohama. There you learned that Welby had discovered the duplicate key. By the way, where did you have it then?" Ross made no reply. "Some clever place, I'll wager," the Scotland Yard man continued. "But it doesn't matter. You sensed somehow that Welby had gone ashore to cable. He'd sent the message before you could stop him, but on the chance that there was no mention of you in it—as indeed there wasn't—you shot him down on the dock when he returned.

"Again you began to feel safe. I don't know much

about what has happened since Yokohama. But I
judge that when you got to Honolulu and met Duff
on the pier, you saw red again. Nearly at the end of
your journey—only a few more miles—and all serene
—save for Duff. How much had he learned? Nothing,
that was clear. How much would he learn on that
final lap of the tour? Nothing again, if you could
prevent it. You removed him from your trail."
Wales glanced at Charlie Chan. "And right there,
Ross," the Englishman finished, "I think you made
the big mistake of your life."

Ross stood up. The boat was now fast to the dock,
and outside the window, the passengers were gathered
about the top of the plank.

"Well, what of it?" Ross said. "How about going
ashore?"

They waited a moment on the deck, until the crowd
on the plank had diminished to a few late stragglers,
then started down. A uniformed policeman appeared
before Flannery. "The car's ready, Chief," he said.

Charlie held out his hand to Sergeant Wales.
"Maybe we meet again," he said. "I have in bag
Inspector Duff's brief-case, my study of which is now
completed."

Wales shook hands warmly. "Yes, you've passed
your examination on that, I fancy," he smiled.
"With honours, too. I'll be in San Francisco until
Duff comes. I hope you'll be here when he arrives.
He'll want to thank you in person, I know."

"I may be—who can say?" Charlie returned.

"Good. In the meantime, you must dine with me
to-night. There are still some details I'm curious
about. Ross's speech at the Minchin dinner, for
example. Can you meet me at the Stewart at seven?"

"Delighted," Charlie answered. "I stop at same
hotel myself."

Wales walked away with Ross in the company of the uniformed policeman. The man whom Charlie had at last brought to justice was wrapped in sullen silence now. His eyes, in those final moments, had studiously avoided those of Chan.

"Be in San Francisco long, Charlie?" asked Flannery, coming up.

"Hard to answer," Chan replied. "I have daughter at college in south California, and I have unquenchable longing to visit her."

"That's the ticket," Flannery cried, relieved. "You go down and give a helping hand to the Los Angeles police. They need it, if anybody ever did."

Chan smiled gently to himself. "You have here no little matter on which I might assist?"

"Not a thing, Charlie. Everything's pretty well cleaned up around San Francisco. But then, we got a mighty able organization here."

Chan nodded. "Under a strong general there are no weak soldiers."

"You said it. Lot of truth in some of those old wheezes of yours. Well, Charlie—drop in and see me before you go. I'll have to run along now."

As Charlie walked over to get his bag, he met Kashimo and the purser.

"Taking this lad aboard the *President Taft*," the purser said. "He'll be on his way back to Hawaii at two."

Chan beamed upon his assistant. "And he goes covered with glory," he remarked. "Kashimo, you have suffused my heart with pride. Not only did you do notable searching on boat, but when you came aboard that night in Honolulu, your suspicious eye was already on the guilty man." He patted the Japanese on the shoulder. "Even a peach grown in the shade will ripen in the end," he added.

"Hope chief will not be angry that I ran away," Kashimo said.

"Chief will be at pier with loudly playing band," Charlie assured him. "I do not appear to make you understand, Kashimo. You are hero. You are, I repeat again, covered with glory. Do not continually seek to push it aside, like blanket on hot night. Go aboard other ship now and wait for my return. I go to city to purchase fresh linen for you. I am inclined to think six days are plenty for that present outfit."

He picked up his bag, and walked a few steps with them towards the plank of the *President Taft.*

"For the present, I say good-bye," he announced. "Will see you again, maybe at one o'clock. You are going home, Kashimo, not only in the shining garments of success, but also in a more hygienic shirt."

"All right," said Kashimo meekly.

As Charlie was leaving the pier-shed, he encountered Mark Kennaway.

"Hello," the young man cried. "Pamela and I have been waiting for you. I've engaged a car, and you're riding up-town with us."

"You are too kind," Charlie replied.

"Oh, our motives are not entirely unselfish. Tell you what I mean in a minute." They went to the kerb, where Pamela Potter was seated in a large touring car. "Jump in, Mr. Chan," the young man added.

Chan did no jumping, but climbed aboard with his usual dignity. Kennaway followed and the car started.

"Both are looking very happy," Charlie suggested.

"Then I suppose our news is superfluous," the young man said. "As a matter of fact, we're engaged——"

Chan turned to the girl. "Pardon my surprise. You accepted this irritating young man, after all?"

"I certainly did. About a minute before he proposed, at that. I wasn't going to let all my hard work go for nothing."

"My warmest congratulations to you both," Chan bowed.

"Thanks," smiled the girl. "Mark's all right, everything considered. He's promised to forget Boston, and practise law in Detroit."

"Greater love hath no man than that," nodded Kennaway.

"So it's turned out to be a pretty good tour, after all," the girl continued. "Even if it did start so badly." Her smile faded. "By the way, I can't wait another minute. I want to learn how you knew that Ross was guilty. You said that night on the deck that I ought to know, too, and I've racked my slight brain until I'm dizzy. But it's no use. I'm no detective, I guess."

"Vivian told us a few minutes ago," Kennaway added, "that it was something Ross said at the Minchin dinner. We've been over that speech of Ross's a dozen times. There wasn't much to it, as I recall. He was interrupted before he'd fairly got started——"

"But not before he had spoken a most incriminating word," Chan put in. "I will repeat for you the sentence in which it occurred. I have memorized it. Listen carefully. 'As for that unfortunate night in London, when poor Hugh Morris Drake lay dead in that stuffy room in Broome's Hotel——'"

"Stuffy!" cried Pamela Potter.

"Stuffy," repeated Charlie. "You are now bright girl I thought you. Consider. Was the room in which your honourable grandfather was discovered

lifeless on bed a stuffy room? Remember testimony
of Martin, the floor waiter, which you heard at
inquest, and which I read in Inspector Duff's notes.
'I unlocked the door of the room and went in,'
Martin said. 'One window was closed, the curtain
was down all the way. The other was open, and the
curtain was up, too. The light entered from there.'
Adding word of my own I would remark, so also
did plenty good fresh air."

"Of course," cried the girl. "I should have
remembered. When I was in that room, talking with
Mr. Duff, the window was still open, and a street
orchestra was playing *There's a Long, Long Trail
A-Winding* outside. The music came up to us quite
loudly."

"Ah, yes—but it was not in the same room that
grandfather was slain," Chan reminded her. "It
was in room next door. And when Ross mentioned
matter at dinner his memory played him sorry trick.
His thoughts returned, not to room in which grandfather was finally discovered, but to that other room
in which he died. You read Walter Honywood's
letter to his wife?"

"Yes, I did."

"Recall how he said to her: 'I entered and looked
about me. Drake's clothes were on a chair, his ear-
phone on a table; all the doors and windows were
closed.' You observe, Miss Pamela—that was the
stuffy room. The room where your grandfather
perished."

"Of course it was," the girl answered. "Poor
grandfather had asthma, and he thought the London
night air was bad for it. So he refused to have any
windows open where he slept. Oh—I have been
stupid."

"You were otherwise engaged," smiled Charlie.

"I was not. Three men knew that Hugh Morris Drake slept that night in a stuffy room. One, Mr. Drake himself—and he was dead. Two, Mr. Honywood, who went in and found the body—and he too was dead. Three, the man who stole in there in the night and strangled him—the murderer. In simpler words—Mr. Ross."

"Good work!" cried Kennaway.

"But finished now," added Chan. "The Emperor Shi Hwang-ti, who built the Great Wall of China, once said: 'He who squanders to-day talking of yesterday's triumph, will have nothing to boast of to-morrow.'"

The car had drawn up before the door of an hotel in Union Square, and when the young people had alighted, Charlie followed. He took the girl's hand in his.

"I see plenty glad look in your eyes this morning," he said. "May it remain, is vigorous wish from me. Remember, fortune calls at the smiling gate."

He shook hands with Kennaway, picked up his bag, and disappeared quickly round the corner.